"WHY ME?"

"I've been keeping an eye on you, Ms. Timberlake, and I've decided that I can trust you. Your mother thinks you're the salt of the earth."

"I pay her to say that."

She waved a hand impatiently. "I need your help and I don't know where else to turn. A cousin of mine was recently murdered. I need you to help me find the killer."

Thank God my hair is short, because it was standing on end. I stood up to keep it company.

"Me? Why me?"

"Because," she said, "my cousin was killed in your shop, The Den of Antiquity. She was killed because of you!"

Den of Antiquity Mysteries by
Tamar Myers
from Avon Books

BAROQUE AND DESPERATE
ESTATE OF MIND
SO FAUX, SO GOOD
THE MING AND I
GILT BY ASSOCIATION
LARCENY AND OLD LACE
A PENNY URNED
NIGHTMARE IN SHINING ARMOR

Coming Soon

SPLENDOR IN THE GLASS

The Ming and I

A DEN OF ANTIQUITY MYSTERY

TAMAR MYERS

AVON BOOKS

An Imprint of HarperCollinsPublishers

AVON BOOKS
An Imprint of HarperCollins*Publishers*
195 Broadway
New York, NY, 10007

Copyright © 1997 by Tamar Myers
Library of Congress Catalog Card Number: 97-93174
ISBN: 0-380-79255-9
www.avonmystery.com

First Avon Books printing: November 1997

Avon Trademark Reg. U.S. Pat. Off. and in Other Countries, Marca Registrada, Hecho en U.S.A.
HarperCollins® is a trademark of HarperCollins Publishers Inc.

Printed in the U.S.A.

10

For Carrie Feron,
Executive Editor at Avon Books

I would like to acknowledge my fourth grade teacher, Miss Enz; my tenth grade English teacher, Mr. Jester; my twelfth grade English teacher, Mrs. Seibert; and my Speech and Creative Writing teacher, Mr. Sodt. Thanks for your encouragement.

1

It took a lot to get my attention that day. The first time June Troyan came into my shop, I barely noticed her. Her subsequent visit was a little more dramatic. I noticed her the second she came hurtling through the plate glass window. My customers noticed her as well. Prior to that rather dramatic and fatal second entrance, June was just one of many nondescript shoppers on the busiest Tuesday on record.

The night before, Channel 9 had done a special on the thriving antique business in Charlotte, and in a rare stroke of luck, my shop was singled out. It didn't hurt that it was azalea season, and the weather was as perfect as it gets this side of heaven. People came out in droves. Then to add to my unbelievably good fortune, a sudden but brief downpour came out of nowhere, trapping everyone inside. The gods were finally smiling on me.

My name is Abigail Timberlake, and I am the overworked owner and sole employee of the Den of Antiquity. I'm not complaining, mind you. I didn't mind having to wait on five people at once. It's just that I couldn't give every customer my full attention, especially those who have obviously come into my shop just to sell something. A mere glance at June and the ugly gray vase she was holding was all I needed to know that she was a seller, not a buyer.

I do my buying at auctions and private estate sales. I never, ever, buy anything "off the street." By sticking to this little rule I have so far managed to avoid buying stolen and fenced goods, and wasting my time with the myriad of wishful souls who expect to make a fortune off their grandmother's trinkets—never mind that the old lady herself was as poor as a church mouse on welfare.

Of course I miss out on some exceptional buys. My friend and fellow shop owner, Wynnell Crawford, once bought an exquisite set of nineteenth-century Meissen figures in mint condition from a little old lady wearing only a babushka and a bathrobe. I would have taken one look at the vendor and concluded that her wares originally came from Kmart, having possibly made several detours through area garage sales.

"What did you notice about the victim when she came in the first time?" Investigator Greg Washburn asked when he arrived on the scene.

Greg, incidentally, is my boyfriend. He is tall, dark, and handsome, with gleaming white teeth and eyes that are Wedgwood blue. Greg is just an ego away from being a cliché. Fortunately he has no idea just how handsome he is. I, on the other hand, am four foot nine, with no outstanding colors. Enough said.

"I didn't notice anything," I wailed.

"Nothing?"

I glanced down at the spot where the very battered and bloody body had come to a rest. Thankfully the body had been removed and a police blanket covered most of the gore. Still, it made me uneasy to speak of the dead so near her place of demise.

"She was mousy," I said.

"Mousy?"

"Well, brownish then. Brown hair, brown clothes. That's all I remember."

"Her shoes and purse were Gucci." The speaker was a tall, leggy blond woman, a customer and fellow eyewitness detained for questioning.

Greg turned to her. "Anything else?"

"Her dress was definitely not off the rack. Christian Dior, maybe."

"Some mouse," Greg said, and gave me a pitying look.

"Oh, her watch was a Rolex, and her earrings were from Tiffany," the blonde said triumphantly.

Greg rewarded her with one of his blinding smiles.

"She was wearing Shalimar," another woman customer said, vying for Greg's attention. "The perfume, not the cologne."

"Which has nothing to do with anything," I said. "She's still wearing all those things. The lab can tell you that. Isn't her behavior more important than her appearance?"

"Exactly," Greg said, but he failed to reward me with a blinding smile.

A distinguished-looking man, a frequent customer, stepped forward gallantly. "I think maybe she was drunk."

Greg turned to him. "Oh?"

"She kept bobbing back and forth."

"She was trying to get my attention," I said.

Greg graciously bestowed a bemused smile on me. "So, you saw nothing, did you?"

I stood my ground. "I saw nothing but a mousy woman who was trying to sell me a hideous vase."

Greg turned to Officer Sullivan, the first of Charlotte's finest on the scene. "That wasn't in the report, was it?"

Officer Sullivan shook his head. "You can see

where she landed, sir. Just a broken chair. No sign of a vase."

"That broken chair is a genuine Louis XIV," I said. "Original upholstery."

"And outside?" Greg asked.

Officer Sullivan shook his head again. "The car came right up onto the sidewalk and hit her. No vase there either—or in the street."

"That's a shame," Greg said.

"One thousand six hundred and twenty-five dollars," I said, "but I would have taken off fifteen percent just for the asking."

They both stared at me.

"The woman is dead," I reminded them. "There's nothing to be done about that. I, however, have a smashed window and a ruined chair."

Greg turned back to Officer Sullivan. "Any witnesses outside the shop?"

Officer Sullivan shook his head. "Everyone was inside because of the downpour, but there are three witnesses who claim to have seen it from the shop across the street."

"Any of them get a make on the car? See who was driving?"

Officer Sullivan grinned. "All three of these people are sure of what they saw. One saw a black Cadillac driven by a middle-aged black man. One saw a beige station wagon driven by a young red-haired woman. The third saw an old white man in a blue Ford van. A large one. Possibly commercial."

"Figures," Greg said. "Which direction was the driver coming from?"

Officer Sullivan glanced at his notes and chuckled. "One said from the north, one from the south, and the third was positive about everything except that."

"I saw the car," the leggy blonde said. Personally I thought she was lying shamelessly just to get Greg's attention.

The Wedgwood eyes focused on her expectantly.

"It was the black man in the black Cadillac. He was going south." The blonde pointed north.

"I don't think so," I said.

The blonde glared at me.

Greg's eyes twinkled in amusement. "Do tell, Ab—I mean, Ms. Timberlake."

"It was the blue Ford van," I said.

"Oh? And how do you know that?"

"Look outside. All the parking places are full. That's the most common complaint we get. But there"—I pointed to the right—"is the loading zone. Only trucks and large vans are permitted to park there, and then for only five minutes.

"My guess is that the driver of the van had pulled into that spot and was waiting for Ms. Troyan to come out. He then accelerated and"—I pointed to my smashed window—"there you have it."

"Likely story," the blonde said, tilting her man-made shnoz skyward.

"Could be true," Greg said.

I felt so proud of myself that I didn't even mind when the blonde slammed my front door behind her, precipitating a second shower of broken glass.

2

"**D**amn good job," Bob Steuben boomed. He is a transplanted Yankee from Toledo, and has a Yankee accent, but his voice would make a bullfrog jealous.

I jumped—higher than a bullfrog, I'm sure.

"We didn't mean to scare you," Rob Goldburg said.

We were standing on the sidewalk in front of the Den of Antiquity. I had started out admiring the window, which had been repaired late the day before, but I had somehow managed to become deeply lost in thought.

"You guys want to come in for coffee? I've got plenty of doughnuts." I waved a white paper bag.

Rob looked at it longingly. Like me, he is a doughnut freak. Bob, his life partner, is a gourmand who eschews any food normally eaten with the fingers. Dunking is a definite no-no.

"Mostly just glazed," I said, "but there is at least one raspberry jelly, and it's yours."

The two men exchanged glances, and the raspberry jelly won out.

"But just for a minute," Bob said. "We came in early to rearrange the merchandise in our front window—just in case."

I smiled and unlocked my door. The odds of another body hurtling through a window on Selwyn Avenue were undoubtedly rather slim. Still, I could understand their concern.

Bob and Rob—the Rob-Bobs, as I like to call them—own The Finer Things, a truly splendid shop just next door to mine. Ever since they bought it, I have found myself upgrading my merchandise. This is an unconscious act, I am sure. However, I am far from achieving the height of sophistication practiced by my good neighbors, and am always willing, if not eager, to learn from them.

I held the doughnut bag aloft like the rabbit at a greyhound race, and the men trooped in after me. While Bob wandered around nervously, Rob and I dug into the breakfast of angels. I was on my third glazed when Bob shrieked.

Since basso profundos seldom shriek, you can imagine my surprise.

"What the—" Rob said, his mouth as full as mine.

Bob shrieked again.

My heart would have been in my mouth had there been any room. That Rob reached his partner before I did is only because he has longer legs. Frankly I didn't know what to expect, but the possibility that it might be another body did cross my mind.

Bob was not anywhere near the window, however, but in the far left corner of my shop, in a space I called The Nook. This architectural oddity was necessitated by the construction of a public toilet last year. It took me awhile to figure it out, but customers are more likely to browse when they are comfortable.

At any rate The Nook is a small space—just six feet square—and it is the only spot in my shop not visible from the cash register. Consequently only small items of relatively little value are displayed there. The previous month it was a collection of carnival glass. On that particular day The Nook was

home to an eighteenth-century pine cupboard, the
shelves of which were lined with spindle toys.

I arrived at The Nook to find Bob standing by the
cupboard, a look of absolute rapture on his face. He
was cradling an ugly gray vase in his hands.

"Shit!" Rob said. Rob is a local boy, born and bred,
and it took him three syllables to say the word.

I could feel the doughnuts and my heart sink to a
spot just above my knees. It was undoubtedly the
same ugly vase June Troyan had tried to peddle. Not
that I'd gotten a close look at it, mind you, but I
certainly would never stock something that hideous.

"Oh no," I wailed, "it's her vase. Now it will look
like I was trying to cover something up. Officer Sullivan will probably think I was flat-out lying."

The Rob-Bobs turned to stare at me. Rob is in his
fifties and devilishly handsome. Tall, muscular, with
a touch of gray at the temples, he looks like Cary
Grant would have, had the actor belonged to a gym.
Bob is slight of build, with a face too narrow for his
generous features, but hey, with a voice that can
calm the Bosporus Strait, who needs looks?

"Abby, fess up," Bob boomed.

"Fess up to what?"

"Don't hold out on us," Rob said with a knowing
smile. "We're your friends."

"So you are. But honestly, guys, I didn't know that
disgusting thing was here."

They burst out laughing. They laughed almost as
hard as the time Bob found a pair of pink plastic
flamingos in my storeroom. The flamingos, incidentally, were a gag gift for a friend. They were not
meant to be sold.

I could feel my face turn red. I know that I have
a lot of catching up to do to reach their league, but
I am not the neophyte they seem to think.

"Give me a break," I snapped. "I've never
touched that disgusting thing before in my life."

They laughed harder.

I snatched the monstrous piece from Rob's hands. I would have smashed it on the floor right then and there, but Rob's right hand grabbed my wrist in a viselike grip. His left hand cradled the vase.

"Abby, this disgusting thing is a Ming dynasty vase. We'd have to clean it up to be sure, but in form at least it appears to be a fine example of the Ch'eng-hua period."

I inadvertently released my grip on the vase. Fortunately Rob was still cradling it in the palm of his left hand. Even then he had to move fast with his right to steady it. A second later and all the king's horses and all the king's men wouldn't have been able to put that Ming together again.

"Bravo!" Bob boomed.

My mouth was still open wide enough for Sherman and all his troops to enter.

"You'll see," Rob said, taking a handkerchief out of his pocket. "There's a real treasure under this grime. All we need is a little soap and warm water."

We crammed into the adjacent rest room I had so thoughtfully provided for my customers. It was meant for one person at a time, not three people about to perform a delicate operation.

I stared, still mute, while Rob gently wiped away with a circular motion what must have been a century of soot, grease, and dust. I can only describe the transformation as a flower bud unfolding in time-lapse photography, as in those nature shows Mama used to make me watch when I was a little girl.

This flower was made out of porcelain so thin, it was almost translucent, like the petals of a gardenia held up to the sun. Unlike a gardenia, however, it was a multicolored flower. The underglaze was a delicate blue, but the design was polychrome, with overglaze shades of red, green, yellow, and even aubergine. Although it was a fairly simple design, primarily flowers and branching twigs, it was beautifully balanced.

"It's what they call *tou ts'ai*," Rob said reverently. "It means 'appropriateness of design.' "

As the unveiling progressed we oohed and aahed like participants at a bridal gift shower. So engrossed were we that none of us heard the phone until its eleventh ring.

"Hello," I said reluctantly. Frankly I wouldn't have answered at all, but it was almost opening time, and a good customer of mine had promised to call and confirm a major purchase. Something in the five digit range!

"Abby—there you are! I let it ring twelve times. I was starting to get worried."

I sighed. "Mama, I'm forty-eight years old, for Pete's sake. And I don't even open for another—"

"Two minutes." I could hear Mama's pearls clicking against the phone receiver. She fiddles with them whenever she's stressed.

"What is it?" I asked as pleasantly as a forty-eight-year-old woman can when her mother has just treated her like a child.

"What are you doing tonight, dear?"

I thought fast. I do enjoy spending time with Mama, but—perhaps I do deserve to be treated like a child—I was miffed.

"Greg and I have a date," I lied. "We're going out to dinner."

That was a mistake. Mama adores Greg, and she is the world's best cook, bar none. As for Greg, sometimes I think he would rather accept food from Mama than anything from me.

"Why don't the two of you come here instead?" Mama asked. "Say, about seven? I'm making saddle of lamb, new potatoes, and fresh asparagus."

Mama is a widow who usually eats alone, but you would never know it by the way she dines. Fresh flowers, a linen tablecloth, and real silver are daily accoutrements at her table. Leave it to Mama to make saddle of lamb for one.

"Greg doesn't like lamb," I said honestly.

Mama was unflappable. "Well, then, how does a nice, medium-rare beef Wellington sound? Of course we'd skip the potatoes then. Maybe an artichoke salad instead. But the asparagus stays. I have a new recipe for hollandaise sauce."

"Artichoke hearts?" I asked hopefully. Mama's menus had mellowed me. I no longer remembered being miffed.

"Of course," Mama said. "You can't put artichoke leaves in a salad."

"All right, we'll be there. But only if we get to do the dishes."

"I wouldn't have it any other way," Mama said, and hung up.

It took me just a second to switch from menus to Ming. I scurried back to The Nook. Rob and Bob were still there, and so was the vase. Rob was gently patting it dry with one of his silk shirttails. Paper towels, he told me, were too rough.

I had been there at the beginning of the transformation; still, I could hardly believe the end product. Just looking at it brought tears of joy to my eyes.

"How much is it worth?" I asked sensibly.

"Five thousand minimum at a dealer's auction," Bob said. "Retail between ten and fifteen."

The tears of joy streamed down my cheeks.

"If you don't mind my asking," Rob said, "how much did you pay for it?"

"Well, uh—actually I didn't. I'm not sure, but I think it might have been put here by Ms. Troyan, that poor woman who was hit by the car yesterday."

"Then of course the Ming's value is only an academic question," Bob said, looking pointedly at me.

"I beg your pardon?"

"Well, it isn't rightfully yours. You just said so yourself."

"But I found it in my shop," I wailed. "What about finders keepers? Isn't there such a law?"

"Well, you have to notify the police, don't you? Then they have to track down Ms. Troyan's heirs, assuming she has any."

"Assuming she doesn't?"

"That's another story, of course. Eventually the vase might end up yours. Unless . . ."

I reverently took the vase from Rob. It was much lighter than I had expected. "Unless what?"

"Well, unless the vase didn't belong to Ms. Troyan in the first place."

The tears slowed. "Who then?"

Bob shrugged. "Maybe it was stolen. Or smuggled into the country. In either case it might take years to sort it all out, and in the end this beauty would probably go up for sale at public auction."

I stared at him with eyes as dry as cotton balls.

"Don't listen to him," Rob said, tucking his wet shirttail back in. "It was all those Toledo winters that made him so negative. He was just giving you one scenario."

"Oh?"

"You could just keep it, you know. Not tell the police. After all, maybe you did buy it at an auction along with some other stuff, and just never noticed it before."

Bob gave his partner a reproachful look. "That wouldn't be right, Robert."

"But we have no proof that the vase doesn't belong to her," Rob protested.

I smiled at him gratefully.

Bob shook his head. It was clear he was disappointed in both of us.

"Anyway, Abby would never do such a thing." He looked at me pointedly. "Would you?"

I shook my head reluctantly. I would never steal anything, of course. Even we Episcopalians still have that commandment on the books. But I wanted to think of this situation as falling under one of those gray areas of ethics, the kind you can debate for hours in a college dorm with a bottle of Boones Farm wine.

Unfortunately my brain is two and a half decades older, and I now drink chardonnay. While it was possible I might have bought the vase as part of a lot, I never would have set it out for display in The Nook. Besides, I had seen Ms. Troyan holding a vase that looked similar to this one while it was yet in its ugly duckling state, and the odds of two ugly ducklings showing up in my shop were not good. Or so I'd like to think.

"All settled then?" Bob asked gently. "I'll make the call for you, if you like."

"No," I said quickly. "It's my responsibility, so I'll call."

He gave me a questioning look.

"I promise," I snapped.

"Let's go," Rob said, taking Bob by the arm.

I meant what I said. I would call Greg, but only to invite him to dinner that night. News about the vase could keep until then. In the meantime I would keep the beauty with me behind the counter. Between customers I could at least fantasize that it was mine.

I put the vase in all its shining glory on a small table against the wall behind the counter that I use as a desk. Then I stepped around the counter to admire the Ming for a few precious seconds before flinging my door open to the public.

In retrospect, I will acknowledge that displaying the Ming, no matter how briefly, was not one of my brightest moves. While it is true that my taste buds prefer chardonnay, on occasion I still think with a Boones Farm brain.

I had just finished ringing up the sale of an Art Deco mirrored console when the phone rang.

"Den of Antiquity," I said cheerily. The console had sold for full price.

"Is this the owner?" someone of indeterminate sex asked in a muffled voice.

"Yes. How may I help you?"

"This is Lock, Stock, and Barrel Security Services," the androgynous voice said. "We're offering a special this week—"

"Thanks, but no thanks," I said politely.

"You'll want to hear this special."

"I bet I won't."

There followed a long and delightful silence. "Hey lady, I'm just trying to make a living," the caller said at last.

"Tell you what. I'm with a customer right now, but give me your number and I'll call you right back."

I felt for the tablet of notepaper I keep by the phone. Unfortunately it was missing. Not that I would have called right back, mind you, but I would have called. I know, it is absolutely puerile of me—perhaps even unchristian—but I enjoy calling phone solicitors at home in the middle of the night. I don't set my alarm especially for that, mind you. I just do it whenever I wake up to use the bathroom.

"It's against company regulations to give out our phone number," the caller said.

"Well, it's against my regulations to talk to companies that won't." I hung up.

Immediately the phone rang again. I let it ring five times before answering. When you are in a retail business, you shouldn't rely on an answering machine during business hours. There are still folks out there who hang up on canned voices.

"Hello?"

"You shouldn't be so rude," my previous caller said.

"Excuse me?"

"I have to make a living, too, you know."

"I know. So give me your home phone number and I'll call you this evening," I said. That almost always works like a charm.

The caller paused only a microsecond, if at all. "I can't. My roommate works night shift. But this will only take a moment, I promise."

"No—"

"Please. Just one minute. Then I get credit for the call."

"One minute," I said crisply. It would be my one good deed of the day.

The salesperson took a deep breath. "We at Lock, Stock, and Barrel Security Services guarantee that we can upgrade your existing security system, and offer you continued protection at half the cost of your current system, or you get a check from us for five hundred dollars for your trouble. Whose system are you currently using?"

"I'm not using any," I said triumphantly. "Will you be sending my check by registered mail?"

This time the party on the other end hung up.

3

"What do you mean Greg couldn't come?" Mama demanded, wiping her hands on a starched white apron dotted with eyelets.

To my knowledge Mama has never even flirted with Greg, but I would bet the Ming—if it were mine—that she has a crush on him. But an innocent crush, I'm sure, like the one I had on Ricky Nelson in the fifth grade. My mama would never step out of line, even in the privacy of her own mind.

"Greg called just before he was due to pick me up at six. There's been a double homicide in Myers Park. Apparently some banker went berserk."

"I thought that was the post office's job," Mama said, and held the door open for me. I was, after all, bearing gifts—a bottle of chardonnay and a pecan pie, both of which I had picked up at the new Hannaford's on Ebeneezer Road in Rock Hill.

I was born and raised in Rock Hill, South Carolina, which is just a stone's throw from Charlotte, North Carolina. Mama still lives there, on shady, dignified Eden Terrace. It is the same house I grew up in. Nothing has changed, not even the mint green drapes hanging desolately from the cornice. Although she would hotly deny it, Mama has kept the house as a shrine to Daddy, who died in a water-

16

skiing accident on nearby Lake Wylie seventeen years ago.

At four foot ten, Mama is only an inch taller than me, but we both have healthy appetites and managed to make a sizable dent in her delicious dinner. In fact, had Greg come there wouldn't have been enough artichoke salad for him. Mama claimed that the Harris Teeter where she shops was plum out except for the one jar.

"Then you should try Hannaford's," I said.

The corners of Mama's mouth twitched, which is as close to a grimace as a true southern lady is capable of making.

"I can't stand the traffic on Ebeneezer Road," she said. "Rock Hill is getting so big. It's growing by leaps and bounds."

"Growth is supposed to be good," I said, but I was obviously not an expert on the subject.

"New stores are popping up all the time."

"Like Hannaford's," I said.

Her mouth twitched. "Other stores, too. All kinds."

"Yeah."

Mama gave me a long, hard look. "Other stores, Abby, if you know what I mean."

I didn't and said so.

"Are you sure?"

"I'm sure. Would you like to split another piece of pie?"

Mama shook her head and sighed deeply. Her fingers drifted absentmindedly up to her pearls, a gift from my father.

"I'm glad we have this chance to talk alone, dear. There's something I've been wanting to tell you."

She had me spooked. "Mama, it's not *cancer*, is it?"

"Oh no, nothing like that." She sighed again. "I'm just not sure it's something I should tell you. You might think less of me."

I patted her arm. "You can tell me anything, Mama."

Mama leaned toward me. "I'm going to finally get one."

I had no idea what she meant. It could have been anything from a pet parakeet to a jogging machine. Didn't both of those things come in avocado green? No, it had to be more personal than that, like maybe an electric razor or one of those depilatory kits.

"You're going to have to be more specific," I said gently.

Mama's face turned the color of pickled ginger. "I'm going to get a tattoo."

"*What*?"

"Don't ask me why, but I've always wanted a tattoo, Abby. Ever since I was a little girl."

"Why?" I wailed.

"Because I'm seventy-five years old, and I want to have a tattoo before I die, that's why."

"You just turned seventy, Mama." My mother is one of six women in this world who actually pad their ages, rather than shave a few years off. That way they are always complimented on their relative states of preservation, rather than given sympathetic looks. In Mama's case, however, this ruse is totally unwarranted, since Mama looks young enough to be my sister, and I must habitually maintain an artificial gray streak in my chestnut brown hair so as not to be mistaken for a teenager.

I stared at her. Her color was back to normal, and she appeared surprisingly composed. Too composed. Mama is a Monroe, and her chin was set in that peculiar Monroe position that could only mean one thing—she was hunkering down to be stubborn.

"Well, I don't see what this has to do with me."

"I want you to go with me. You know, in case I'm too uncomfortable to drive myself home."

"Can't one of your friends go with you?"

Mama gave me a horrified look. "Gracious, no! They must never find out. Promise me you won't tell them, Abby."

"I promise." Of course I meant it. Far be it from me to start rumors that my mother was fast slipping into her dotage.

"Good. I'd just die if they found out."

Something terrible occurred to me. Mama's friends have eagle eyes to go with their rabbit ears. They were going to see the bloody thing unless . . .

"Mama, *where* are you getting this tattoo?"

"Tiny Tim's Tattoo Palace. It's that new place on Cherry Road I was trying to tell you about."

"Not where in Rock Hill," I practically screamed. "Where on your body?"

She looked away and mumbled something.

"What?"

She turned reluctantly to face me. "Okay, if you must know, I was thinking of getting it where the sun doesn't shine. After all, I still swim when we go to Pawleys Island. It has to be someplace it doesn't show."

I stared at her, seeing a stranger. "What if the tattoo artist is a man?"

She sighed. "That's why I really need you to go with me, Abby."

"Let me get this straight, Mama. You want me to go with you to some sleazy tattoo shop to safeguard your virtue?"

Mercifully the phone rang.

Mama answered it in the kitchen and was back a minute later to get me. "It's Greg, for you," she said. "Just think about it, dear."

The double homicide in Myers Park had not taken as long as expected to deal with. It turned out that the berserk banker was bogus—there were bodies all right, but they belonged to two store mannequins

that someone had dumped in the front yard of a
banker's house. Probably just a teenage prank.
Would it be okay with me if he dropped by my
house for a nightcap when I got home?

I said it was. Don't get me wrong. I am not sex
crazed like my mama. Greg and I have been dating
less than a year, and we're building on our relationship slowly. I am not about to just jump into bed
with a man because I feel lonely now and again.

Once was enough. I got married right out of college to a snake named Buford Timberlake. I met him
on the water slide of an area amusement park just
days after I broke with my college sweetheart Del-
bert Dewimple. I suppose that I was your classic re-
bound case, whereas Buford no doubt was just
horny. At any rate Buford had just finished his first
year of law school, and he had the same glib tongue
then that he has now. By that I mean he could talk
a politician into telling the truth—even a Republi-
can.

I found myself walking down the aisle with Buford in less time than it took to go down the water
slide. Unfortunately our sex life was like that, too.
On the plus side, it did produce two lovely children:
Susan, now twenty and in college, and eighteen-
year-old Charlie, who is a senior in high school.
Susan lives in a dorm; Charlie lives with Buford and
his new wife, Tweetie.

As for me, I live in a newly acquired house in
south Charlotte, alone, except for the company of my
yellow tomcat, Dmitri. All in all, I am very happy
living alone. Of course I miss the children, and there
are times it would be nice to have a man around,
but I don't need a man in my life, as I did on that
water slide.

Greg was waiting for me in the double carport. I
pulled up beside him, got out, and we kissed hello.
I was, of course, standing on my tiptoes. Greg is six

feet tall, and I'm afraid that one of these days he's going to wrench his back bending down so far.

"You missed a great dinner," I said.

"I'm sure I did, so I brought this." He held up a bottle of Bailey's Irish Creme whiskey, my favorite after dinner drink. "To help me forget the taste of that burger I had. McDonald's is trying to market a new flavor."

We went inside to the den—as we call our family rooms in these parts—and Greg poured us each a drink. We took off our shoes and settled onto my oversize Federal Period sofa, me with my legs across his lap. Incidentally the sofa isn't nearly as comfortable as it is attractive, but since I wear high heels regularly, who am I to complain?

"Tell me about your evening," Greg said, just as comfortably as if we were happily married.

Despite a fairly active sex life, Buford and I were never as intimate as that.

"Well, Mama—no, you go first this time. Tell me all about the bogus bodies on the banker's lawn."

Greg took a sip of Bailey's and licked his lips appreciatively. "First let me tell you about a real body."

"Do tell." Because of his line of work, Greg has some fascinating stories.

"I just saw the lab report on the Troyan woman. You were right, Abigail. She was hit by a blue vehicle."

I sat up quickly and almost knocked the glass out of Greg's hand. "A van?"

He chuckled. "I can't tell that from just the paint. I'm not Columbo. But I can tell you a little bit about Ms. Troyan."

"Please do." You might think that my interest was macabre, but just you wait until a body comes hurtling through your window. Then you'll whistle a different tune.

"For starters, her full name was June Gibbons Troyan. She was originally from Indiana, but lived in Lake City, Florida, until two years ago. Moved here shortly after the death of her husband. Mr. Troyan died of natural causes. Some kind of heart trouble."

I had heard the story before—similar stories really, but all pretty much interchangeable. Couple moves to Florida, lives there for several years, and then one of them—usually the husband—dies. What then is the survivor supposed to do? Move back north after burning all her bridges, or hang on in a community of transplants, where memories of her loved one linger? In a surprising number of cases the survivor decides to relocate elsewhere in the South, usually in the Carolinas. Perhaps our slower pace reminds them of the good old days, but I like to think they find a sense of community here that helps them through their grief.

"Anything else?"

"Ms. Troyan was no spring chicken."

I was not especially surprised. I had not taken a close look at June Troyan while she was alive, and as for after— Well, going through plate glass does nothing for one's complexion.

"How old?"

"Seventy-eight."

"Is that all you have?"

He laughed. "Is this an interrogation?"

"Just curious, dear."

"Well, she was volunteering part-time as a docent at Roselawn Plantation. You know, giving guided tours and that kind of thing."

I swung my legs off Greg's lap. This was the most interesting piece of information, one that needed to be considered in a normal sitting position.

Roselawn is an antebellum plantation that is just a Yankee hoot and a Rebel holler from Rock Hill. In the days before the Civil War—Mama and her generation call it The War Between the States—Roselawn was one of the premier cotton-producing plantations in the state. It supported hundreds of slaves—rather, they supported it.

The plantation house, which still stands, is atypical of upcountry plantation houses in that its style is Greek Revival, with a Tuscan portico and cast iron balustraded decks. It would be more at home in Natchez, Mississippi, than in York County, South Carolina. The mansion escaped the ravages of Sherman's army in The War of Northern Aggression (as my friend Wynnell calls it) only because it occupies a narrow spit of land on a hairpin turn in the Catawba River. The Yankees simply did not know it was there.

James L. Rose VI, a widower and the last descendant of the original owners, died only last year. According to the newspapers, the entire estate was sold off to pay back taxes. Farmers bought most of the fertile river bottom land, and the house ended up in the hands of a private historical group that calls itself the Upstate Preservation Foundation.

I was pretty sure Mama knew at least one person on the foundation, since Mama knows everyone of any consequence in Rock Hill. And I mean that humbly. Through no effort of my own I am well connected, and am usually privy to all the important gossip. But it was news to me that Roselawn Plantation was now open to the public and had, in fact, docents.

"How long did Ms. Troyan work there?" I asked.

Greg took a small piece of paper out of his pocket and unfolded it. "I knew you were going to ask tough questions. Let's see—just three weeks. They've only been open to the public that long."

It was time to resume my subscription to *The Herald*, Rock Hill's newspaper. I had let it lapse because of the way its book editor treated local authors. But it was clear now that Mama was no longer a reliable conduit of hometown information. The time had come to sacrifice principle for knowledge.

"Hmm, let's see," I mused, no doubt running my fingers through my short dark hair. "Ms. Troyan had only lived in the area for two years, correct?"

"Correct."

"And already she was volunteering as a docent at a privately owned historical foundation. That can only mean one thing."

"What?" Greg is both handsome and smart, but he's not brilliant.

"She had—"

"Money?"

"To the contrary. She might well have been dirt poor."

"I don't think so."

"That's because you don't know life in a small southern town."

Greg was born and raised in Atlanta, and had spent all his adult life in Charlotte. Both places are booming metropolises as far as I'm concerned. Thanks to the recent rust belt invasion, Rock Hill may now be pushing fifty thousand people, but it is essentially a small town at heart.

Greg crossed his long legs at the knee. "Enlighten me."

"I'm talking about position, dear. Breeding. Dollars to doughnuts Ms. Troyan has a lineage that would make a Daughter of the Confederacy turn green with envy."

He chuckled. "I don't think so. Not in this case. She was originally from Indiana, remember? Fort Wayne, to be exact."

"Her parents, then, or grandparents. In Rock Hill it's not what you have, but who you know. And believe me, Ms. Troyan had some connection to someone on the Upstate Preservation Foundation."

He had the temerity to laugh. "Maybe, but I still say it's money. Off the record, Abby, this old gal was loaded. She and her husband owned FarmTec Incorporated, the largest manufacturer of combines and tractors in the Midwest."

I gasped. "Oh! Then she could easily have afforded that Ming."

"What mink? She was wearing a rather plain brown dress."

"Did I say 'mink'?" I asked with all the innocence of a babe.

The Wedgwood blue eyes locked on mine. "Out with it, Abby."

I took my foot out of my mouth. Fortunately it is only a size four, and I've had a lot of practice. Besides, I was going to tell him anyway—sooner or later.

Greg remained remarkably calm during my brief account of the day's highlight, but as soon as I was finished, he exploded like a badly made firecracker. After a few minutes of banging and popping he settled down to a sporadic sizzle and became relatively coherent.

"Damn it, Abby! Goddamn it to hell. Withholding information is an obstruction of justice. You could get in big trouble for this. You know that, don't you?"

My heart was pounding. I hadn't meant to obstruct justice, and I certainly hadn't meant to tick Greg off. All I had wanted was a little time to appreciate the Ming that had magically appeared in my shop.

"We don't know that the Ming was hers," I said quietly.

"But you said you saw her carry it into your shop."

I swallowed. "I said I saw her carry an ugly gray

vase into the shop. The Ming is definitely neither ugly nor gray. So we can't be entirely, one hundred percent sure it's the same vase, can we?"

Greg rolled his eyes in exasperation. It was the first time I had seen the Wedgwood blues put to such poor use.

"Where is the damn thing now?"

I jumped up hotly. "I didn't sell the damn thing, for Pete's sake, if that's what you're driving at. You want it? You've got it. Just follow me—in your own damn car!"

I snatched my key ring off the hook by the front door, but purposefully left my purse behind. If Greg wanted to ticket me for speeding and not having a driver's license on my person, so be it. But if that was the case, he could count on never having one of Mama's home-cooked dinners again. Or anything from me.

4

Greg didn't follow me. He took a different route altogether, and he must have done some pretty fast driving himself, because he was waiting in front of the shop when I arrived. His time behind the wheel must have been therapeutic for him—he was actually smiling when I got out of my car.

"Hey, maybe I came off sounding a little angry back there," he said, reaching for my hand.

"You were obnoxious."

He withdrew his hand. "You got the keys?"

I glared at him, which was, alas, a wasted action because my face was in the shadows. "I am not a total idiot," I said, and fumbled for the right key.

We both stomped our way back to the back of the shop. Of course Greg can stomp harder than I can, but I made up for it with my loud, drawn-out sighs of disgust.

"There, you see"—I pointed to the table behind the counter—"there's your precious Ming. You happy now?"

"Hell no," he said childishly. "I don't see anything but some damn papers."

That was it. I had lost all patience. I marched around the counter.

"Here—" I started to point, but my hand dropped

27

to my side in horror. The Ming was missing. There was nothing on the table but a stack of bills.

"Damn you, Abby, is this some kind of a game?"

My mouth opened and closed rhythmically, like a baby bird begging for its supper. Unlike the baby bird, I was mute.

"I don't have time for this," Greg said, and turned.

I found my voice. It was a couple of octaves higher than where I'd left it.

"The Ming was here, Greg! I swear!"

He turned halfway around. I could see that his hands were balled into fists, pressed up against his chest. Greg has never hit me. He has never even punched a pillow in my presence. But I must have driven him perilously close to the edge.

"This is a serious matter, Abby," he said in measured tones. "You can't be leading me on."

"I know it's serious," I cried, "and I'm not leading you on. The vase was right here when I locked up this evening. I looked at it—touched it even—just before I left."

I knew he believed me when I saw his posture change. His shoulders, which had been rigid, relaxed and his hands came down to his side. He faced me.

"Who else has a key?"

"Lots of people," I confessed.

"What do you mean by 'lots'?" he asked calmly.

I could feel the tears welling up in my eyes. They were hot. No doubt they would scald my cheeks when they rolled down, scarring me for life. I was so stupid I deserved such a fate.

I looked away. He was just a blur anyway.

"I lose keys easily. You know that. That's why I keep them on a ring by the front door. But sometimes I still lose them. So I keep extra car keys hidden under the hood of my car, and my friends all have house keys."

"And your shop keys?"

"Just Wynnell, C.J., and the Rob-Bobs."

I hung my head in shame, and the tears began dropping on my shoes. They weren't that hot after all.

Greg, bless his soul, walked over and put his arms around me. I fully expected him to apologize for having yelled at me, but he didn't. Which meant he was still mad. That's true love, if you ask me—being able to comfort someone when you're mad as hell at them.

"Tomorrow you talk to them. Find out if any of them—for any reason—might have borrowed your Ming."

My tap shuts off easily. "My Ming! You mean I can keep it? I mean, if we find it?"

"Not very likely," he said, and kissed the top of my head.

But he didn't apologize. Not that night at any rate.

I approached the Rob-Bobs first, of course. After all, they were the only ones beside Mama and Greg who knew about the Ming.

"*Mais non!*" Bob boomed. He sometimes resorts to French when he's highly offended.

"Abby, Abby, Abby," Rob said, and I felt as if a cock had crowed three times.

"Not that I thought y'all had," I said, beating a hasty retreat.

It was still ten minutes until nine, so I wandered over to Wynnell's shop, Wooden Wonders. Wynnell and I met in the business, and we have only been friends for a couple of years, but I like to think of her as the older sister I never had. I do have a brother—Toy Wiggins—but he lives in California, where he works hard to look like he's playing. Last we heard he was parking cars at Planet Hollywood at night, and patrolling the streets of Malibu by day, in both cases hoping to pick up a starlet.

We shop owners are generally very busy in the minutes just prior to opening—straightening stock and such—so Wynnell was both pleased and surprised to see me.

"Is something wrong?" she asked, pulling me into the shop and locking the door behind me.

I nodded. There was no need to tell Wynnell that the homemade outfit she was wearing had given me a sudden fit of nausea. I had never seen such a conglomeration of patterns and colors—even Joseph's coat of many colors would have paled by comparison. Don't get me wrong. I am not putting down those less fortunate than myself. Wynnell can well afford to buy store-bought clothes—even the best—but suffers from the delusion that she is both a seamstress and a designer. Picasso might have agreed.

"Are you sure you're all right?"

"*I'm* fine," I wailed. "It's the Ming!"

Wynnell's shrub-size eyebrows fused in confusion. "What's amazing?"

"Not amazing—a Ming! A genuine fifteenth-century Ch'eng-hua period Ming vase. A *tou ts'ai!*"

The eyebrows remained fused. "You aren't making a lick of sense, honey! Are you sure you're all right?"

I spit out my tale of woe. Wynnell has a face that law enforcement departments should copy and patent if they really want a foolproof lie detector. It was clear that I couldn't have stabbed her any worse had my words been pitchforks and her heart a block of warm butter.

"So you think that I might have taken it?"

"Of course not!"

"Then why are you here, Abigail?"

"Well, uh—I—"

She glanced at her watch. "It's almost opening time, and I still have work to do."

"Wynnell, I'm sorry, I really am! I don't know what got over me. Panic, I guess. I'll do anything to make it up to you. Please, Wynnell, forgive me."

What began as a bushy-browed glare dissolved into a warm, slightly gap-toothed smile. "Help me do inventory next month?"

"Do we have to move those around?" I gestured at the jumble of heavy dressers, beds, and armoires that make up the bulk of the merchandise that packs Wooden Wonders.

"You bet you do."

"Deal," I said, and gave her a quick hug.

"You speak to C.J. yet?" she asked sensibly. C.J. was the youngest of Greg's suspects and the most likely to borrow something without permission.

"Unh-unh. What if she doesn't have it?" I wailed.

"Don't worry, she'll have it," my pseudosister said, and patted me encouragingly on the back.

"But if she doesn't?"

Wynnell scowled, hopelessly snarling her brows, I'm sure. "Then it's the Yankees. I saw this TV documentary about a band of roving thieves—"

"I saw that same show, Wynnell, and the thieves were from South Carolina. Besides, my shop was locked when we arrived last night. What thief is going to break in, and then lock the shop behind him?"

Wynnell shrugged, unconvinced. The dear woman spots a Yankee behind every bush. If she had her way, the North Carolina Highway Department would erect barriers at the state's northern border and screen all motorists. Perhaps make them say their vowels.

"Well, I don't think it was stolen," I said. "Just borrowed. I'm sure you're right, though—C.J. must have it."

Wynnell patted me again. "She has it, honey. But good luck all the same."

*   *   *

C.J. said she didn't have it.

"Are you sure?" I asked. "I mean—if you did, it's all right. Just give it back. No more questions asked."

At twenty-three, C.J. is the youngest, and incidentally newest, dealer on this street. She's just a kid, really, a fact that I often overlook, because she is so precocious. After all the tears I'd shed, I certainly had no intention of making her cry.

"There, there," I said, patting her back awkwardly. I am no Wynnell.

"How can you blame me, Abigail, after all I've done for you?"

"I didn't blame you," I said, patting harder.

And I hadn't. I had only intimated that she might have the vase. Whereas she had concluded that I thought her a criminal, just one cell away from death row. This was pure C.J.

Jane Cox is her real name, but we call her Calamity Jane behind her back—hence the initials. She thinks—at least we all hope so—that we have bestowed upon her a fond nickname, using her reversed initials. No doubt she is unaware that she jumps to conclusions faster than a cat leaps from a red-hot stove. But she not only jumps to conclusions, she runs with them. To the extreme.

"As long as no one trusts me, I should turn to a life of crime," she said, still weeping.

"I trust you, dear," I said, patting even harder.

"Folks didn't trust my cousin Erval, either."

"You're not your cousin."

She looked down at me with red-rimmed eyes. "Erval wasn't really my cousin, just an orphan boy my church took in. But we were as close as twins, Abigail. Anyway, one day when we were about ten, a dollar bill got stolen off the offering plate at church.

"Deacon Cauldwell swore he'd seen Erval take it.

Miss Emma put it in, and by the time it got to Miss Cory, the dollar was gone. Erval was the only non-tithing suspect sitting between the two of them.

"What can a ten-year-old say to an accusation like that, Abigail?"

I stopped patting long enough to shrug.

"Well, there was nothing for Erval to say. The next thing we knew, Erval took off—left Shelby plum behind, and headed up over the mountains. Nobody heard from him again." She took a deep, much-needed breath.

"Until four years had passed. And then there it was—right there in the *Shelby Gazette*. Erval Snicker had been arrested for murder in Tennessee! Not just one person, but three. The youngest mass murderer in the state's history—and all because Deacon Cauldwell accused him of stealing a dollar he didn't take."

I stopped patting altogether. "I didn't accuse you of anything, dear. I'm terribly sorry I even brought the matter up. Please forgive me."

C.J. rubbed the tears from her eyes with fists twice as big as mine. "I might not have stopped at just three," she said. "Seventeen is my lucky number."

I apologized again and scooted back to my shop lickety-split. In the future I would be careful to stay on C.J.'s good side.

Greg called around ten. "Any word on the Ming?"

"No. They all swear they haven't taken it. In fact, I may have made a few enemies."

"Is there anyone else who might possibly have a key?"

His tone was so formal, it nearly broke my heart. And all because I wanted to fantasize that some stupid vase was mine. How could I have let my daydreams get in the way of common sense? Who knows; if the damn thing had been an Etruscan urn of exceptional beauty, I might have sold out my children.

"No one, Greg."

"Not even your mother?"

"Mama's time warp doesn't go back past Victorian, and she's not into Oriental."

"But does she have a key?"

"I don't remember. I'll ask her."

"Do that," he said, and hung up. Just like that. No good-bye, no lip smacks. Nothing but a dial tone.

5

Mama picked up on the first ring. "My nose was twitching," she said smugly.

My mother claims her proboscis is capable of smelling the future. There have been enough coincidences for me to keep an open mind, although I won't be totally convinced until she takes her shnoz to Vegas and comes back a millionaire.

I asked her about the key.

"You gave me a key once, Abigail, but for the life of me I wouldn't know where to lay my fingers on it now. It may be in my box at the bank. You did say it was in case of an emergency—in case something happened to you. Are you all right, dear?"

"I'm fine, Mama."

"It isn't cancer, is it, dear?"

"No, Mama. There's just been a little mix-up, and a rather valuable Ming vase seems to be missing."

"Is that the vase you were telling me about at supper, dear?"

"Yes, Mama. You didn't borrow it, did you?"

There was a stunned silence.

I should have slapped myself, asking my own mama a question like that. After all, I had just offended three friends, and all but alienated the fourth with the same question, and none of them had suf-

35

fered through thirty-four hours of painful labor on my behalf.

"Mama, I'm sorry," I said quickly, "I shouldn't even have asked."

More silence, but I could hear her pearls clicking against the receiver, which meant she was angry but had at least come out of shock.

"It's just that I'm in big trouble, Mama. That Ming may have belonged to June Troyan, the woman who was killed by that hit-and-run driver yesterday."

The pearls stopped clicking. "June Troyan?"

"Yes, Mama. Did you know her?"

"Of course I knew her. Why didn't you tell me her name last night?" Mama was back to normal.

"I didn't know anything about her last night. Did she live in Rock Hill?"

"She lived in Tega Cay," Mama said, referring to a lakeside community about fifteen minutes north of town, "but she was a member of the Apathia Club."

Apathia is a social club to which Mama tried for years to gain entree, but when she was finally admitted, she had turned the gals down. It was her way of snubbing them back. But Mama still saw many of the members on a weekly, if not daily basis. They all lived in her neighborhood, shopped the same stores, and attended the same cluster of churches. A few of them were even in her bridge club. In Rock Hill politeness is a given, and dirty laundry is never aired in public. Back stabbing is relegated to the privacy of one's home, and then only shared with one's closest friends or spouse. A voodoo doll vendor could make a killing in my hometown.

"Did you know she was a docent at Roselawn Plantation?"

"Yes, I guess I did."

"So you knew that Roselawn was already open to the public?"

"Of course, dear, everyone in Rock Hill knows that. You really should move back to town, Abby. Then you'd know everything that's going on. You could have your old room back."

"Thanks, Mama, but I have my own house now, remember?" I tried not to sound as sarcastic as my own kids, but for a brief moment I empathized with them.

"I saved all your stuffed toys, Abby. They're in the attic, all sealed in airtight bags. Next to your prom dresses."

"Mama, do you know anyone at the Upstate Preservation Foundation?"

A sudden, furious clicking told me my question had offended Mama. She probably not only knew them, but had undoubtedly turned down invitations to their homes.

"If I wanted to become a docent, Mama, who would I speak to?"

The clicking slowed.

"I'm serious, Mama."

It stopped.

"Okay, Mama, so I want to snoop around a little. I won't get into any trouble or make a pest of myself. I promise."

"What do you hope to find, dear?"

"I don't know. More about June Troyan, I guess. Maybe I'll learn something from the other docents. Roselawn Plantation is the only clue I have."

"That's only part of it, isn't it?"

"Excuse me, Mama?"

"You're miffed, aren't you? Your feelings are hurt because you're a Rock Hill native and an expert on antiques, and yet no one from the foundation even as much as asked for your advice."

"Mama!"

"Admit it, dear. And believe me, I understand totally. Imagine the Apathia Club taking all those years to invite me to join, when our ancestors were among the very first settlers in Rock Hill."

"Okay, so I'm unhappy that the place is already open for business and I didn't even hear about it. Just tell me who's in charge, Mama."

"I forget," Mama said, but I knew she was lying. It was a mother's lie of protection, however, which is almost always justified.

"They could at least make me a docent," I said doggedly. "Even an honorary one."

"It would have to be an honorary position," Mama said, "because your shop is a full-time job, Abby. I hardly get to see you as it is."

"I could help out part-time, Mama. Is it open in the evenings?"

"I'm pretty sure it is not. But I could ask."

I smelled a favor in the asking.

"In exchange for what, Mama?"

"You know quite well, dear. Tiny Tim's Tattoo Palace on Cherry Road."

It was another incredibly busy day at the shop. I hate to have to say this, but the hit and run was definitely good for business. Although the day had started out sunny, it was drizzling by noon. Still, the customers continued to pour into my shop.

The *Observer* had carried a rather graphic description of the incident, and a number of folks wanted to know the exact spot where June's body had come to rest. I had, of course, removed the Louis XIV chair that June had inadvertently dismantled, but the rest of the display remained the same—that is, until I discovered that the items in the immediate vicinity sold like hotcakes. Thanks to a ghoulish public and my own lack of good taste, I spent the bulk of the day hauling merchandise over to the window display area. The rest of my day was spent at the cash register.

I even went so far as to unplug my phone—a first in my shop's history—but not soon enough.

"Hello," I said breathlessly, having just returned from the window display. "Den of Iniquity here—I mean, Antiquity!"

"It's me."

It was a familiar voice, but I couldn't place it. "Me who?" I asked politely.

"You don't need to know who I am. But I know who you are."

"Ah, you're the Lock, Stock, and Barrel person," I said. "I recognize your voice."

"You do not!"

"You bet I do, dear. Androgynous, muffled—what's not to recognize?"

There was a long silence, but no sound of pearls clicking, so I knew it wasn't Mama. "I want my Ming," the caller said at last.

"Excuse me?" I felt my heart drop down into my stomach. If it wasn't for my small pelvis, it might have hit the floor.

"You heard me. I said, 'I want my Ming.' Do you want me to spell it for you?"

I took a couple of deep, cleansing breaths, courtesy of Lamaze. "Describe it."

"The same vase Ms. Troyan carried into your shop the day before yesterday."

It is times like this I could kick myself for not subscribing to the caller ID service my phone company offers. I should, at the very least, keep a cassette recorder by the phone, and record these kinds of calls. By replaying them when I am not so stressed, I might be better able to pick up on clues. Not that I get many mysteriously ominous phone calls, mind you.

"I don't have your stupid vase," I said loudly, my dander rising. Fear and anger are the flip sides of the same coin, and in my case the coin was spinning like a whirling dervish.

There was a muffled gasp. "What did you do with it?"

"I didn't do a damn thing with it, because I don't know what the hell you're talking about."

"Listen," the voice growled, "if I don't get my vase back, the same thing that happened to Ms. Troyan might happen to you."

"So you're the hit-and-run driver," I said stupidly.

Androgynous hung up.

I hung up as well, but was still staring stupidly at the damn machine when it rang again. I snatched up the receiver, angrier than the day Buford announced he was trading in my forty-plus years for Tweetie's forty-plus bosom.

"Your calls have been traced," I spat. "No doubt the police are right outside your door, waiting to pounce on you."

"Mama?"

"Charlie!"

"Mama, I didn't make all those 900 calls. Phil made at least half of them. Derek made some, too."

"Charlie—"

"Mama, please don't tell Daddy. I promise I'll never make them again, and I won't let the guys make them, either. I'll even help you out at the shop this weekend, but please don't tell Daddy."

"Charlie, dear, he'll see them on the phone bill."

"He will?"

I consider myself to be reasonably intelligent, and my kids more so. But why it is my kids just assume they can get away with their many misdemeanors is beyond me. Surely they know about such things as phone and credit card bills, and that the school does call and report their absences. I like to think that they have always gotten caught. Still, I shudder to think of the possibility that they might, in fact, be getting away with oodles of things—so many things that the few times I catch them misbehaving aren't even worth remembering.

"Charlie, dear, the best thing you can do is to tell your daddy right away. Tell him before the phone bill comes. You'll save yourself a whole lot of grief."

I could hear Charlie gulp. "But I can't, Mama. He's already pissed at me."

There were three customers lined up at the counter, waiting to buy. One was actually waving a fistful of money. I recognized the man, fat but well-groomed, always a big spender. What was a mother to do?

"Why is Daddy angry?" I asked.

"Because I don't want to be his clone, that's why!" Ironically when Charlie is angry he sounds just like his father.

I glanced at the man waving the money. In his other hand he was holding a sixteenth-century Castelli painted porcelain box with a lid. One slip of his pudgy middle finger and the lid would shatter on the counter, along with the box's value.

"You're not his clone, dear. You are your own person," I said as patiently as I could. "You're free to be whoever you want."

"So I don't have to be a lawyer like Daddy, do I?"

I bit my tongue. Buford is the prototype lawyer of all the lawyer jokes. I should have checked him for a dorsal fin when we were on that water slide. That Charlie wouldn't become a lawyer like his daddy was my daily prayer.

"You want my money or not?" the cash customer called.

I nodded and gave him a little wave. "You had talked about becoming a teacher," I said to Charlie. "Winthrop has a good education program. You could stay with Grandma."

"Uh—I don't think so," Charlie said.

"No, of course not. You should experience dorm life. I'll talk to your father tonight."

"Mama, I don't want to go to Winthrop."

"Where then?"

"I don't want to go to college at all."

There were now five people lined up at the counter, and the boor in front was now waving the box instead of his money.

"What do you mean you don't want to go to college? Charlie, in today's world a college degree is a must. It's like high school used to be."

"Mama, you don't need a college degree to be a vacuum cleaner repairman."

"What?"

"That's what Derek's going to do. He says there's big bucks in it. Everyone has to vacuum, right? And with the economy like it is, people are going to want to hang on to their old vacuum cleaners longer. Right? Derek figures that we can make eight dollars an hour easy. Maybe more if we move to a really big city like Atlanta."

The fat-fingered, cash-carrying customer said it was my scream that made him drop the porcelain box along with its lid. Since I do have a "You broke it, you bought it" sign prominently displayed, he had no legal recourse but to pay. I did agree to meet him halfway, which paid for my cost. Nonetheless, I lost a customer forever.

6

It had been a long, hard day. I had managed to strain all my important relationships and lose a good customer, and now my only son was eschewing college in order to overhaul Hoovers. I would have to resort to drastic measures if I was to avoid a plunge into a virtual slough of despondency.

I locked up early, treated myself to a supper of chicken cordon bleu, took a relaxing soak in a gardenia-scented bubble bath, and settled down to watch a taped episode of my favorite sitcom, "The Nanny," with Dmitri purring contentedly in my lap. Life, if not redeemed, was at least manageable.

Lord only knows why I answered the phone when it rang.

"Yes?" I said, somewhat tersely.

"This is your mama!" When it comes to terseness Mama can give tit for tat.

"Sorry, Mama," I said quickly. "What is it?"

"You know our little agreement, Abby?"

"Mama, I haven't yet agreed to go with you to Tiny Tim's Tattoo Palace."

"Nonsense, Abby, you all but promised. Anyway, I want you to know that I have already lived up to my half of the bargain."

"Oh?"

"I found out what you wanted to know, dear."

"Oh?"

"It turns out that Anne Holliday, who is a member of my bridge club, is also on the board of directors of the Upstate Preservation Foundation. She filled me in."

"Oh?" Dmitri had stood up and was beating me around the face with his tail.

"Is that all you can say, Abby?"

I spit out a mouthful of fur. "What exactly did you find out?"

"Why, how to become a docent, of course. That's what you asked."

"And how do I become a docent, Mama?"

"By showing up at meeting room number one at the Rock Hill Library."

"When?"

"Tonight at eight," Mama said with just a hint of mirth in her voice.

I glanced at the clock above the TV. It was seven-thirty on the dot.

Under the best of conditions, it takes me forty minutes to get from my house to Mama's down in Rock Hill. The library is five minutes farther. Usually when I drive that route I am fully dressed, not lounging about in flannel pajamas with wet hair and a face scrubbed as clean as one of my mama's copper pots.

It took me half an hour just to get presentable, so I hope you understand why it is that I barreled down I-77 at more than ten miles over the speed limit, passing all the cars going my way except for that unmarked state trooper's car just past the border in South Carolina.

"Where's the fire?" Smoky asked.

I thought it would be clever to answer a cliché with a cliché. "My wife's having a baby, officer. Would you escort me to the hospital?"

Officer Belinda Daniels was not amused.

"My boyfriend is Investigator Greg Washburn," I

said desperately. "He's with the Charlotte Police Department, Division of Homicide."

Officer Daniels was even less amused. She vehemently assured me that she was not in cahoots with the CPD or any other police department. When she had made that perfectly clear, she laboriously wrote out the longest traffic citation I had ever seen (not that I've seen that many, mind you). Another lecture followed.

So it was that a thoroughly chastised Abigail Timberlake showed up at meeting room number one a full hour late. I may even have perspired a little. The door was tightly closed, and I knocked timidly.

"Come in," a muffled voice said.

I opened the door slowly and stepped in as gracefully as I could. Believe me, I could not have been scrutinized more intensely had I been strolling down the runway at the Miss Universe pageant.

There were five people sitting at a round table in the room, four women and one man.

"Yes?" the man said. His eyes in particular were giving me the once-over. In the short time it took me to respond, I could feel him undress me, reject me, and dress me again.

"My name is Abigail Timberlake. I am a native of Rock Hill. My mother is Mozella Gaye Wiggins. I believe she spoke to one of you about the possibility of me becoming a docent."

They looked at one another accusingly. Finally one of them, a little old lady who looked like the Queen Mum, waved perfunctorily.

"That might have been me," she said in a high, girlish voice. Apparently the Queen Mum and Anne Holliday were one and the same.

The man, who was seated next to her, raised his eyebrows. "Well, it's a moot point, isn't it? That part of our meeting has been concluded."

The Queen Mum turned to the neighbor on her

right. "Well, Madame Chairman," she chirped, "it's your call. I was only doing Mozella a favor."

Her neighbor considered this, and I considered her neighbor. I knew the woman from somewhere. The newspaper, that was it. The *Herald* doesn't have a society page per se, but society does have a knack for finding its way into print, sometimes even as far as the *Charlotte Observer*. This woman's face had been reproduced in ink enough times to make it indelible. If only her name had stuck. Some kind of color perhaps.

But of course—Lilah Greene. *The* Lilah Greene. Miss Lilah, as she was known around Rock Hill. Quite possibly the oldest money in Rock Hill. Perfect manners, of course. Impeccable taste. Exquisitely groomed. Even as a child she must have stayed out of the sun; after threescore years the milk white skin was still seamless. Her silver hair was pulled back into a flawless chignon. Her lavender-blue silk suit complemented her eyes. The pearls in her choker were at least nine millimeters across, and were an exact match for the simple studs that graced her ears. Lilah Greene is the kind of woman who would make a social climber want to puke (not that I am one), except for the fact that she is exceedingly nice. A true lady in every sense of the word.

"Frankly none of the other candidates seemed quite suited," Miss Lilah said, musing aloud. "What do you think, Shirley?"

Dr. Shirley Hall, PhD, as I later found out, had recently retired from Winthrop University as a full professor of history. Supposedly she had a national reputation as an expert on the Civil War. She looked, however, more like my idea of a retired chef—sort of a cross between the Campbell's soup twins and the Pillsbury doughboy. Put a tall white hat atop her curly gray hair and tie a crisp white apron around her ample middle, and she would be all set to whip up a late supper for us. Her eyes, which were mere slits, managed to sparkle above her dumpling cheeks.

"Well, she is a native, after all," Shirley said in an accent that was anything but native. "She might lend sort of an authentic air."

"But the costumes wouldn't fit her," said the fourth woman present. "She's way too short. We'd have to have new ones made, and that simply is not in the budget."

Miss Lilah smiled at the last speaker. She was far too well-bred to chide the woman for speaking out of turn.

"Well, Gloria, you certainly have a point. But we might could squeeze a little extra out of petty cash, if we tried really hard." Please don't misunderstand. "Might could" is perfectly proper speech construct in Rock Hill.

Gloria glared at me. I tried to stare placidly back. It was difficult. Gloria Roach, I was to learn, had perfected that glare in the courtrooms of York County, where she practiced as a defense attorney. Gloria's glare aside, it was hard to look at the woman and not react somehow. She was heavily into bodybuilding and looked as much like Arnold Schwarzenegger as any woman I'd ever seen. Except for her face. Gloria Roach had an itty-bitty ferret face, replete with beady eyes and remarkably pointed teeth. Throw in the personality of a piranha, and she was a strange bird—to mangle a metaphor.

"What are your credentials besides being a native of Rock Hill and a friend of Miss Holliday?"

"Oh, she isn't my friend," the Queen Mum protested. "I merely play bridge with her mama."

I cleared my throat. "Well, I am an antique dealer—I own Den of Antiquity up in Charlotte. I'm not an expert yet, but I am learning. And I assume there are antiques in the Roselawn collection. Perhaps I could help you catalog them. Maybe even appraise them."

"There is nothing of substantial value at Roselawn," Anne Holliday—alias Her Majesty—said quickly. "I really don't think we need to have anything appraised."

Miss Lilah gave her an inquiring look, and then turned to the lone man.

"Red?"

He gave me a smarmy look. "If you have a shop up in Charlotte, how do you expect to volunteer down here?"

I met his smarm with what I hoped was a penetrating gaze. I had figured out who the skinny little bastard was. Red was a nickname because of his carrot-colored hair and the blizzard of freckles that nearly obliterated his features. His real name was Angus Barnes. When not undressing potential docents with his grass green eyes, he was busy as a beaver building Rock Hill. Half the new subdivisions around town were supposedly Red Barnes's developments. Mama's friend Mattie has a daughter who moved into a Red Barnes home that, like her marriage, began to crumble immediately. Still, Red has made millions from his business.

"I thought I might help out in the evenings and on my days off," I said coolly.

Red smirked. "We aren't open in the evenings, and I doubt if you get that many days off in your business. What we're really looking for is someone younger. Someone with more time on her hands."

"Like a buxom college girl?" I asked pointedly. Red had a reputation of using and then discarding young women, which is a polite way of saying he didn't use all his tools responsibly. Mattie's daughter was one of his victims.

"The best tour guides are attractive," he snapped.

"Zing," Shirley Hall said, and wet an index finger

on her tongue and pretended to mark the air.

Miss Lilah gave us all her Stern Look, a slight puckering between the eyebrows and a firmly closed mouth.

The others may have recoiled in fear, but, as yet, I had nothing to lose. "He's got a point about my time being limited, but I would like to contribute in some way. Even if there is nothing worth appraising in the mansion, you still need it cataloged, don't you? Suppose there was a fire? And anyway, if I'm just there at night making an inventory, I won't need a costume, will I?"

"But we have our own historian, dear," the Queen Mum said, and bestowed a gracious, albeit brief, smile on Shirley Hall.

It was Miss Lilah's turn to bestow a smile, and the unlucky recipient was Anne Holliday. The Queen Mum visibly shrank in her folding metal throne.

"Well, it's all settled then, isn't it?" Miss Lilah clasped her immaculate hands in a decisive gesture. "We can have the contents of Roselawn cataloged, and it won't cost us a penny, thanks to Mrs. Timberlake's generosity." The lavender eyes fixed calmly on me. "When can you start?"

"Anytime."

"I'll give you a call, then," she said, and I knew that I had been graciously dismissed.

I stopped at Mama's on the way home. Through her front window I could see the flicker of her television screen, but she turned it off when I rang the doorbell. Mama denies that she watches much television, eschewing the tube for books and little literary magazines. That night, for instance, she had *Dreaming in Color*, a book of short stories by Ruth Moose, on the end table beside her favorite wing chair. The book was actually open.

Mama answered the door fully dressed. Changing

into her nightgown is the last thing she does before falling asleep. Unless she dies in her sleep, Mama will be found dead someday in a dress with a full circle skirt puffed out by crinolines, high heels, and of course her ubiquitous pearls (I honestly have no idea what, if anything, she wears in the shower).

"Did you go, dear?" she asked needlessly.

I nodded.

"And?"

"Miss Lilah has agreed to let me catalog the contents of the mansion."

"But you won't be a docent?" The disappointment in her voice was clear. No doubt "my daughter the docent" had a better ring to it than "my daughter the cataloger."

"I don't really have the time, Mama. Anyway, I'll still be able to poke around a little, and I got to meet all the board members. Maybe I'll figure out a way to meet some of the docents."

"I could throw a party," Mama offered graciously.

I chewed on that. Mama can throw a party that would make Martha Stewart turn the color of limes. The year I turned sixteen, the debutante reception was held at our house. Mama outdid herself and made more enemies than Fidel Castro. Nobody likes a perfect hostess, and the reception that year created a mountain impossible for future hostesses to scale. Socially we would have been better off taking the group out to supper at Burger King. Maybe it was time Rock Hill got stood on its ear again.

"How many kinds of hors d'oeuvres?"

"A dozen," Mama said without a second's hesitation.

"Warm or cold?"

Mama rolled her eyes. "Warm, of course. There will be two dozen cold finger foods."

"Well, I'll certainly think about it, Mama. Thanks for the offer."

"The baked ham and roast beef for sandwiches don't count toward either."

"Thanks, Mama, but I said I'll think about it." I started for the door.

"You didn't tell me who all was there," Mama said accusingly. "Besides Anne Holliday, of course."

"Well, Lilah."

"Yes," Mama whispered reverently. "Lilah is the crème de la crème of Rock Hill. No, make that York County. The Upstate Preservation Foundation was her idea. Most of the worthy projects in the county are."

I told her the rest of the names, and she had something pointed or revealing to say about each person. Being Mama, all her comments are true—you could bet the cotton gin on that—but they weren't necessarily flattering.

"Gloria Roach beat her ex-husband to a pulp last year. Abby, did you know that?"

I hadn't, but unless Gloria's husband was Arnold Schwarzenegger, it wasn't hard to imagine. "Did he press charges? Was she indicted?"

"No, ma'am. Ed Roach mows grass and cuts down trees—when he's working. Gloria is his meal ticket." It was only a slight exaggeration. Roach Tree & Service was not a one-man operation. Its ad in the yellow pages took up a quarter page.

"I see. Why do you think she's on the board, Mama? Because she's a lawyer?"

"Undoubtedly. Old Mr. Rose died without a will, which in effect left the plantation to the state of Carolina—"

"Which it in turn sold off to collect back taxes," I said, proud of my knowledge.

Mama's look told me to climb down off my high horse. "So I'm sure you're aware then that Mercedes-Benz was hoping to acquire the property for their second Carolina factory."

"Uh, no."

"And they might have, except for Ms. Roach. But she found an old law that required the state to give preference to a historical foundation—even a private one—over a foreign company. She donated her legal services for free."

"Well, I'll be." I could respect the muscled shark, but I didn't have to like her. "And Red Barnes? What's he doing on the board?"

Mama shuddered. "That Red should keep his barn door shut. Mattie Markham is still traumatized by what happened to her daughter."

"Her daughter Phyllis Sue had an affair," I said. "She wasn't raped."

Mama gave me a glare worthy of Gloria Roach. "The only reason Red Barnes is on that board is because he has money. Ill-gotten, of course, but it's still green. Red Barnes figures he can bolster his social standing by flinging wads of money around. Did you know that Rock Hill Country Club won't let him join?"

I confessed that I didn't. "And I can guess why Shirley Hall is part of the team," I said.

Mama shuddered again. "That woman may be a history expert, but whose history is she an expert on? Did you know she calls it the Civil War?"

I shook my head sympathetically. "And your buddy Anne Holliday?"

Mama grimaced. "Please, Abby, she's not my buddy. Anne and I play bridge together, that's all. I hope you appreciate the call I made to her on your behalf to find out about tonight. The meeting date had already been advertised in the paper. Apparently they were looking to train more docents before that unfortunate incident in your shop on Tuesday. I felt like such a fool when she told me that."

"Thank you, Mama, but you haven't answered my question. Why is Anne Holliday on the board?"

Mama rolled her eyes for the second time that night, prompting me to ponder the possibility that she was on the threshold of her second childhood. When my daughter, Susan, was a little girl, she rolled her eyes so often that I actually took her to an ophthalmologist for fear that something was wrong. The diagnosis was, of course, simply that Susan thought I was stupid.

"Abby, don't you know any Rock Hill gossip?"

I knew some. I knew that the frizzy-headed blond author who lives in town supposedly spent Christmas Day with David Bowie on a Bali beach, watching a Hindu cremation.

"Do tell," I begged.

Mama took a deep breath. "Anne Holliday was Jimmy Rose's—mistress." If she had been holding the word, she would have held it at arm's length, like a dirty diaper.

"What?" I was honestly surprised. James L. Rose VI had to have been in his nineties when he died.

"You heard me, dear."

"Mistress," I said maliciously. "So she was his mistress."

Mama shook her head while her hand reached up to caress her pearls. I had succeeded in annoying her.

"So it's a courtesy position then, is it?"

Mama continued to caress her pearls in silence.

"But she looks like the Queen Mum," I said.

A smile tugged at the left corner of Mama's mouth.

7

I woke up flat on my back, with Dmitri on my chest. His right front paw was jammed between my lips. I pushed it away and spat. Dmitri thinks I was put on this earth to feed him, sift his litter, and scratch under his chin. He has learned that a surefire way of getting his chin scratched is to sit on me and pat my face. I like to think he tries to pat my chin and isn't a very good aim. While I love my cat dearly, a paw that's been pawing around in a litter box is not welcome in my mouth.

I was out of milk, so breakfast for me was a bowl of Cheerios with half-and-half. I'm one of those people who has to eat the second I wake up. I get the shakes unless I do. Some people have to have their caffeine; I have to have my carbs.

The jitters satiated, I was just stepping into the shower when the phone rang. A saner person would have let the machine pick up, but it was only six-thirty in the morning. It had to be Mama with bad news.

"Is it Charlie or Susan?" I demanded.

There was a long pause, which should have tipped me off. "The vase wasn't here, so where is it?"

Androgynous again. Maybe I should have hung up immediately. But Mama raised me to be a well-

54

mannered southern belle, one who answers when questions are asked.

"It's in the kitchen garbage," I said, "under the coffee grinds, but above the fish heads."

"Don't mess with me!"

"Exactly! I don't know where the damn Ming is, and if I did— Hey, what do you mean by it wasn't *here*? Where are you looking?"

The line went dead.

I sorrowfully surveyed the shambles that was my shop.

"He—she—whoever was calling from here," I said to Greg.

Greg had his arm resting on my shoulder, and he gave it a quick squeeze. It was at least a small comfort to know that his professionalism took second place to his feelings for me. Not that everything was hunky-dory between us again. He was still ticked, I'm sure, as was I, although we were undoubtedly angry on different levels. He was still mad about the Ming, and I was mad about him still being mad, which, at least in my frame of mind, made my anger a little more righteous.

"Did they say they were calling from here?"

I swallowed my irritation. "They didn't say the name of my shop, but they said 'here.' "

"We'll check the phone for prints," he said casually. Too casually.

I shrugged his arm off my shoulder. "They took the goddamn phone."

He had the audacity then to walk over to my little desk and check for himself. As if I might have accidentally misplaced a plugged-in phone. It might happen in movies, but I assure you it has never happened to Abigail Wiggins Timberlake.

Greg ran strong fingers through his head of thick brown black hair. "You're right, it's gone."

"No shit," I said. I don't usually swear, but under extreme stress I revert to patterns learned during all those years of living with Buford Timberlake. "Whoever it was realized they didn't have time to wipe off the prints, and just unplugged the goddamn thing."

"Are you sure—"

"Don't you dare ask me if I'm sure I even had a phone," I snapped.

"But there is no sign of breaking and entering, Abigail. Whoever took the phone and did this to your shop had to have a key."

"Don't start down that road, Greg. It wasn't Mama or my friends."

"Well, it had to be somebody."

"Exactly. And it's your job to find out who."

He raked his hair again, and I found it intensely annoying. "Can you give me a damage estimate?"

It was a fair question. Although my shop was in total disarray, remarkably nothing was broken except for one small Depression glass bowl that had apparently fallen off a shelf. I mentioned the bowl.

"Nothing else?"

"Maybe a few new scratches here and there. Nothing major, although it's going to take me all day to set things straight again. I told you, Greg, this isn't a case of vandalism. They want the Ming."

"Ah yes, the old Chinese vase that I have yet to see—even though there is a direct connection between it and the victim of a homicide I'm investigating."

"There's the door," I said. "Lock it behind you."

"I don't have a key—ha, ha, Abigail. Very funny."

He stayed another fifteen or twenty minutes, dusting the doors for prints and just generally poking around. During that time he completely ignored me, and I was happy to oblige his little tantrum. No doubt he would find a sympathetic listener in

Hooter Fawn, his old girlfriend, provided her attractive parts hadn't been recalled by the surgeon general.

Abigail Wiggins Timberlake did not need a man in her life to be happy. A pint of Hunter's Dixie Delight ice cream would do just fine. Chocolate and peanut butter were the only perfect combination.

"Abby, I can't afford to be your secretary," C.J. said breathlessly. "I've got my own shop to attend to."

"I didn't ask you to come running over here with messages," I snapped.

"Your mother sounded desperate. She said she let the phone ring twenty times and you didn't pick it up."

"That's because I have no phone. Someone stole it."

"Oh." C.J. glanced around the room. "That explains the mess."

I had been slaving all morning to put things back in order, and I didn't appreciate her observation. But, in deference to her tender age and the fact that I was mad at Greg, not her, I held my tongue.

"Mama's always desperate about one thing or another. What is it this time?"

"She just said to call her."

"And the other message?"

"It was your boyfriend. You know, the one with those sexy blue eyes."

"He's not my boyfriend anymore."

Her eyes lit up. "Really? Well, he must have known you didn't have a phone, because he didn't sound upset at all."

"What did he have to say?"

"He wants you to call him back."

"If he calls again tell him I've taken a slow boat

to China. I hear that Beijing is the place to buy antiques these days."

"Does this mean what I think it means?" She actually sounded hopeful.

"I just found out that, although he's never been married, he has six children," I said. "All of them by different mothers."

Her eyes widened, but she didn't seem in the least bit deterred. "Oh, my. There was a man back home in Shelby who had ten children by ten different mothers. The Woman's Club had a fund-raiser and bought him a vasectomy. But during the surgery the knife slipped, and the man could no longer— Well, you know."

"Imagine that! The very same thing happened to Greg," I said without batting an eyelash.

C.J. swallowed. "Oh, my!"

"But it was finding out about this secret society he belonged to that really did our relationship in."

C.J. took the bait. "You mean he's a Mason?"

"Close," I said. "He's a Dixonite. He wanted me to become one, too. Every month I would have had to dress up in a choir robe, wear a colander on my head, and recite the pledge of allegiance in Japanese—in front of four hundred people!"

"You poor dear." She shook her head in sympathy. "My daddy was a Dixonite—"

"C.J.! Stop it. There's no such thing."

"Are you sure? Because if not then my daddy lied an awful lot."

I didn't know C.J. had a sense of humor. The woman was good—she wasn't even cracking a smile—or else she was loonier than a night on a Maine lake.

"Yes, well, finding all that out was painful, but I'll get over it. C.J., may I use your phone?"

She shrugged. "Why not, if it will save me from

having to run back over here. I'm not as young as I used to be, you know."

I told her she looked young for her twenty-three years, and followed her back to her store.

"Lord, child!" Mama said. "You had me scared half to death. My nose has been twitching like a rabbit in heat."

"It was only a glitch in my phone line, Mama. The phone company will have it repaired by tomorrow," I said. There was no use worrying Mama with the truth. "What is it you wanted?"

"Oh, that. It's all set for Saturday evening. Here at my house."

"What?" Now I was scared half to death. Knowing Mama, she had arranged a wedding reception for Greg and me, or something equally as preposterous.

"Why, the soiree, of course."

"What soiree?"

"For the docents, silly. You said you wanted to meet them."

"But Mama—"

"Of course I had to invite the board, too. Even that awful Red Barnes and his wife."

"He's married?" Do you see how easy it is for me to get sidetracked?

"Some society girl from Chester."

"I didn't know Chester had any."

"Now, Abby, I didn't bring you up to be catty," Mama said, and rightly so. After all, who am I to talk? Buford was the muck beneath the ooze beneath the sludge beneath the slime on life's scummiest pond. That shows you just how much taste I had.

"How many hors d'oeuvres?" I asked.

"A dozen hot, and two dozen cold, just like I promised," she said indignantly.

"What time?"

"Seven till ten. And Abby, don't wear that polka dot outfit you're so fond of—it makes you look short."

"Yes, Mama."

"Oh, Abby, I took a call for you this morning, since your phone wasn't working. It was Miss Lilah Greene. I wrote everything down. I hope you don't mind."

"No, Mama. Thanks. What was the message?"

"She said you could start cataloging tomorrow night, if you want. She said to meet her at the front gate at Roselawn at seven-thirty. If you can't make it, give her a call."

"Thanks, Mama. Really."

"Don't mention it, dear. But don't forget the favor you owe me, either." She hung up.

I dreaded calling Greg. Most probably he wanted to apologize, or he wanted me to apologize. In either case I wasn't ready. There was only a slight chance it was business, and if so I was sure to be harangued.

"Investigator Washburn here."

"You wanted to speak to me."

"I thought you might want to know that we're releasing June Troyan's remains to the custody of her daughter."

"She has a daughter?"

"Lots of folks do," he said dryly. "This daughter lives in Reno, Nevada. She'll be flying in tonight, and flying back tomorrow."

"Oh."

"That should help some with closure, I guess." As if he were a psychiatrist.

"Yeah, right."

"Also, I was able to lift six sets of prints from the doorknobs and two from the phone table, but they don't match any in our files." Did he expect my customers to have mug shots?

"Uhn-hunh."

"There was no point in interviewing any of the other merchants on Selwyn Avenue, since none of them were at work when you got your call."

"You're probably right. But back to June Troyan. Can I assume that you have already launched a thorough investigation down at Roselawn Plantation?"

I could hear Greg fiddling with something, probably a chain of paper clips. Thank God he didn't wear pearls.

"Abby, I did send a man down there yesterday to ask a few questions."

"And?"

"We didn't get anything. None of the docents—or board members for that matter—drive a blue van, and no one remembered seeing one around."

"What does this mean?"

"It means we look elsewhere."

"Where?"

The paper clips were more annoying than Mama's pearls. "Abby, let us handle the investigation."

"Frankly it sounds like you're stumped. Well, I have news for you, Greg. I want my phone back, I want to stop being harassed, and I want whomever—"

"Abby, unless this thief strikes again, there's not much we can do."

"You mean the case is closed? You can't just close a murder case because the body is being picked up tomorrow! Not when my life is at stake."

He sighed dramatically. "Abby, you're being dramatic," he had the gall to say. "So you had an annoying call, Abby, and someone stole your phone. But there's nothing substantial enough to tie this in with the hit and run."

"Oh yes there is, buster," I said, my dander rising. "He threatened to kill me, too."

"What? When was this?" I could practically feel

Greg's energy leap at me from the receiver.

"Yesterday. He said he'd run me over if he didn't get back the Ming."

"This happened yesterday? And you're just now telling me?"

"I was too upset this morning. I forgot."

"Withholding information that pertains to the case is an obstruction of justice, Abby. Just like when you and your friends cleaned up that vase."

I slammed down the receiver.

He must have known I was calling from C.J.'s, because he called right back.

As a favor to C.J., who was with a customer, I picked up. "Feathers 'N Treasures," I said cheerily.

"Cut the crap, Abby. This is serious stuff."

"I've been trying to tell you that."

There was a long silence. I hoped that he would go easy on the tongue biting, in case we got back together someday.

"Abby, a moment ago you referred to this caller as 'he.' I thought you didn't know the gender."

"I don't. That just slipped out. I really couldn't tell."

"If anything comes to you, Abby, anything at all, give me a call."

"I will."

"And be careful."

"I promise."

"Okay, then. 'Bye."

He took an excruciatingly long time to hang up, during which I was sure he was going to say something else. I'll confess that when I finally hung up, there were tears in my eyes.

8

I bought a new phone for the shop and three new phones for the house. I subscribed to caller ID, but I still panicked every time I got a call.

You can bet I watched my back when crossing the street. My front and sides, too. I nearly gave myself whiplash just crossing Selwyn Avenue. Just the sight of a blue van was enough to strike terror in my heart, which accounts for why I swerved up onto the bank in front of the Black-Eyed Pea on Tyvola Road in Charlotte.

Given my state of mind, it would have made sense to forgo my meeting with Miss Lilah and spend the evening at home, my doors barricaded, watching "Seinfield." But Mama didn't raise me to make sense. I would like to think she aimed for "plucky." Even as a girl, I never lay trembling in bed, waiting for the bogeyman to come out of my closet or reach up from under the bed and grab my feet. Not little Abby Wiggins. Mama thought I kept a broom in my room because I was a clean freak. Little did she know that as soon as she turned out the light and closed my door, I turned my light back on again and ferociously jabbed every remaining shadow with my wooden lance.

If Greg and his staff weren't going to poke under the bed for me, I would have to do it myself. This time I was better armed, with a can of pepper spray, a fistful of keys, Buford's old fish scaler (how I ended up with it, Lord only knows), and a long-handled shovel. The bogeyman wasn't going to get me without a struggle.

Lilah was true to her word. At precisely seven-thirty, just as the sun was starting to set, she pulled up to the gate and lowered the window of her mint green Cadillac.

"I'm sorry to have kept you waiting. I hope it wasn't too long."

"I just arrived myself," I said. It was a white lie. I'd been lying in wait for the bogeyman for at least twenty minutes. But except for a skunk family crossing the road, there had been no traffic.

"We'll park in back," Lilah said. "The back door is easier to open."

She raised her window and drove ahead of me between the massive brick pillars of the open gate. I watched her silver chignon grow smaller for a moment while I entertained some rather silly thoughts. If Lilah was the bogeyman then she was a stupid one, because Mama knew exactly where I was, and with whom. But Lilah, the Rock Hill legend, was anything but stupid. Her degree from Winthrop aside, the woman was brilliant—so smart, in fact, that several U.S. presidents have picked her brain while ensconced as houseguests at her vacation home on Kiawah Island.

I shifted into drive and followed the shrinking chignon down a long, narrow dirt lane. Old live oaks arched overhead, shutting out the last of the fading light. It was like driving through a tunnel, and I immediately put my lights on. The chignon and Cadillac disappeared around a bend, and I had to brake hard to avoid smashing into an oak. Miss Lilah, it seemed, had a heavy foot. It took some fancy driving to keep up with her and still stay intact.

Even at that rate it took us several minutes to reach the clearing where the mansion stood. It was, of course, lighter in the clearing. I hadn't seen the main house since I was a child. It took my breath away then; it took it away now. The set designers for Tara should have done their homework in Rock Hill.

The first thing one notices are the Ionic columns. They are two feet in diameter at the base and twenty-two feet tall—twenty-four of them in all. There are three aboveground floors to the mansion, although from the outside the top floor appears to be merely a jumble of gables, chimneys, and eaves. The two lower floors are separated by a wide veranda, which in turn is guarded by a black wrought iron fence. Scores of tall windows, each with its pair of black wooden shutters, punctuate the white walls.

But the most important feature, in my book at any rate, is the pair of stone staircases that curve away from the massive front door and sweep around to meet each other on the front lawn. They give the impression of embracing arms, that Roselawn in its heyday welcomed visitors.

I reluctantly followed Miss Lilah around the back of the house. There I saw a cluster of buildings—a small village, really—that I had forgotten about. Summer kitchen, washhouse, storage sheds, slave quarters, barns; Roselawn had required a large supporting cast, most of whom were there without their consent and received no pay. And if half the stories told around the fire at local Scout meetings were true, Old Man Rose, the Civil War plantation owner, had been an exceptionally evil taskmaster. Virtually every building on the premises was said to be haunted by the souls of his anguished victims. It was a wonder the freed slaves didn't burn the place down after the Yankees missed it.

"Are any of those buildings open to the public?"

I asked. "I mean, just imagine the stories they could tell if walls could talk."

"I'm afraid we haven't had time to get around to them yet. Maybe next year."

I wondered aloud if the teenagers of Rock Hill knew about all those empty buildings. It looked like make-out heaven to me.

Miss Lilah was clearly shocked. "They are all locked," she said firmly, "and I am the only one who has a key. I would never tolerate a situation like that."

My face was still stinging from her aristocratic rebuke when she—ever the lady—softened.

"For some reason, this back stretch of lawn gets unusually dark at night," she said, producing a flashlight. "We've seen to the indoor wiring satisfactorily, but the paving lights we installed are always shorting out. We've had four electricians out here, and not one of them can find the problem."

"Ghosts?" I suggested lightheartedly.

Miss Lilah had a laugh like porch chimes in a gentle breeze. "That would be Samson's fault, then."

"Samson?"

She pointed into the gathering gloam at the nearest outbuilding.

"Samson was a house slave who jumped the broom with Rebecca, a kitchen girl." By that she meant the pair had gotten married, slave-style. "According to the story, Rebecca was beaten for some minor infraction, and she foolishly tried to avenge herself by poisoning the dinner guests one night when the Roses were entertaining. Rebecca had no lethal poisons in her possession, and it's doubtful she meant to kill anyone. However, she was able to lay her hands on some noxious herbs and give everyone a proper bellyache.

"Unfortunately Rebecca confided her misdeed to another kitchen slave named Uma. It turned out that

Uma was a stoolie. Rebecca was sold to a rice planter in the low country, and Samson never saw her again. One night when it was much darker than this, and the Roses were away, Samson killed Uma. Slashed her throat with one of the kitchen knives. Right here where we're standing. Supposedly it's Uma's blood that shorts out the wiring, even with the proper grounding."

I glanced down at the ground that Uma's blood had cursed. It seemed inordinately dark, considering we were still in red clay country.

"Do you mind if we go inside?" I asked. "It's getting rather cool."

My heart sank when Miss Lilah flipped on the lights in the dining room, the first room we entered. Anne Holliday was right. At least to a precursory glance, Roselawn was no treasure trove of priceless antiques. No English Chippendale appeared to have survived the treacherous Atlantic voyage, no hand-carved rice beds and sideboards had been hauled up from Charleston, no family heirlooms brought south from Virginia.

Oh, it was furnished, and amply so, but everything was Victorian. Late Victorian. True, the pieces were authentic and in good, if not excellent condition, but it was not the kind of collection that normally produced a fifteenth-century Ming vase of exceptional value. Granted, one cannot judge an entire mansion by just one room, but those first pieces I saw would, if sold individually, bring in only hundreds of dollars at an auction, not thousands. Certainly not millions.

Miss Lilah read my mind as clearly as if it contained the headlines on a supermarket tabloid. "The good stuff is upstairs, dear. So far only the ground floor is open to the public. We're using the upstairs rooms for storage."

"I see. Then Miss Holliday—"

Miss Lilah waved a manicured hand. She was too much of a lady to interrupt vocally.

"Miss Holliday is not an expert on antiques. But you are. That's why I took you up on your kind offer."

Flattery will get you anywhere you want to go with me—well, almost. It worked for Buford. But I would like to think I have matured at least a little since the water slide. At least I didn't throw myself into Miss Lilah's arms and nibble her ear.

"Thank you, Miss Lilah. You don't know how good that makes me feel, especially coming from you. You're a legend around Rock Hill, you know that? I've been a great admirer of yours my entire life!"

She smiled graciously. "That's very kind of you, dear."

We walked from the dining room into the drawing room, and came to a stop in front of an enormous fireplace. I caught my breath. The carved oak mantel was worth all the furniture that I had seen so far put together.

"Irish?" I managed to ask.

She nodded. "Dublin, 1758. Old Man Rose's great-great-great-great-grandfather brought it over from the family seat. It should be worth a pretty penny, I imagine."

"A drop-dead-gorgeous penny."

"That's what I thought. Miss Timberlake?"

"Yes."

"Would you mind terribly keeping two lists when you do the inventory?"

"*Two* lists?"

She smiled awkwardly. It was the first imperfect thing about her.

"Yes. You see, we need a very detailed list with replacement values. That would be for insurance

purposes. I think Polaroid shots of the more important pieces would be in order, don't you?"

"Yes, ma'am."

"Good. I'll see that you are supplied with a cam-
era."

"And the second list, ma'am?"

She laughed, and this time the chimes rang a little
off-key. "Yes, that. Well, we think it would be helpful to have a list of liquidation value prices—in case
we find ourselves in the position of having to sell
off a few of the redundant pieces."

"I see."

I didn't. If Miss Lilah and the board wanted to sell
a few of the pieces, liquidation was not the route
they wanted to go. Ten to twenty-five cents on the
dollar was all they could expect to get. I was screw-
ing up my nerve to tell her so when I was distracted
by a thump upstairs. This was not imagined; the
crystal chandelier above our heads was swinging
back and forth like the pendulum of a giant clock.

It's possible I took a step closer to Miss Lilah. "Is
there someone else here?"

"That would be Maynard."

"A resident caretaker?"

The chimes rang clear again. "In a manner of
speaking, I guess. Although Maynard doesn't have
a social security number, and never gets a pay-
check."

"Another ghost?"

"A very active ghost, I'm afraid. One who dates
to the Late Great Unpleasantness. You see, although
officially the Yankees never made it to Roselawn,
unofficially a young soldier named Maynard stumbled onto Roselawn during a reconnaissance mis-
sion. He was discovered in the house, and never left.
Old Man Rose supposedly had him sealed up somewhere inside a wall. Sort of like 'The Cask of Amon-

tillado,' by Edgar Allan Poe. Have you read that story?"

"Yes, in high school. You don't think the story about Maynard is true, do you?"

Even her shrugs were elegant. "Of course there are no documents to support it. But there are plenty of unexplained noises, as you will soon find out."

I could hardly wait.

That night I woke twice during nightmares. In the first my bed was floating on a river of blood, bobbing along like a huge piece of driftwood. In the second there was a Yankee soldier—a quite live specimen—living between my bedroom walls. Every day I had to remove the wall plate around an electrical socket and stuff bread and small vials of water into the hole.

I rarely have such bad dreams, but those times when I do, I would settle for any warm human body—even Buford's—lying next to me. Abigail the Fearless, the tyke who poked a broomstick under her bed, can be rendered into a bowl of jelly by her subconscious. I must have lain awake for an hour or more after each dream. After all, I couldn't very well poke a broomstick into my walls, although I came mighty close to removing the screws on my wall plate and peering inside.

Suffice it to say I arrived at work tired and out of sorts. "Yes?" I snapped at the man waiting for me at the front door of my shop.

It was Frank McBride, an antique dealer whose shop, Estates of Mine, is just down the street. Frank is about my age and of medium height. I have the feeling he was once fairly muscular, but it has long since turned to flab. Even his face looks, to put it kindly, like that of a shar-pei. What little hair he has is bleached, pale blond, while his skin is the color of walnuts. Frank is originally from North Myrtle

Beach, and still spends a lot of time there, so he probably owes at least some of his bizarre appearance to the sun.

"I heard about your break-in," Frank said. "Is there anything I can do to help?"

"Thanks but no thanks," I said, not even having the decency to regret my waspishness. "Only a phone was stolen, and it's been replaced. I've got caller ID now."

He blinked several times. His faded gray eyes were undoubtedly solar damaged as well.

"Everyone should have caller ID these days. And a good security system."

"That's next on my list."

"I could recommend a good company. In fact, I have a cousin here in Charlotte who has his own security systems company. He could get you a really good deal."

"That would be very nice, but I prefer to just browse through the yellow pages." Let him think me strange, but I didn't want to be beholden to him in the slightest. I was just plain too stressed to worry about returning favors.

"Well, let me know if you change your mind."

"Thanks. I will." I turned away to unlock my door.

"Abigail?"

I swallowed my sigh. "Yes, Frank?"

"Some friends of mine refurbished an old Tudor-style mansion in Myers Park and are having an open house on Saturday evening. I hear they have the entire place done in authentic fifteenth- and sixteenth-century English antiques. Even the textiles. It's supposed to be really something. *Architectural Digest* and *Southern Accents* are both hot to do stories on it."

"Oh?"

He definitely had my interest. In a country as

young as the United States, anything over a hundred years old is an antique, and anything over two hundred years old is as rare as a bikini top on the Riviera. On the other hand, a one-hundred-year-old chair in England would barely qualify as used furniture. Many dealers I know cross the great pond annually and buy containers of quality antiques at incredibly low prices. But fifteenth-century furniture and textiles, now that was stretching the envelope! Even for England.

"They say there's a possibility that the Duchess of York will be there," he said, sweetening the pot for me.

I will confess to being a royal watcher. I am especially fond of the House of Windsor. Since only Pat Conroy could invent a more dysfunctional family, the Windsors make my own seem normal by comparison.

"You're kidding, aren't you?"

He was blinking with the regularity of a caution light by now. "I kid you not. She's great friends with the family. And even if she doesn't show, the Countess of Worchester will. She owns a decorating firm, and acted as a consultant."

"What time exactly?" I asked.

"The open house officially begins at eight, but it has no scheduled ending. I suppose it will continue through the rest of the weekend. I wouldn't be surprised if it's already begun. You know how that crowd is."

"Boy, do I ever," I said, absolutely clueless. "Unfortunately, Frank, I already have plans." I tried not to sound too disappointed, but it must have been obvious.

"If it involves somebody else, bring them along," he said gallantly. "The more the merrier. How about I pick you up at seven?"

"Well, uh, you see, my plans are down in Rock

Hill. I'll be occupied until at least eight," I said, which was true in its own way. "Maybe even nine."

He shrugged. "No big deal. I'll pick you up at nine. Oh, and wear something snazzy."

I arched my eyebrows. "But of course."

"It's a date then?"

Believe me, I was torn between an evening of hors d'oeuvres with Mama and the docents, and partying with the rich and titled. Throw in the opportunity to gaze at a house full of exquisite treasures, and the chance to thumb my nose at Greg and thereby make him jealous, and I was suddenly willing—no, make that eager—to ditch the docents. Of course, I would have to speak to the docents sometime. But you only live once, right? Putting my quest for June Troyan's murder on hold was not going to make her any more dead than she already was.

I told Frank to pick me up at Mama's at nine, and then immediately called Wynnell to see if, by chance, she knew the proper way to curtsy.

9

Wynnell hadn't the foggiest idea how to curtsy, but she was amused by my call. Mama was not amused.

"You can't do that to me, Abigail. I already made all the cold hors d'oeuvres, and I'm having the house professionally cleaned."

"What?" To my knowledge, even Mama's toilet bowls have never been scrubbed by anyone not wearing pearls.

"Scrub A Tub-Tub. It's a new cleaning service out of Lake Wylie. They're very particular. They're here right now. I think I'm going to like their work."

"Are they wearing pearls?"

"Heavens!" Mama said. "They're all men."

"I suppose they wear cute little outfits, though," I said sarcastically.

"Black shorts and little white half aprons," Mama practically cooed.

"No shirts? No shoes and socks?"

"Naked toes and naked torsos." There is probably nothing as disgusting as the sound of one's parent drooling libidinously. And who knew what Mama would be like after she got her tattoo!

"Anyway, Mama, something's come up—"

"Don't you dare, Abigail Louise Wiggins Timberlake. After all the work and expense I've gone to just for you."

"I'll pay you back, Mama. Every penny."

"Not to mention thirty-nine hours of excruciating labor, and Dr. Grady wouldn't even let me have a spinal."

"Please, Mama—"

"And then since you were allergic to formula, I had to breast-feed you until you were weaned. You got your teeth early, Abigail, and they were as sharp as a rat's."

"They have breast pumps, Mama," I said futilely. I'd heard the story a million times, but there was no stopping it once it started.

"Those things hurt more than your teeth."

"As a consequence you lost your figure forever," I said, helping the story along. "What little remains of your breasts somehow manages to hang down to your knees. And since you haven't lost your abdominal pooch, you're convinced I still have a twin inside. Let's not forget your stretch marks. They look like the remains of a taffy pull on a hot summer day."

"You forgot my hemorrhoids and varicose veins," Mama said dryly. "But never mind any of that. Just go ahead and abandon me. I'll survive. Lord knows, if I could survive your daddy's death, I can survive this, too."

That did it. Mama as martyr was something I refused to deal with. And the nerve of her, dragging Daddy's death into this. That made me really angry.

"Feed the goddamn hors d'oeuvres to the scrub squad," I snapped, and hung up. It was the rudest I'd been to Mama since I was fourteen and convinced I'd reached the zenith of mental maturity. I can't tell you just how much I regretted saying that.

*   *   *

I was still charged up—filled with lots of angry energy—when I closed my shop that day; so after changing clothes and grabbing a quick bite at Bojangles, I headed straight to Roselawn. It wasn't even dusk yet when I arrived, but already the back of the house was in deep shadow.

It wasn't ordinary shadow, either; everything seemed to have a magenta tinge. And although it had been an exceptionally warm day, the minute I stepped out of my car, I felt chilled to the bone. Even if I hadn't heard the horrible story about Uma, I would have thought the place weird. Thank God I had remembered to bring an industrial-size flashlight with four extra batteries and an extra bulb.

The back door, which had been easy for the lithe Lilah to open, was tighter than Buford's fist at alimony time. Only by pretending that it was Buford was I able to summon the necessary strength to force it open. I flicked on the flashlight, found the overhead light switch, and turned it on.

"Anyone here?" I called.

Call me superstitious, but I believe in the possibility of ghosts. As Albert Einstein said, it takes a tremendous amount of energy to run the human machine in life, and it is reasonable to believe that it just doesn't disappear once we die. Albert believed in an afterlife, and so do I. But I have read that in some cases this energy—call it a soul, if you choose—is unable to leave the world behind. This phenomenon is most commonly associated with murder victims or with those folks who, for whatever reason, had important emotional business to attend to at the time of their deaths. At any rate I thought it only polite to announce myself on the chance, however slight, that I was disturbing the specter's supper hour. Even a Yankee ghost deserves that consideration.

Maynard didn't answer, so I proceeded with confidence—more or less. Frankly I did feel a little nervous, all alone in a deserted mansion off a lonely road in the hinterlands of York County. However, Miss Lilah had permitted me a brief but tantalizing look at the items in storage, and I was eager to get to work. Motivation can go a long way in combating the willies.

I paused at the bottom step of the grand stairway that connected the drawing room and the second floor with a sweeping arc. A flip of a switch illuminated a dusty chandelier at the top. I turned it off and on a couple of times. It worked fine. Quite stupidly I stashed my rather cumbersome flashlight in my rather sizable pocketbook, and then, because there was no Lilah present to censure my behavior, I virtually sprinted upstairs. In my haste I didn't even think about turning out the drawing room light.

Some truly lovely things were stored on the second floor, which was itself a work of art. There were six bedrooms in all, each with its own fireplace. The mantels were all carved oak, presumably Irish like the one downstairs. The friezes, moldings, cornices, and wallpaper were all original to the house and, except for some serious fading in one room, were in remarkably good condition. Either the Rose family raised their children out in the slave cabins, or they were strict and effective disciplinarians. In just one hour my children could have "distressed" that house to a far greater degree.

The only real concession the Roses had made to the twentieth century was the installation of a single bathroom. Apparently they simply renovated a large closet, cramming in the necessary features as space permitted. The result was a jigsaw puzzle of ceramic pieces. Theoretically (I did not try it!) one could sit on the john, dangle one's feet in the tub, and brush one's teeth over the sink all at the same time. Admittedly it would take a tall contortionist, but it could be done. Since the bathroom would be used henceforth only by staff, and only sporadically, there were no plans to improve the space.

I can't say enough how impressed I was with Lilah Greene. "The good stuff," as she put it, had all been tagged, specifying the room in which it had been found at the time of occupancy. Any known history, oral or written, had been meticulously noted on the back of each tag.

Alone now, without her looking over my shoulder, I felt free to browse and poke around the goodies at my own pace. A child alone in a video arcade could not have felt so happy. I picked up a tag on a rather sturdy brown desk. It read:

> *Desk from bedroom #3 (floral wallpaper). Cherry? 1800s? Probably came from Boston. Used by Old Man Rose to conduct plantation business. Some old papers still inside.*

I shook my head. I had some serious work to do. The desk in question was Chippendale, but from Philadelphia, not Boston. The blind fret carving on the frieze, a feature favored by Thomas Affleck and other Philadelphia masters, told me that. The date, therefore, had to be between 1770 and 1780. As for the wood, it was definitely mahogany, not cherry.

With great anticipation I opened the drawers and peered into the cubbyholes. Alas, they were as empty as a schoolboy's head on the last day of summer vacation. Perhaps Miss Lilah had relocated them to an area just for documents.

At least an hour passed, during which I was so engrossed in my pleasurable task that I forgot all about my troubles, and ghosts for that matter. But as I was reading the tag on a bowfront dresser, I not only heard but felt a thud. I could feel it vibrate through my feet.

"All right, Maynard," I said, dropping the tag. "If this dresser is yours, I'll leave it alone. How about this? Is this yours?"

I ran my fingers lightly along the slanted front of a George III bureau, circa 1750. It was walnut, inlaid with satinwood and oak. I could scarcely believe its state of preservation. It almost looked new. If Jimmy Carter, president of the United States, could lust after women in his heart and then announce it to *Playboy* magazine, then Abigail Timberlake had every right to lust after a piece of fine furniture. Especially if she told no one.

My soul filled with lust, and I stood there in a trance caressing the warm, hard wood as if it were a lover. My fingers lovingly traced the sides of the piece and started on the back. Suddenly my fingers stopped, as did my heart. Was that a metal screw I felt?

I peered closely at my lover, then recoiled in horror. It was a phony, a reproduction. A good one, mind you, and it was undoubtedly worth a pretty penny, but not top dollar.

I dashed over to the Chippendale desk from Philadelphia. I swear I held my breath for the time it took me to give it a thorough examination, and when I was done my sigh of relief would have blown out a birthday cake full of candles twenty paces away. The desk, at least, was the genuine article.

It was a mixed bag. I reexamined every piece, and I am ashamed to say that only about half were the real McCoys, the other half just stunning imitations. At least the late Old Man Rose knew where to shop for the latter, because believe you me not all fakes are created equal.

Still, what was I going to say to Miss Lilah? The woman was expecting good news. She was going to be devastated, maybe even angry, to find out that half of Roselawn's furniture had been manufactured within the decade.

And what about my feelings? I had never felt like such a fool. I actually felt worse than the first time I discovered Tweetie's hot pink lipstick along the waistband of Buford's boxer shorts.

Even we Episcopalians are taught that God is omniscient, but ghosts? How did Maynard know what I was thinking? And who gave him the right to laugh?

That's right! Maynard was laughing, alternating between low guttural sounds and high-pitched squeals, like pigs grunting at a trough.

It's true what they say; one's hair does stand on end. But I have short hair, and I had been having a bad hair day all along. My point is that I was scared, but not reduced to a quivering mass of jelly. I was, after all, Abigail the broom-wielding shadow slayer. Still, I was unnerved enough to head straight downstairs, out of Maynard's territorial claim.

I was so intent on my departure that at first I failed to notice the light in the drawing room had been extinguished. It wasn't until after I had tripped over my own pocketbook, and was almost sent sprawling, that the situation became clear.

"Damn you, Maynard," I said, fumbling for the light switch.

To my great relief, the lights came on, but I had reason to be horrified nonetheless. There, right in the middle of the drawing room, practically centered on the antique Aubusson carpet, was a huge, rhythmically undulating white mass. No, it wasn't Maynard, or Casper, or any other denizen of the spectral world. It was nothing more than Red Barnes's bare ass.

"Oh my God—"

"What the hell?" Red glanced at me over his

shoulder while the tart beneath him continued to squeal in ecstasy.

"Mr. Barnes!"

Red rolled over and sat up, in the process revealing something even more grotesque than his naked butt. I averted my eyes.

"What the hell are you doing here?" he roared.

Shakespeare was wrong. Hell has no fury like freshly converted fear.

"You bastard!" I screamed. "How dare you scare me like that?"

Red had managed to snatch up some piece of clothing—a shirt, I think—but the tart was still as naked as Eve before the fall.

"Me? What I do here is none of your goddamn business, missy. But you—"

"I'm here at the invitation of Miss Lilah," I said, and I think I managed to say it rather regally.

"Hell. You could at least warn a body that you were here."

"My car is parked out back," I snapped. "And I had the lights on, and my purse was sitting right here on the bottom step. How much more warning do you need?"

"We always park in front," the tart said.

"Shut up," Red growled.

"And I suppose you always find the lights on, Mrs. Barnes?" I asked.

"Oh, I'm not Mrs. Barnes. I'm—"

"I said 'shut up!' " Red smacked her with the back of a ham-sized fist.

The girl squealed, this time in pain.

"You son of a bitch," I said.

There is one advantage to carrying a large, overloaded pocketbook. Especially one that contains a heavy flashlight. Red Barnes got tit for tat.

He stared at me stupidly, too stunned to react. I stretched a hand out to the girl.

"Come on, I'll get you out of here."

"I ain't going nowhere with you, missy," she hissed.

"My name isn't Missy," I said calmly, and scurried from the drawing room through the dining room and out the back door. Just as it was closing behind me I heard Red Barnes bellow with rage. But I was out of there, halfway down the oak-lined lane before he had a chance to get his pants on.

"Please, Mama," I said. "Pretty please with sugar on top?"

I had foolishly asked Mama if she minded postponing the party. Although Frank had agreed to pick me up at nine, I didn't want to miss a minute of the royal bash.

Her necklace whirled through her fingers. It amazes me that despite constant and vigorous use, Mama's pearls look none the worse for wear. Daddy must have bought her cultured pearls with exceptionally thick nacre, or else they were natural and worth a fortune.

"What if I said I'd taken all those hors d'oeuvres and donated them to Pilgrim's Inn?"

There was only one answer. "I'd say you were the saint I always knew you to be."

"Ha!" The pearls slowed to a pace reminiscent of worry beads.

"Have you?"

"Well, I should have. After all that hard work, and then you turned on me like that!"

"Mama, I didn't turn on you. I just foolishly accepted an invitation to a party. There's a rumor that royalty will be present—"

Mama dropped her pearls and grabbed my hand. "Who? Not *him*?"

My mother is absolutely smitten with the Prince of Wales. Our birthdays—his and mine, Mama is much older—are only a few days apart, and Mama pegged me as his bride the day I was born. Nothing that Charles has done in the interim has shaken her faith in the suitability of our match. When Diana came along, Mama was livid. Even though I was already married to Buford and had two children, Mama saw the new princess as an interloper who had to be stopped. As far as I know, her letters to Buckingham Palace on my behalf have never been answered.

"No, Mama, not him. But possibly the Duchess of York, and some countess of somewhere. She has a steak sauce name."

"A-1?"

"No. It doesn't matter. The point is, I used you, and I'm sorry. Will you forgive me?"

Mama is nothing if not generous, so she gave me a warm hug. "Of course I will, dear. Now, Abby, just hold your horses, because I have an idea."

I braced myself against a team of wild horses—hers, not mine.

"Yes?"

"What time is this party?"

"It starts at eight, but it's open-ended."

Mama's eyes sparkled like the cubic zirconia in Tweetie Timberlake's engagement ring. "Why, that's perfect. I'll call up our guests and tell them that the time of the soiree has been changed. I'll tell them to come at six instead of seven, and to leave by eight instead of ten. Then, as soon as the last one leaves, we can head straight over to your party. We'll only be fashionably late."

"But Mama," I wailed, "I have a date."

"Oh, Greg won't mind if I tag along." Mama is truly fond of Greg, but only as a stand-in until Prince Charles comes to his senses.

"It's Frank McBride."

Mama took the news calmly. "Well, in that case I'll bring a date, too."

I stared at the woman whose body had given birth to me, but whose soul had been replaced with that of an alien from outer space.

"You will? Who?"

"Stanley."

"Stanley Steamer?" I asked, laughing.

She smiled smugly. "Nope. Stanley Morris from Scrub A Tub-Tub."

10

"**M**ama! That's ridiculous. You can't date your maid, even if he is a male."

"He's positively buff," Mama said in all seriousness. "I'll tell him to come at eight o'clock to help us clear things away before your date picks us up."

"But you don't know anything about him."

"He's twenty-two, and he has pecs like Sly Stallone."

"Important stuff," I shouted. "For instance, who are his parents?"

Mama stared at me insolently. "I don't know, and I don't care."

"You see, he's got you brainwashed already. Does he have an education?"

"Who needs an education with a body like that?"

"This is asinine. You know that, don't you? What are you going to do someday when you're old and wrinkled, and he dumps you for a younger woman?"

"I'm already old and wrinkled. He doesn't care."

Now I stared at her. "Mama, you and Stanley didn't—uh—well, you know what I mean."

"No, frankly I don't."

"Are you doing the horizontal mambo, Mama?"

"Why, Abigail Timberlake! You should be

85

ashamed of yourself!" She shook her finger at me, as if I were a little girl again. "That would be wrong. A sin even, outside the bonds of marriage."

I breathed a sigh of relief. If only tattoos were morally off limits as well.

"Does he think maybe you have money?" I asked casually.

Mama's expression reminded me of that time I forgot her birthday. "He thinks I'm intellectually stimulating, Abigail. He called me witty. Do you think I'm witty?"

"You're a barrel of laughs, Mama."

"Now you're making fun of me." She sighed. "Just wait until you get to be my age. I hope your children treat you like a child."

I cringed. When I was a teenager Mama wished two stubborn, rebellious teens on me. She got her wish. It was time to change the subject.

"Do you know how to curtsy, Mama?"

"Of course!"

"Could you teach me?"

She looked at me incredulously, as if I'd just admitted I couldn't walk.

I was perhaps overdressed for Mama's soiree, although frankly it is hard to be overdressed in Rock Hill. It was the last city in the United States to give up gloves for indoor daytime wear, and every now and then in the supermarkets you will spot one or two blue-haired ladies with mink heads bobbing over their shoulders. Stockings and heels are de rigueur, even at picnics. The first and only woman to wear pants to the Episcopal Church of Our Savior was pelted with wadded up bulletins (discreetly, of course), and made to double her pledge for the following year. Or so I am told.

"You look lovely," Mama said, who just happened to be wearing an identical outfit.

"Thanks." I stroked the soft skirt of my floor-length, off-the-shoulder black velvet gown. "If only I had some pearls to wear with this."

"Nothing doing," Mama said, her hand flying protectively up to her neck.

I had to make do with the faux diamond necklace Buford bought me for our fifteenth wedding anniversary. Apparently it was the same store where he bought Tweetie's engagement ring. At least Buford told me at the time that my gems weren't real. Poor Tweetie was going to be in for a shock if she ever tried to hawk that ring. Real diamonds have a higher refractive index and do not display dark areas when the table facet is tilted. Besides, the Buford I know would never spring for a ten carat diamond, even to possess the man-made treasures Tweetie has to offer.

Mama stayed in the kitchen while I greeted the guests. Believe me, my mother is not a wallflower, nor was she gallantly giving me center stage. She simply wanted to take all the credit for the food.

In Rock Hill everyone knows his or her place, and the docents all arrived precisely on time, and well before any of the board. The first two brought husbands. I dutifully allowed the men to peck my cheek—as is our custom in the South—and turned my attention to the women. I wouldn't say that I pounced on them, but by the time they had drinks in their hands and were seated, I had ascertained that they knew no more about June Troyan than I did. Quite possibly they knew less.

"Oh, was she the one who got an Elvis tattoo on her calf?" one of them asked.

Her companion laughed, spraying good red wine on Mama's white carpet. "No, that was Irma, silly. That's why they fired her. June is the one who looked just like Oprah before she went on her diet."

All my interviews went similarly. There were an even dozen docents, and only one woman (the docents were all female) remembered her.

"June and I volunteered on the same days," she said. "Thursdays. She was a real nice lady, but very quiet. Oh, don't get me wrong. She had a strong voice, and was a great tour leader, but between visitors she didn't say much. And never a word about herself."

My interviewee was not at all the quiet type, nor was she what I expected in a docent. Amanda was a gaunt woman with stringy hair, small but intensely bright eyes, and enormous ears that had been pierced many times. In her left nostril she wore a discreet nose ring. Call me a snob if you will, but the woman neither looked nor sounded particularly well educated. Buford would have pronounced her "rode hard and put away wet."

"Did she seem to know her antiques?"

Amanda scrunched her nose in concentration, and the ring glinted. I wondered if it hurt to have it installed, and if it was inconvenient during a bad head cold.

"Not so that I noticed. We have these fact sheets to memorize, see. Everything we need to know is on them. All the history, all about the stuff in the house. But we aren't allowed to say anything that isn't on the sheets."

"What if someone asks a question?"

"Well, then you can answer it, if you know your stuff. But people almost never ask questions, and when they do they're always about silly things, like where's the bathroom and do you enjoy your job."

"To your knowledge, did June have any enemies?" I asked, trying another tack.

Amanda shrugged her bony shoulders. "Like I said, she never talked about herself."

I thanked her and turned away.

"Oh, there is one thing," she called.

I whirled. "Yes?"

"One time I showed up a half an hour early on account of I had to drive my husband to work that morning—he works over at Bowater, you see."

I waved at her to speed up.

"Well, anyway, her car was already there, but I couldn't find her anywhere. Then at nine o'clock, just when we are supposed to open the place, she shows up out of nowhere."

"Oh?"

"And boy howdy was she ever dirty!"

"You mean dusty?"

"Yeah. She looked like she'd just crawled out of a chimney."

"Where had she been?"

"I dunno. Like I said, she didn't say much. She just asked me to cover for her while she went and cleaned up. But I can tell you one thing."

"What's that?"

"She seemed mighty excited about something. Kept humming to herself all day. Even when she was taking a group around."

That was all Amanda was able, or willing, to divulge. Nonetheless I thanked her profusely, and then took advantage of the moment to ask her how she got her job.

The dark marble-sized eyes regarded me unabashedly. "Miss Lilah Green is my auntie. By marriage," she added, perhaps sensing my incredulity.

Just as I said. In Rock Hill it isn't necessarily who you are, but who you know.

The board began their fashionably late trickle at half past six. I'm not claiming that they coordinated their arrivals, but Shirley Hall was the first to arrive, and as a Yankee she was at the bottom of the totem pole. I breathed a loud sigh of relief. I hadn't expected Miss Lilah to be the first to show up, but with my luck you never know, and I was dreading her arrival.

"Hi," she greeted me cheerily.

"Hey. Glad you could come," I said, and stepped back so she could enter. Shirley Hall is not someone with whom to share doorway space.

But Shirley had her own agenda and stepped back as well. Her appraisal was quick and ended with a warm smile.

"I love your dress, Miss Timberlake. I have one identical to it."

I sincerely hoped her dress was several sizes larger. "Thank you. Won't you come in, Dr. Hall?"

"Shirley. Only students call me doctor, and half of them don't anymore."

I liked the woman. "In that case, you needn't call me bachelor."

She laughed. "Winthrop?"

"Yes. But way before your time."

"Before I retired last year, I'd been at Winthrop twenty-five years."

"I graduated thirty years ago," I said, and could scarcely believe it myself.

We chatted amiably about this and that, but before I could get around to zeroing in on important issues, Mama came in bearing the first tray of hors d'oeuvres. Mama owns enormous sterling silver English trays, large enough for a roast pig, and this one was definitely a sight for hungry eyes. Mama got the round of applause she expected—and deserved— but before I could get back into my conversation with Shirley, the doorbell rang again.

Since Mama is vertically challenged, the peephole on her front door is much lower than most, and I was able to peer through it. I liked what I saw. Despite—or perhaps because of—his male appendage, Angus "Red" Barnes ranks just above a Yankee on the Rock Hill totem pole. All his money, while useful to the foundation, cannot buy him the box seat in society that he desires. Backfield upper bleachers are all he's ever going to get. One does not diddle Mattie Markham's daughter and get away with it. Especially when one is married to a Sunday School teacher at the First Baptist Church.

I was surprised that Red had the nerve to show up at the docents' party, but frankly I would have been more surprised if he hadn't. Staying away would have given credence to any rumors I might be spreading. Of course I wouldn't have spread any—telling Mama and Wynnell doesn't count, nor does the Rob-Bobs—but Red, given his principles, would assume that I had.

It took me a minute to realize that he had the little woman in tow. His lawful bedmate, Marsha Barnes, was standing a full step behind him. Perhaps she didn't like being seen with him, either.

I flung the door open and forced a big smile. "Hey y'all! Come on in."

Red stared at me suspiciously. "Ms. Timberlake?" he asked, as if there might be another short, perky woman who looked like me at the same address.

"Yes. And you're Mr. Barnes. We've met before."

He blushed, a color that was incompatible with his orange freckles. "How's that?"

"At my interview, remember?"

"Ah, yes!"

His relief was pitifully evident. But this cat had only begun to play with her mouse.

"Mrs. Barnes?" I pushed past him and all but dragged his wife into the house. "I'm Abigail Wiggins Timberlake. It's so nice to meet you."

That she regarded me suspiciously was understandable. I am, after all, not unpleasant to look at, and she was undoubtedly aware of her husband's reputation.

Red looked around the room. "Miss Lilah here yet?"

I laughed appropriately. "Heavens no, you're only the second board member to arrive."

I had yet to let go of Marsha's arm, and with only minimal tugging I steered her to the table. Red was right on our heels, probably the first time he'd stuck so close to his wife.

"What a terrible thing, Miss Troyan's death," I said, shaking my head. "Did you know her well, Mrs. Barnes?"

"Of course she didn't know her," Red growled.

"But I did know her," Marsha Barnes said.

Red and I stared in surprise. "How?" he asked.

"She came to one of our Newcomers Club meetings."

I was confused, and said so. I knew there was a group called Newcomers in town, but surely Marsha Barnes didn't belong to it. She was as local as the trees on Mama's lawn.

"But I'm originally from Lancaster," Marsha protested. "I moved here only eighteen years ago, the year I met Red. As long as you renew your membership, they don't care how long you've lived here."

Now I understood why Marsha was in the Newcomers Club. Lancaster, South Carolina (not Pennsylvania!), is the next county over. It is also the name of the county seat. But for we South Carolinians—who are, by and large, a very sentimental lot—twenty miles may as well be two hundred. Any farther than that and one is, ipso facto, from out of state, in which case one would be inclined to join the Foreigners Club instead.

"Did you know her well?" I asked, trying not to lose track of my agenda.

She shook her head. "She seemed nice enough, but she only came once or twice. I remember her because we have a birthday drawing each month and she won the centerpiece. She was sitting next to me, but Judy Farewell was on my other side and we kinda got carried away talking about miniatures. But I could tell June was really moved, because she actually started to cry."

"Women," Red snorted.

I patted Marsha, who seemed pretty choked up herself. "Do you know if she made any friends?"

"I haven't the slightest idea. I invited her to come to church with me, but she wasn't a Baptist."

"What was she?" Trust me, this is a perfectly acceptable question south of the Line.

"A Buddhist, I think. Like I said, we didn't talk much."

"No damned way," Red snarled. "She was as white as grits."

I was beginning to like the mousy, mysterious women who had come hurtling through the plate glass window of my shop. She obviously had been plucky, moving to a new state by herself. And intriguing, appearing out of nowhere as she did, covered in grime. Of course she was exotic, since Buddhists don't grow on trees in Rock Hill. And then there was the thing with the Ming. If only I had waited on her out of turn.

The doorbell rang again, and I shoved the Barneses toward the dining room.

"The food is in there. Eat as much as you can and make my mama a happy woman."

Marsha smiled, and I sensed that she was grateful to be here. The poor woman was clearly in need of social acceptance, if not friends. When I got all my ducks in a row, I'd give her a call. Maybe even sooner—before she came hurtling through my window as well.

Red must have sent his wife on ahead. Just as I

reached for the door, he grabbed my elbow. His grip was much harder than necessary.

"Why the nice act?"

"Because I'm a lady."

The doorbell chimed again, and a couple of guests glanced over, no doubt wondering what was going on.

"Say anything to anyone and you'll be sorry," he hissed.

I flung open the door.

11

It was the Roach, the third board member, which put her smack-dab in the middle of the totem pole. I honestly endeavor to be a good Christian—or at least a proper Southern lady—but I have to get this off my chest. From the very first moment I lay eyes on her, I could not stand Gloria Roach. She brought out the worst in me.

Maybe it was her name, maybe it was her occupation, maybe it was the weight lifter's body crowned by the ferret face, but I just wanted to slap her. Almost as much as I wanted to slap a mime once in Charleston. That man followed me for three blocks, despite my demands that he get out of my face. Then he had the nerve to ask for money—in mime language.

"Good evening," I said cheerily. If hypocrisy in the name of decency is an art form, then Mama is Michelangelo. I had studied at her feet.

Gloria gave me a swift, appraising look. "Well, well, we're a bit of a sycophant, aren't we?"

"I beg your pardon?"

"It means one who is fawning and obsequious."

"I know what it means, dear; I just can't believe you said it."

"Miss Lilah is not going to be impressed by your

dress. It's a bit too much for a soiree of this sort, don't you think?"

I glanced at her dress. It was knee length, navy with white piping, and had cap sleeves. Even with long sleeves, there would have been no way to disguise those bulging muscles. But physique aside she was more appropriately attired.

"I'm going to another function later," I felt compelled to say. "A reception for the Prince of Wales." If one is going to embellish, do it in a grand way, I always say.

"Here?" Only a dog could tell her laugh from a bark.

"No, in Charlotte."

"Funny, but I don't recall hearing anything about it. It wasn't in the papers."

"It's all very hush-hush. For security reasons."

"I have many clients in Charlotte. Important people. I would know if there were any royals in town."

"This is an unofficial visit. Charlie is just visiting some close personal friends."

That part wasn't a lie. My son, Charlie, was spending the weekend with a buddy.

The ferret face was awash in skepticism. "Would you swear to that under oath?"

"I have sworn many oaths," I said, and left her standing at the door. I had other guests to attend to, and a quick glance at my watch told me that Mama was about to make her second appearance.

No matter who was at the Charlotte party, it was not going to be a night *sans* royalty. Anne Holliday showed up right on cue, placing her fourth from the bottom on the pole. She was dressed in a pink-and-blue pastel floral dress, a pink hat the size of a basketball hoop, matching shoes, and a blue purse every bit as large as an attaché case. She came alone. Apparently there was no prince consort.

"Miss Timberlake?" she shrilled.

"Yes, ma'am. We met at the interview, remember?"

"I haven't the foggiest recollection," she said. "All I know is that Mozella asked me to come. Is she here?"

"Yes, ma'am. Please come in."

She staggered in and stood blinking while I breathed in her fumes. It took me a minute, but I figured it out. Anne Holliday was a tippler. Mama must have had a hard time holding her tongue on that one.

"There is some nonalcoholic punch over there," I said kindly, pointing to the dining room, where the crowd had gathered around Mama's treats. "Would you like me to get you some?"

She was staring at me. "You look familiar. Are you and Mozella kin?"

"Yes, she's my mama, and we've met before." I reminded her of where and when.

"That's right," she said. "And I told you we didn't need an appraiser, because there is nothing out there worth appraising."

"Bingo."

"No thanks, but I play bridge. Do you need a fourth?"

"We're not playing bridge tonight, dear. This is a party for the docents."

She looked like a sheep that had been asked an algebra question.

"The Upstate Preservation Foundation docents," I said patiently. "The guides at Roselawn."

She swayed, but not dangerously so. "That's right. And you wanted to be one."

"And you didn't want me. Now how about that punch? Or would you prefer some nice strong coffee?"

She swayed again, and in an attempt to steady

her, I was nearly decapitated by the brim of her hat. It was with risk to life and limb that I got her seated in the nearest armchair, whereupon she immediately began to snore. I have very little experience with drunks, and none at all with women drunks of a certain age. Mama was going to have to hustle her bustle out of the kitchen and take over.

I tried to slip away discreetly, but was able to take only one step before finding myself jerked backward like a toy on a string. Somewhere along the line Her Majesty had managed to grab the skirt of my gown and was clinging to it with a bony talon.

"And you didn't find anything out there of value, did you?" she demanded.

"I beg your pardon?"

"At Roselawn, child!"

I peered under the hat brim and found her eyes. She was definitely wide awake now, and full of fire.

"Well, actually there are a number of nice pieces. No—make that excellent pieces. Upstairs." I wasn't about to confide my horrible discovery to her until I had had a chance to speak with Miss Lilah.

"Liar!" she croaked.

Everyone except Mama, who was still in the kitchen, looked our way. What's a gal to do at a time like this, except to lie through her teeth?

"She said she passed a big fire on the way here," I called out.

Several folks nodded, but that was it. Frankly that ticked me off. It might have been their own houses burning to the ground for all they knew, but they couldn't tear themselves away from the food long enough to ask questions.

"I didn't say anything about a fire," Her Majesty said, but her eyes had closed and within seconds she was snoring again. I tilted her hat so that it hid her face and muffled the snores. Then I found Mama.

*   *   *

"Of course she drinks," Mama said as she triumphantly took a cookie sheet of golden brown sausage rolls out of the oven. "Everyone drinks."

"Not some Methodists," I said. I reached for a sausage roll, but Mama slapped my hand.

"What do you want me to do, Abby?"

"I don't know—call her a cab, put her to bed. What does one do with drunks?"

"Tsk, tsk," Mama said as she slid a new sheet of snacks—cheese puffs, I believe—into the oven. "Anne Holliday is not a drunk. She's just fond of drinking. And you'd drink, too, if your husband had neglected to write a will."

"She was his mistress, Mama. You said so yourself."

Mama cringed. "So I did, but she stood by that old goat for thirty years. Kept house for him. Helped him nurse his wife through the last years of her Alzheimer's. He should have left her something."

"Nonetheless, she's sitting out there in your living room, sawing logs. We've got to do something."

Mama wiped her hands before removing the crisp white apron that covered the lap of her black velvet dress. "Okay, Abigail, I'll go out there and do something, but you watch those puffs. Check them every couple of minutes or so. As soon as they get as dark as the back of your hand, yank them out and put them over there to cool. Then pop those salami roll ups in. Think you can handle that?"

I rolled my eyes.

And I would have done a fine job, too, if Shirley Hall hadn't strayed into Mama's inner sanctum.

"Can I help?" she asked sweetly.

I shook my head, despite the fact that Shirley obviously knew her way around a kitchen. "How's the food holding out in the dining room?"

She held up an empty tray. "Your mother's a good cook. Did you help her?"

I suppose I could have taken credit for watching the cheese puffs and said yes, but I didn't. I gave Mama all the credit.

"You know, you two look very much alike," she said. "Almost like sisters."

"My mother thanks you."

"My mother and I don't look alike at all."

"My father was six foot and blond. If I didn't know Mama better, I'd suspect the milkman. Although come to think of it, my brother, Toy, is six foot four and looks like a Viking."

She laughed. "Family traits are funny things, especially given the mix of genetics we have in this country. My grandmother was pure Cherokee, but I don't think I look Native American at all, do you?"

I shrugged. It seemed like half the people I knew claimed to be part Cherokee. Why was it nobody claimed to be part Navaho? Or Sioux? Perhaps it was a regional thing. At any rate, if all the part Cherokee in the eastern half of the United States were given full tribal membership, the Native Americans could have their country back in a flash.

"Are you into genealogy?" Shirley seemed to have an agenda.

"Not much, but Mama is. She did a thorough job of researching her family tree to see if she could get into the DAR."

"Did she?"

"No. Mama won't join any group that will have her as a member. Except for church. She sings in the choir every Sunday, but if you ask me the only reason she really goes is because her granddaddy's name is on one of the windows."

She laughed again. "Anyway, I find genealogy fascinating. It's a form of history, you know. Take Miss Lilah, for instance—"

"Damn!" I shouted.

She recoiled in surprise.

"Not you," I cried, and flew at the oven.

They weren't smoking yet, but Mama's puffs had browned to the color of my hair.

It wouldn't even begin to cross Mama's mind to throw a hissy fit in public. With lips as tight as a clam at low tide, she went to work on a new batch of cheese puffs while I mingled with the guests and awaited the arrival of the grande dame. Miss Lilah Greene, the real queen of Rock Hill, showed up at precisely seven o'clock, one hour late. Given her position, however, she was exactly on time.

We pecked cheeks and complimented each other on perfume choices—we had, after all, spent an entire evening together in a plantation house. After she had made her courtly rounds and was comfortably ensconced in one of Mama's easy chairs with a plate of sausage rolls and a glass of cranberry punch, she got down to business.

"Have you had a chance to look things over more carefully?"

I braced myself to tell her the awful truth of my discovery. "Yes, ma'am—"

"Well, I think it's a stupid idea!" Red's voice drowned my words like rain on a corrugated tin roof.

"They do it at Brattonsville." Shirley Hall was referring to another plantation and historic site near Rock Hill. "They even have Civil War reenactments there."

"The War Between the States," Red corrected her. "And the NAACP isn't going to sit still for folks dressed up like slaves parking cars."

"That's not what I meant," Shirley said calmly. "The white docents would dress up like southern belles and the black docents—"

"We don't have any black docents."

"But that's my point; we should. Plantation life is

their history, too." She looked appealingly at Miss Lilah.

Miss Lilah took a sip of the cranberry punch but said nothing.

"Fine," Red said, "let's advertise for black docents, but we can't have them dressing up like slaves. Nobody will stand for it."

"We can't keep revising history," Shirley said firmly. "Roselawn had black slaves, and if we're going to show it as a working plantation, we need to be as authentic as possible."

"With whips and slave auctions? It won't fly for one thing, and for another thing it just isn't right."

I must confess that I was stunned. As despicable as he was, Red was apparently not a racist.

"What do the docents wear?" I asked Miss Lilah.

"Why, whatever they like, dear." She meant that while dresses were mandatory, style, within reason, was up to the individual.

It was a generous policy, and I told her so. I also sided with Red on the issue of adopting costumes, particularly slave costumes. Frankly I belabored my points, anything to delay delivering the truth. But Miss Lilah did not maintain her position on top of the cream by being stupid.

"What are you not telling me, child," she said bluntly.

"Well, Miss Lilah, uh—I—"

She stood up. "Out with it, dear."

"You know all those lovely pieces you have stored upstairs?"

Her back stiffened, and the empty punch cup trembled. "Yes?"

"At least half of them are reproductions, Miss Lilah."

She took the news calmly, then fainted.

12

It takes a great deal of panache to appear calm and collected when the grande dame of Rock Hill is lying spread-eagle (modestly, of course) across one's living room floor.

"More canapés?" Mama said brightly, proffering a silver tray to her guests that was almost as large as a surfboard.

In the meantime I set about reviving Lilah Greene. Not having smelling salts handy, I removed my right shoe and held it, sole side up, over her nose. It worked like a charm. In no time at all I had her fully conscious and sitting in a chair. Some folks, like Anne Holliday for instance, weren't even aware of a disruption.

"What do you mean they're reproductions?" Miss Lilah managed to ask, gasping between each word.

I explained that they were, in fact, very good reproductions, and that as such, they were still worth a good deal of cash, although of course not nearly as much as the originals.

"But," I added, "don't take my word alone for it. By all means, get a second opinion. Rob Goldburg and his partner, Bob Steuben, at The Finer Things in Charlotte are the area experts on antiques. And there are lots of others, too. I won't be at all insulted if you bring in someone else."

Good breeding will tell, as Mama often says, and during my brief explanation Miss Lilah had managed to compose herself. Except for a few hairs that had managed to escape the confines of her chignon, she appeared as cool, calm, and collected as ever.

"I appreciate your candor, Miss Timberlake."

"Please, call me Abigail."

"Thank you, Abigail. But it won't be necessary to get another opinion. I have taken the liberty of doing some background checking, and I am quite satisfied with your knowledge and, most importantly, your ethics. Everyone I spoke to thinks very highly of you."

I was both flattered and annoyed. The idea of someone doing a background check was reminiscent of my college days during the Vietnam War. My best friend, Lorrie Anderson, took part in an antiwar demonstration in Washington, D.C., and as a consequence the FBI opened files on us and for months followed us around the Winthrop campus in their gray suits and fedoras. It was a horrible and humiliating experience. Actually I have no proof that the FBI even heard of us, much less harassed us, but Lorrie swore it was true.

I frowned to show that I was annoyed. "Do you mind if I ask who these people were?"

"Oh, just everyone. The two gentlemen you just mentioned, a Miss Wynnell Crawford, and a delightful young woman who tells the most fascinating stories."

"That would be C.J."

"No, I thought her name was Cox, or something. Yes, that's it, Jane Cox. Oh, and a Mr. Frank McBride."

"Frank? What did he have to say?"

Miss Lilah's aristocratic lips pressed briefly together in an approximation of a smile. "Well, of all the people I spoke to, he was perhaps the least effusive in his praise."

"Oh? Do tell."

"Now, that wouldn't be ethical of me, would it Miss—Abigail?"

"Indeed not. I'll ask him myself."

She gently placed a reproving hand over mine, and I nearly jumped. Her hand felt just like the pet lizard Charlie used to keep. Cold-blooded, that's what she was. It was about seventy-three degrees in the room, and that's exactly how she felt.

"He just said that you exhibit a tendency to jump to conclusions."

"I do no such thing! And I categorically deny his other charges as well."

She produced a genuine smile. "There were no other charges, Abigail. Anyway, I would like to continue to use your services, for a fee, of course."

"But why?"

"It would still be useful to have an inventory, don't you think? You did say those are quality reproductions, didn't you?"

"Yes, ma'am. The best."

She shook her head ever so slightly, barely more than a tremor. "I don't understand it. It wasn't like the Roses—even Jimmy—to decorate with reproductions. Well, it just goes to show you that the old cliché is right. You can't judge a book by its cover."

"Indeed it does," I said smugly.

Had I known what lay ahead, I wouldn't have bothered to turn any more pages.

It wasn't just wishful thinking on Mama's part. She did have a date with a guy from Scrub A Tub-Tub, and he was a hunk. Unfortunately his brain seemed to be a hunk as well. Concrete maybe.

"Hey, I'm Stanley," he said when I opened the door. "You ready to party, babe?"

"Yes, but not with you, dear," I said gently. I glanced at my watch. It was five until eight. At least he was on time.

He stuck his lower lip out in an exaggerated pout. "But you said we was going to party. You was going to show me the time of my life."

"That was my mother. She's in the kitchen. Why don't you go on in and surprise her."

He stared at me, obviously bewildered. "But you said—"

"We look alike," I said kindly, "but Mama is twenty-one years older. You sure you still want to go on this date?"

"Oh man! She's your mother?"

I nodded.

"Far out. I ain't never been out with no one that old before. How old is she?"

"Eighty-two, but she's well preserved," I said.

"Wow!" He seemed absolutely delighted at the prospect of dating an octogenarian.

"This is a double date," I said sternly.

His face lit up like a sheep who'd answered his algebra question correctly. "Cool."

"You do not understand," I said, enunciating each word. "There will be another person on this date. A man."

"I ain't never dated no man, either." He shrugged. "What the hell."

I sent him into the kitchen. I have to admit it: when Mama picks a man based on his physical appearance, she does a damned good job. This man had everything she said he had, and a pair of buns so perfect, they didn't need caraway seeds. He was dressed, of course, but I can barely remember what he wore. A tux, I think, but without a shirt, because I remember seeing a swath of hair rising above the cummerbund and spreading across a massive chest. He was blond, blue-eyed, and either had caps or his parents had married each other because of their teeth. If I'd been of breeding age, there's no telling what kind of a fool I would have made of myself.

Except for Miss Lilah, all our guests were still there, and believe me, every female head turned to watch those buns disappear behind the swinging doors. I wouldn't be surprised if a few male heads turned as well.

"Who was that?" Gloria Roach demanded. It is hard, however, to appear imperious when one is drooling.

"Just one of my mother's students," I mumbled.

The ferret face regarded me suspiciously. "I didn't know your mother taught. What does she teach?"

"Well—"

"None of my students ever looked like that," Shirley Hall said, and giggled.

I smiled at her gratefully. "Well, it was very nice having y'all here. Thanks for coming."

They were slow to take a hint, or maybe it was us. At any rate, it wasn't until after we yanked all the food off the table that they began to trickle out. Even then, it was almost eight forty-five before the front door closed on the last of them. Even with Stan's help—he really was sweet—we were barely able to get things squared away before Frank arrived.

I introduced Frank to Mama.

"Who's this?" he asked pointing to Stan. Frank lives up to his name.

"This is my mother's date, Stan A Tub-Tub," I said.

Mama glared, but Stan smiled sweetly.

"Where are they going?"

I smiled winsomely up at Frank. "They're going with us, of course. You said the more the merrier."

Frank frowned. "I didn't mean gigolos."

I looked him in his faded eyes. "Now who's jumping to conclusions."

He winced and opened the car door for me, which prompted Stan to do the same for Mama. If Mama was confused by Stan's wince, she didn't let on.

I wouldn't say we were a congenial foursome, but I had been on double dates that were far less pleasant. At least no one threw up, and to my knowledge there was no urinating from open windows.

I will admit to being just a mite nervous when we pulled up in front of the pseudo Tudor house. There was valet parking, for one thing. And on the way over, Frank had confirmed that the duchess was indeed expected.

At the door it became apparent that she was already there. A tall, thin man with a walkie-talkie in his right hand took our names, and then started patting Mama down with his left hand.

"Touch me there again, and you'll need headphones," Mama said sweetly. She wasn't kidding. My mother has an orange belt in karate, thanks to a burglar who paid her an unwelcome visit the year after my father died. She would, no doubt, have her black belt by now, if they had only seen the light and relaxed the rules a little. Pearls, if properly strung, are not a hazard in the martial arts.

Tall and thin stared at Mama. "Identification," he snapped in a heavy British accent.

Mama opened her black velvet clutch bag and whipped out her South Carolina driver's license. The man recoiled, and understandably so. I hear that only the Pennsylvania DMV is capable of producing pictures more ghastly than those taken in the Palmetto State.

"Blimey!"

"You're not so much to look at, either," Mama said peevishly. "If I had two of you, I could string some clothesline and hang my sheets up to dry."

Tall and thin got on his walkie-talkie and had a

long, tiresome conversation with an unseen party. Every now and then he glanced down at Mama, as if he fully expected her to attack. At last he shut off the damn walkie-talkie.

"Go ahead," he said grudgingly.

We sailed on into the mansion without further incident, which was really disappointing, if you ask me. I could have been a terrorist carrying grenades in my bra, or maybe even a land mine in my panties.

I was even more disappointed when Frank immediately abandoned our little group to engage in some dirty gossip with the host and hostess. From the few snippets I overheard, I managed to gather that the duchess had just left through the back door. Apparently there was a lot more to the story, but the three backs turned to us made it quite clear that if we wanted to learn more about the latest scandal, we would have to read about it in the tabloids. Either that or bribe one of the kitchen staff.

Missing the duchess was a bitter disappointment for me. And by only a matter of seconds! If Mama hadn't put up a fuss at being frisked, I would have had the opportunity to practice my curtsy.

"You see," I hissed. "I knew I shouldn't have brought you. I can't take you anywhere without you making a scene."

Mama was not amused. "Don't you get fresh with me, Abigail. You burned the cheese puffs, remember?"

"How perfectly charming," said a female with a very British accent.

I turned around, then did a double-take. Right behind me stood a woman who appeared to be regarding us with amusement. She was tall and angular, with a horsey face and a mane of coarse dark blond hair. Her overbite would have been a challenge to even the best orthodontist, but she didn't mind exposing it in a broad, gummy smile. It wasn't her body or her face that captured my immediate attention, however, but her dress. She was wearing a black velvet gown identical to the ones Mama and I had on. Her gem of choice was emerald.

"Sorry," I said quickly. "I suppose we're out of sorts because we missed the duchess. She's a good friend of ours, you know."

"I'm Caroline," she said, her eyes twinkling, "and I'm talking about your dresses. R. K. Belmont of Trafalgar Square?"

I shook my head shamefully.

"Don't tell me! Off the rack at Harrods?"

"Jacque C. Penné of Rock Hill," Mama said without missing a beat.

"Tell Mr. Penné he has my compliments," she said quite seriously.

"Oh, I will," Mama said without cracking a smile. "Tell me, dear, which one is the Countess—"

Mama was interrupted by a liveried butler with a tray of goodies. Think of us as simple folks, but it has always been a fantasy of both Mama and me to be waited on by someone who looks like Jeeves. Apparently it was a fantasy shared by Stan, because he immediately began making goo-goo eyes at the butler. It must have been lust at first sight for the butler as well, because he almost dropped the tray of canapés. As it was, I ended up with three stuffed mushrooms and one pâté-spread cracker down the front of my dress. A fourth stuffed mushroom rolled between my meager cleavage and lodged in my bra.

Caroline gasped on behalf of the butler, who still hadn't taken his eyes off Stan.

"Oh, I'm so sorry," she said.

"Think nothing of it," I said graciously. "It happens all the time."

"You Americans are such a delight, always taking things in stride."

"Not always," Mama said as she shot daggers at Stan A Tub-Tub, who had clearly forgotten she even existed.

"Rawlings!" Caroline said sharply to the butler.

Rawlings, suddenly realizing where he was, snapped to attention. "Yes, your ladyship?"

"Circulate, Rawlings. But first bring this lady some club soda and a serviette."

"Yes, ma'am." Rawlings bowed slightly and left at once. Without so much as a by-your-leave to Mama, Stan trotted off after him.

"You're the Countess of Worchester?" I asked, no doubt a bit wide eyed myself.

"Yes, but please call me Caroline."

I crudely attempted my curtsy. Unfortunately my nervous brain short-circuited, and I gave her an Episcopalian genuflection instead.

The countess laughed heartily. "Please, introductions all around."

We did as we were bade, and in a few minutes the three of us became fast friends. I realize that may sound absurd to men, but we women have a way of establishing intimacy in a heartbeat, particularly if there is a crisis to deal with. In the time it took to dig the mushroom out of my bra and sponge the stains off my dress, I learned that Caroline had suffered from scoliosis as a girl, was deathly afraid of spiders, was divorced, and was deeply in love with a married Anglican priest.

The countess fingered her emeralds. They were lovely, remarkably clear stones, the kind found only in Muzo, Colombia. They were undoubtedly worth a king's ransom.

"Only an earl's ransom," she said, reading my mind. "They belonged to Harry's mother, but I made him give them to me as part of the settlement. You wouldn't believe the hell that man put me through."

"Oh, yes I would!" I told her all about Buford and the angst I was still experiencing as the mother of young adults.

We both learned far more than we ever needed to know about Mama, too.

"What about that deeply tanned man you came in with?" Caroline asked me in a wise attempt to turn the conversation away from my mother.

"Oh, that's Frank McBride. He's a friend of our hosts."

"Ah yes, the antique dealer I've heard so much about."

"You have?"

"He is practically all Bea and Jerry ever talk about. This Mr. McBride and the wonderful deals he gets them. Ancient treasures from all over the world. Tell me, do all Americans have this fascination with old things?"

"Not if his name is Stan," Mama said bitterly. "And to think I almost let him use my toothbrush."

"Mama!"

"Oh, it's not what you think, Abby. It's just that I fed him lunch one day, and he brushes after every meal."

I think it should be permissible to clamp a hand over your mother's mouth, don't you? Not as retribution for all the times she did it to you when you were a little kid, but merely as a means of preserving your sanity.

"I can't take her anywhere," I said, shaking my head sadly.

"Oh, but she's absolutely delightful," the countess cried. "You both are. As a matter of fact I'd like to arrange dinner with you two before I leave this wonderful city."

"At my house," Mama said. "I make a beef Wellington that is to die for. And not your wimpy English version, either. I put Tabasco in mine."

"Mama, please!"

"Have you ever tasted better, Abby?"

"No."

"It sounds delicious," the countess said, showing me far more gum than I cared to see.

"Beef Wellington it is," Mama sang out victoriously. "How about supper tomorrow night? Say seven?"

"Wonderful!"

"It'll be casual," Mama said a little too casually.

The countess fingered her emeralds. "Casual?"

Mama patted her pearls. "Well, not too casual, of course."

I wandered off while Mama gave the countess directions to our house. I couldn't believe she had the nerve to invite an English aristocrat to visit her on Eden Terrace down in Rock Hill. How did she expect the countess to get there? Turn a pumpkin into a coach?

Rock Hill was going to be emerald green with envy. The minute they found out about Mama's coup, the shakers and movers were going to beat a path from the 'burbs to her door. Come Christmas, Mama's house would undoubtedly be featured on the candlelight tours, and the chair in which Countess Caroline sat would have a red cord strung across the arms to protect the seat.

Well, let Rock Hill be impressed by an English countess. I was impressed with Bea and Jerry. Not by them personally, because they had yet to say a welcoming word to me, but by their house. It was exquisitely, if not authentically—I am certainly not an expert on fifteenth- and sixteenth-century furnishings—appointed.

The walls were hung with monstrous unframed tapestries, the likes of which I had only seen in museums. I guessed them to be Flemish. The floors were bare, polished wood—carpets used daily would not last that long. The furniture was predominantly English, but here and there, adorning the tops of tables, commodes, and various stands, were objets d'art from around the world.

A bigger woman would have wept for joy, whereas I merely lusted in my heart. Although I'm a God-fearing Christian, I might well have lifted one or two items had my purse been larger—that and the fact that I didn't want to share a cell with a woman named Brunhilde who called me her girlfriend. After all, there is only so much temptation a body can stand.

Then I saw the ewer. It was Chinese. Blue underglaze porcelain with polychrome overglaze, looking for all the world like a first cousin to the Ming vase that had found its way into my shop. It wasn't the same piece, of course, since the ewer had handles, and it was perhaps only three quarters the size of my Ming. But—and this is going to sound very unprofessional of me—it had the same look.

I found Frank and dragged him away from our rude hosts and the even ruder jokes about the duchess.

"Is that a Ming?" I asked, pointing to the ewer.

Frank had the audacity to chuckle. "Oh, Abby, how clever. Anyone else would think you were serious."

"But I am."

"Yeah, right."

"What is it?" I snapped.

"You're not kidding, are you? Oh, my, my." Frank shook his head in pity, and the brown wattles at his throat flapped from side to side. "That, my dear, is from the Yüan dynasty."

"I see."

He laid a flabby arm across my shoulder. "Oh Bea," he called, "oh Jerry! Guess what just happened here?"

I ducked the flab and fled.

* * *

I was ready to split long before Frank and Mama. Antique gazing aside, there wasn't anything for me to do. Frankly the food wasn't nearly as good as Mama's, and with the exception of the countess, the people were either obnoxious or boring. After ten minutes it wasn't even fun watching the courtship of Stan and the butler. As for that bald man in a banker's suit who offered to suck my toes, I told him to go straight to hell. What did I care if the duchess had rated him a ten?

So it was that I was bone tired and perhaps a bit cranky by the time our threesome (Stan had elected to stand by his man) made it to the door. But I was raised to be a true lady, a southern lady, so I graciously thanked my rude and obnoxious hosts. I also bade adieu to the delightful, but now slightly cloying, countess.

"The pleasure has been all mine, Abby," she said. "Your mother has told me so much about you."

I glared at Mama. "Then I'm sure she has told you I now have a night job—of sorts—and won't be able to join you for supper tomorrow evening."

"You weren't invited," Mama said.

I glared again for good measure. "Well, have a safe trip back to merry old England, and say 'hey' to the queen for me."

"Her Majesty—" the countess said, and then dropped dead at my feet.

13

"And then what happened?"

Greg balanced his notebook and pen on his knees while he fished in his pocket for a handkerchief. Bea and Jerry had kindly allowed us the use of their kitchen, but apparently they didn't believe in stocking facial tissues, and Mama had my purse.

"And then she just fell. It was awful." I cried a little and dabbed my eyes and nose before continuing. "Greg, I could see her falling, but I didn't move fast enough to catch her. In fact, I didn't move at all. I couldn't. It was like I was watching her fall in slow motion, but I was frozen in time."

Greg snatched the handkerchief from me and caught a large drop that was about to dribble off the tip of my nose.

"It happens like that," he said, "even to seasoned pros. Something totally unexpected happens, and you don't react. It's nothing to be ashamed of."

"But it seemed like forever between the time I heard the shot and when she started to fall. I should have reached out. I should have done something."

"You're too hard on yourself," he said kindly. "There was nothing you could have done to help her. Abby, please remember, what happened wasn't your fault."

"I didn't even scream. I just stared."

"Your reaction was normal, Abby." He picked up the notebook and pen, and crossed his legs at the knee. "Tell me about your relationship with the victim."

"Victim? She had a name. Even a title! Her name was Caroline."

"How well did you know her?"

"I met her tonight. But we hit it off immediately."

"So you had only just met her."

"Yes, but we talked about everything. She was so nice!"

"I'm sure she was."

He waited patiently while I caught the next drop on my own.

"She and Mama were supposed to have supper together tomorrow night."

"Where?"

"At Mama's. Only I wasn't invited." I was babbling like a crazed idiot.

"I see. Abby, try and picture how it was just before she got shot. How were you standing? How was she standing?"

"We were facing each other, of course, because we were saying good-bye. She had her back to the house. I had my back to Mama's car. Mama was standing between us on the left."

"And Mr. McBride?"

"He was behind me someplace, I guess. He was supposed to be getting the car. The valet parking was only to impress the duchess."

"I see. Were there any other people around outside that you were aware of? Your hosts, for instance?"

I crinkled my nose, and not to stop it from running. "They didn't even walk us to the door. Wynnell would call them Yankees."

"Any unexplained movements in the periphery of your vision?"

"No."

"Do you remember any cars driving by at about that time?"

"No."

"Anything at all that you can remember that you haven't told me?"

"I remember Caroline's left eye exploding," I sobbed, and threw myself into Greg's arms.

Mama stayed with me in Charlotte. Neither of us could go to sleep right away, so we sat up and drank a pot of decaf and picked at a jigsaw puzzle I keep on my breakfast room table. There's nothing like putting together a puzzle to help sort out the mind.

"This was the worst evening of my life," Mama said simply. She was trying to cram a blue center piece into a green edge.

"Worse than when Daddy died skiing?"

She tossed the piece back on the pile. "No, that was worse. I saw that seagull dive-bomb your daddy, but there was nothing I could do. Your uncle Gooch stopped the boat as soon as I yelled, but not before your poor daddy smacked into that pontoon boat and— Oh well, you know the rest. He had a brain tumor the size of a walnut, you know."

"Uncle Gooch?" I knew Daddy didn't.

"No, the seagull. According to a state biologist, that damned seagull shouldn't even have gotten airborne."

I patted Mama's hand. After eighteen years, talking about Daddy's death still brought tears to her eyes.

"But tonight might have been worse," she said, picking up that same damn blue piece.

"How?"

"It might have been you instead of Caroline. If I'd

lost you, too, Abby, I wouldn't have been able to take it."

It was a sobering thought I had yet to dwell on. "Oh, Mama, you're right! If the killer had been off by just a couple of inches, that might be me in the morgue."

Mama jammed the blue piece into the green border. "No, Abby, you've got it wrong. It's because the killer was a lousy shot that you're still alive. Whoever it was most certainly was aiming for you, dear."

"Me?"

She jammed a predominantly yellow piece in next to the blue one.

"Why would anyone in the Carolinas want to kill an English countess? Who even knew she was here?"

"I don't know! But why would anyone want to kill me?"

"Think, dear. You don't suppose it could be Buford, do you?"

Buford a killer? That was too much for even me to fathom. Murder was not Buford's style; torment was. Buford was the type to send a suicidal person a gift-wrapped loaded pistol, complete with instructions on how to use it. My ex-husband did not pull the legs off flies when he was a boy. He did, however, keep an open jar of honey in a little screen box in his bedroom.

"It's not Buford," I said. "I can't think of a single reason someone might want to kill me."

Mama cleared her throat, and then patted the pearls as if to apologize to them.

"But someone was killed in your shop recently, dear."

"Yeah, so?"

"And it wasn't an accident, was it?"

"The possibility hasn't been ruled out, Mama.

There were no reliable witnesses, and of course there hasn't been a confession."

"But what if whoever killed—what was her name?"

"June Troyan."

"That's right. Well, if Miss Troyan's killer thought you might have seen—"

"The shop was packed, Mama. They know I didn't see it happen."

"They don't know that for sure."

I got up and checked the kitchen door. It was locked. I pulled the blinds closed.

"What is the killer going to do? Kill everyone who was in my shop?"

"No, of course not. I just feel that there is a connection. I can smell it."

"Leave your nose out of this," I snapped.

It was fear speaking. They say animals can smell fear, so why not someone with a highly developed proboscis like Mama's?

"I'm sorry," I said. I meant it. She was only voicing her concern.

Mama waved off my apology. "Forget it. But you need a gun, dear."

"No, I don't. You know how I feel about guns."

"Maybe it's time to rethink your position."

"What kind of a message would I be giving Susan and Charlie?"

"They wouldn't need to know," Mama said coolly.

"What if I panicked some night and accidentally shot one of them? Or you?"

"You would use the thing for self-protection. Not to pop someone sight unseen."

"A lot of people who keep guns end up being victims of their own guns."

"Liberal poppycock," Mama said stubbornly.

"You don't think Caroline's killer will bring along his own gun?"

"Mama, I just don't believe it's the right thing to do. It makes me a part of the problem. It's against my principles."

"Phooey on principle," Mama said. "Do you think Caroline's killer will take that into consideration? I'm not saying you should buy yourself a cannon and join the NRA. But you should have something to protect yourself with in this house."

"I have you, Mama. At least for tonight."

Mama hugged me. We were pals again. But when she tried to cram another blue piece into the green border, I slapped her hand.

The next day was Sunday. By convention, area antique shops remain closed during church hours (a vestige of the old Sunday blue laws), and open at noon or one. Since I am a churchgoer myself, I open at one. That particular day I should have just kept the shop closed. But I hate to disappoint customers, and Captain Keffert was planning to come in and buy a birthday present for First Mate Keffert, his wife.

The Kefferts are an eccentric couple who live in a boat-shaped house in Belmont, North Carolina. They are exceedingly rich. Periodically one, or both, of them will drop a huge bundle into my coffers in exchange for a one-of-a-kind piece. I had recently acquired an eight-foot-tall wooden statue of an Indonesian *garuda*, a mythical creature that is half eagle and half man. Believe it or not, but a good *garuda* is hard to come by in the Charlotte area, and Captain Keffert was looking for one, so this fellow was a sure sale.

I did skip church, however, and paid for that sin all morning long. A wiser woman would have disconnected the doorbell, or at least refused to answer it.

"Good morning," the Rob-Bobs said in unison with practiced cheer.

I glanced at the ship's clock I keep on the mantel. It was nine o'clock. Mama was still sawing logs.

"Morning."

Bob held out a towel-wrapped tureen. "We brought you this to help you start your day."

"He brought it; I didn't," Rob said.

I cautiously took the tureen. "What is it?"

"Moroccan ambrosia. Couscous, chopped dates, raw brown sugar, and goat milk."

"You can get goat milk in Charlotte?"

"Harris Teeter sells it in cans. But fresh is better, of course."

"Of course." I invited them in, then minded my manners by serving three bowls of the warm concoction. My portion, incidentally, was very small.

"Delicious," Bob said, "isn't it?"

"Indescribably so," I said. Actually it wasn't half bad. It was certainly better than the emu egg omelet he cooked last time he made breakfast for me.

"Abby," Rob said, mashing his ambrosia with his spoon but never actually taking a bite, "you should get yourself a gun."

"I've been over that with Mama," I said calmly, "and the answer is no. Hey, how did you two know about what happened, anyway?"

"We heard it on the radio last night, and it made this morning's paper."

"But it was too late to make the front page," Bob said, and gave me a sympathetic look.

I sat up straight with a start. "Oh shit, this means that Susan and Charlie know."

I gently evicted the Rob-Bobs and called my children. Both of them were royally pissed at being awakened at such an hour, and both of them thought it was cool of me to be so close to a murder.

"I can't wait until tomorrow," Charlie said. "The kids at school are going to love this."

"Did she, like, scream when she fell?" Susan asked.

It was almost a relief when the doorbell rang again. This time it was C.J.

"Oh, am I disturbing something?" she asked, looking past me into the dining room, where the Rob-Bobs still sat.

She was cradling a cardboard box that said Mr. Coffee on the sides. I already had a coffee maker, but hey, one never knows when an emergency wedding present might come in handy.

"Not at all, dear. Please come in. Bob brought over something called Moroccan ambrosia. It's made with goat milk."

C.J. blanched. "Ooh, Abby, I wouldn't eat goat milk if I were you. My granny Wiley used to keep goats at her place just outside of Shelby. She used goat milk in everything. Even poured it on her cereal. Then one day she noticed that her toenails were getting real thick and brown, kind of like little hooves."

"That's toenail fungus, dear. It has nothing to do with goats."

"That's what we all told her—at first. But then she started growing whiskers on her chin."

"Many older women do."

"Yeah, but then Granny Wiley started butting people with her head. When Pastor Andrews came to call on her, she butted him from behind and sent him flying across the lawn. Poor pastor had to wear a neck brace for a month."

"Sounds like it was your granny who should have worn the neck brace," I said pleasantly. "Perhaps one attached to a straitjacket."

"Why, Abigail Timberlake! I didn't come here to be insulted."

"Why did you come, dear?"

"To give you this." She thrust the cardboard box at me.

"Oh, C.J., you shouldn't have."

"I didn't." She opened the box. "I found it by my front door this morning."

Inside was the missing Ming.

14

"It's definitely the same vase," Rob Goldburg declared ex cathedra.

"How can you be so sure?"

He tilted the Ming. "There is a hairline crack in the glaze here, just to the left of this flower. It's the only flaw on the damn thing."

"Have y'all heard of the Yüan dynasty?" I asked casually. I didn't want them to think I was challenging their expertise.

Rob and Bob exchanged modest glances. I should have known. If it was older than the expiration date on the milk in my refrigerator, they not only had heard of it, but were undoubtedly world-class experts.

"Well, anyway," I said, "at that party Frank took me to, there was a ewer that looked a lot like this. The colors and design, I mean. But Frank said it was Yüan, not Ming."

A scowl distorted Rob's handsome brow. "The Chinese weren't using polychrome overglazes during the Yüan dynasty. Blue and white was their big thing."

"Wow, I go my whole life without seeing a Ming, and in the same week I see two of them." I shuddered. "This is really creepy. First this one gets

125

dropped off at my shop by a woman just about to be killed—"

"I'm doomed," C.J. wailed. "Just like Granny Ledbetter!"

"You have enough grannies to fill a nursing home," I said, not unkindly.

"This is serious, Abby. Granny Ledbetter found a pair of bright red shoes on her back porch one day."

"Had Dorothy stopped by on her way to Oz?" Rob had a twinkle in his eye.

"If she finds an oil can, let me know," Bob said. "My Power Master has been squeaking lately."

C.J. was not amused. "Granny died because of those shoes!"

"Please, go on," I begged politely.

C.J. glared at each of us in turn and then took a deep breath. "Granny had no idea where the shoes came from, but they fit her perfectly. One day she wore them into town on a trip to the doctor—she'd cut her hand on a piece of baling wire and it wouldn't heal up.

"Well, her regular doctor was away on vacation, but his substitute was there, only he didn't bother to read Granny's chart thoroughly, or else he would have known she was allergic to penicillin. He gave her a shot, and she died that same day."

"Sounds like a lawsuit," Rob said sympathetically.

"I'm sorry about your granny," I said gently, "but I don't see how the mysterious red shoes had anything to do with her death."

"That's because I didn't get a chance to finish my story!"

"Please, finish," we chorused.

She took her time before speaking. "There was an article in the paper the very next day about a woman over in Polk County whose body had been found in the woods. She'd been missing for two weeks. Her husband said that when they found her, she was wearing the exact same clothes he'd last seen her wearing—except for her shoes. Her shoes were gone, and they were bright red shoes!"

"Well, uh—but, C.J.," I said, "I already had the vase, and nothing happened to me."

"Wrong, Abigail! Something did. Last night you almost got shot. It was in all the papers. I even heard it on the radio on my way over here. The curse isn't over, Abigail, it's just begun. You and I are both doomed!"

I will admit that for a couple of seconds I felt that proverbial goose do a soft-shoe (red, of course) on my grave.

Greg handled the vase like Buford handled newborns. I'm surprised Greg didn't drop it.

"So this is a Ming vase?"

"A particularly fine one. Rob said this one is over three hundred years old and in almost flawless condition."

"And you're positive it is the same one that was left in your shop the day June Troyan was killed?"

"The Rob-Bobs have declared it so."

"I'd like to take it back with me to the lab," he said reverently.

"Just give it a bottle every four hours, and check now and then to make sure it's dry."

Greg has a smile that could light up New York City in a blackout. "I'm glad you're feeling better."

"Shakespeare was right; sleep really does knit up the raveled sleeve of care."

He looked around. "Where's your mother?"

I pointed to the guest bedroom. "Still knitting, I reckon."

"I got the ballistics report."

"And?"

"The countess was killed by a Colt Model 1860." He paused.

"Yes?"

"It is a cap-fired .44 caliber percussion piece."

"So?"

"So, the revolver in question dates to the Civil War."

"No shit!" There are times when one is just too shocked to be a proper southern lady.

Greg nodded. "A real antique. Doesn't that guy across the street sell antique guns?"

"Major Calloway? That's all he sells—that and military paraphernalia. Some of it rather bizarre. Last year he sold a pair of Hitler's pajamas."

Greg laughed. "Civil War guns?"

I shrugged. "That's one area of the business I know nothing about. All guns look the same to me."

"Perhaps I'll have a little chat with the major."

"He's a feisty old goat; he'll probably chew you out. Anyway, I don't think it will do you any good."

"Vee haf our vays," Greg said.

"I'm sure you do, but that's not what I mean. I'm guessing that this revolver and the Ming come from the same place, and it isn't Major Calloway's Antique Gun Emporium."

Greg raised his eyebrows. Unlike most men I've dated, he has two of them.

"You know a dealer who carries both?"

"No, it's not a dealer. It's a plantation."

"Whoa, Abby. Now you've lost me for sure."

"Roselawn Plantation," I said patiently. "You know, the place where the late June Troyan worked as a docent. You have checked out everyone involved with that place, haven't you?"

"Now Abby—"

"You at least interviewed the docents and the board members?"

His eyebrows plunged. "We are professionals, Abby. We know our job. How often do I give you advice?"

I stood up. I was livid. My raveled sleeve had come all the way undone and hung in tatters from my wrist.

"Gregory Wayman Washburn! Any idiot can put this two and two together. Docent from old plantation drops off an old vase and gets killed. Vase disappears. Then someone tries to shoot me, and the next day vase reappears."

"Who was trying to shoot you, Abby? When?"

I whirled. Mama was up, and by the look on her face I had managed to unravel her carefully knit sleeve all to hell.

"Not now, Mama, I—"

"Out with it, Abby! I'm your mother. I have a right to know."

"I'm talking about the party, Mama. The shot that killed Caroline was really meant for me. You said so yourself."

Mama blanched, swayed, and steadied herself by leaning on an end table. Then she turned to Greg. "So I was right? Someone really wanted to kill my baby girl? My precious little Abby?"

I blushed, undoubtedly deeper than the time Mama brought my lunch bucket to school. I hadn't really forgotten it. It took me the rest of the year to live down the pearl-encrusted doilies and pink satin bows.

Greg, thank the good Lord, didn't even grin. "It's beginning to look like that."

Mama's color returned. "Well, I've reconsidered," she said, "and I think the idea of anyone trying to kill my Abby is ridiculous."

Greg swallowed hard, his Adam's apple a cork dragged underwater by a big bass. "Well, actually, it's not."

"The bullet didn't have her name on it, for Pete's sake."

"No, but this did." Greg pulled a crumpled piece

of paper from his vest pocket and smoothed it out along the palm of his hand. It was a sheet of note-size paper with a business logo at the top. *Den of Antiquity,* it read. It was definitely mine.

"So?"

"We found this on the sidewalk in front of the Tudor mansion."

"That doesn't prove anything." Mama was as stubborn as a grounded teenager trying to borrow the family car.

Greg turned the paper over. On the back someone had scrawled Bea and Jerry's address.

"This isn't your writing, is it?"

I shook my head.

"We calculated the distance from which the revolver was fired by taking into account the size of the projectile and the entry wound. This paper was found within a five-foot radius."

"I see. Were there fingerprints?"

"Yes. We got several good sets."

"And? What did you learn?" I wanted to shake the information out of him.

"Well, the prints weren't yours, for one thing, meaning that this sheet of paper was not the first or last one in the tablet."

"What else?"

"The paper was handled by a right-handed person."

"How can you tell?"

Greg gave us a complicated explanation of radial and ulnar loops, whorls and tented arches.

"That's as clear as Catawba River mud," Mama said crossly. "We'll have to take your word for it."

"Male or female?" I asked.

He shook his handsome head. "Race and sex are two things you can't tell from prints. There are some slight statistical differences between prints taken from the various races, but they are not reliable or significant enough to go on. As for sex, a large woman will have larger prints than a small man. And vice versa."

I chewed on that for perhaps three seconds. "Well, get on down to Rock Hill and fingerprint everyone connected with Roselawn Plantation."

Greg chuckled. "You're serious, aren't you?"

"You bet I am! Round them up and print away."

Greg folded the paper and returned it to his pocket. "On what grounds?"

"Murder." I started to cry for the second time in as many days. I do not cry easily. To my knowledge I have never cried from physical pain. Emotional pain has brought tears to my eyes upon rare occasions, but it was utter frustration that made the damn burst for me.

"Now see what you've done," Mama said. She rushed over and threw her arms around me, which just made things worse. I can't stand to be comforted, especially not in front of a third party.

I boo-hooed and blubbered like a tired child whose favorite doll has been snatched from her hands. I slobbered and sniffled as well. No doubt my nose turned cherry red and giant blotches appeared on my cheeks. Thank God that I had at least applied waterproof mascara the day before and had been too exhausted to remove it the previous night.

Poor Greg. He looked as if he'd rather be in Shanghai eating a live snake than watching me cry. He crossed and uncrossed his legs several times and made jerky, haphazard movements with his hands. I chose to interpret that the latter were intended to be helpful.

"Well, don't just sit there like a big dumb ox," Mama said. "Bring that box of tissues from the kitchen."

Greg sprang to his feet, eager to do her bidding.

Retrieving a box of facial tissues was a lot easier than eating a live snake.

"There, there," Mama said when he was gone.

"There, there what?" I wailed.

"Beats me, but that's what one says at a time like this."

We looked at each other and started laughing simultaneously, and by the time Greg returned with the tissues, we were all but rolling on the floor. Not that the tissues weren't needed, mind you, because the dam was still overflowing.

Greg stared at us, trying desperately to comprehend. After a moment he shook his head.

"Women," he growled. "Go figure."

I calmed down enough to repair to the bathroom for some major repairs. When I returned, Mama and Greg were having coffee. Mama was fully dressed.

"Greg has offered me a ride to Rock Hill," she announced.

"Ah, so you are going to interrogate that bunch!"

"Interrogate is putting it a little too strongly, Abby. But I am going to poke around and ask a few questions."

"Poke hard," I said, jabbing the air with a forefinger.

Greg smiled. "I'll poke as hard as I legally can. Now, in the meantime, you have to do something for me."

"Yes?"

"Stay away from those folks. Stay away from Roselawn. You got that?"

"Aye, aye, sir."

"And there is one more thing I want from you—"

"I just said yes, and I already said you could take the vase. What else do you want, the rest of my life?"

There was a stunned silence. I could not believe I had been so flippant. Loose lips might sink ships sometimes, but mine were capable of capsizing the entire Spanish Armada. Even Mama was horrified, too upset, in fact, to reach for her pearls.

"Well," Greg finally said, "that might not be such a bad idea."

Never accuse Abigail Louise Wiggins Timberlake of not being able to turn on a dime.

"Not such a bad idea?" I barked. "Is that all you can say?"

I heeled and stomped from the room, slamming the door behind me. When I got to my bedroom, I slammed that door as well. My blood was boiling so noisily I didn't even hear Greg and Mama drive away.

15

Captain Keffert was a no-show. The least he could have done was call. I waited patiently all afternoon, and for practically nothing. This is a funny business; one day it's feast, the next day it's famine. That Sunday afternoon my cash register was so hungry, it would have gladly taken payment in pennies.

"How much is this?" a well-dressed, obviously well-heeled patron asked. She was referring to a six-by-four-inch seventeenth-century Russian icon in a silver case embedded with semiprecious stones.

"Forty-five hundred," I said.

Her reworked nose tilted upward. "I saw one just like this in St. Petersburg, Russia. They wanted only two thousand for it."

"How much were your airfare and your hotels?" I asked pleasantly.

"Tell you what, I'll give you twenty-five hundred."

I am always open to any reasonable offer, but that wasn't one of them. I smiled sweetly.

"Four thousand is the best I can do."

Actually I was prepared to go as low as thirty-five hundred. There isn't a whole lot of call for icons in Charlotte, and valuable items that small can be a pain in the neck. You have to keep them locked up behind glass, or they'll grow legs, a peculiar side effect of sticky fingers.

Moneybags had the gall to call me a tightwad, so I graciously showed her the door. I was seriously toying with the idea of locking it behind her and closing early, when the phone rang.

"Den of Antiquity."

The ensuing pause should have tipped me off.

"Yes?" I snapped.

"Did you get the vase?"

An entire flock of Canada geese abandoned their favorite lake on the golf course to dance on my grave. It was Androgynous again.

"What vase?" I wrote down the number displayed on my caller ID panel. Unfortunately my service does not show the caller's name.

"Don't play dumb with me, Abigail. I sent it to you this morning, in care of one of your friends."

"Well, it hasn't arrived yet, dear," I said sweetly. "I'll call you when it does."

Androgynous obligingly hung up so I could call Greg. Unfortunately, tall, dark, and handsome was off in Rock Hill jousting dragons on my behalf. Melody Brzezinski, a coworker, picked up for him.

"I need to trace a number," I said, then briefly described the situation.

As it turned out, Greg had already filled her in. She told me to hold the line, that it might take a few minutes because they were understaffed on Sundays. However, she got back to me in a matter of seconds.

"That one's easy," she said. "It's a public phone on Selwyn. It must be only a block or two from where you are."

"Damn!"

"Sorry, Abby. Do you want me to have Greg call you back?"

"You can tell him to go to hell," I said.

"If it's any comfort, that's one confused puppy you have there. He absolutely adores you, you know, but he has trouble understanding you at times."

"His skull is thicker than an oak plank."

"You're talking about that offhand proposal this morning, aren't you?"

"He told you about that?"

"I think he'd like to rip his own tongue out," she confided.

Melody is single, but she has never shown the slightest interest in Greg. She has her own boyfriend, Tom.

"He said that?"

"I think he'd propose all over again, correctly, if you'd only give him a chance."

"Drop him a few hints about candlelight dinners, soft music, and, of course, a ring."

"Of course. What size?"

"Six. And my preference is oval-cut diamonds."

"Will do," she said, and I knew she would. Now all I had to do was sit back and see if Knucklehead would take her hints. If he didn't I might be forced to propose to him myself. It was the nineties after all, even in the Carolinas.

I needed to work off steam, and I could think of no better way than driving down to Roselawn and working on Miss Lilah's inventory. I decided to take the back way, and avoid Rock Hill and the possibility of running into Greg—until I was good and ready. My route took me down U.S. 521 across the border into South Carolina as far as Andrew Jackson State Park, and then right past Van Wyck and across the Catawba River. Between the towns of Catawba and Lesslie, I made a sharp right turn on Live Oak Road.

This road is the plantation's only vehicular access,

and it is nothing more than a private, single-lane dirt track. From the very beginning the Upstate Preservation Foundation had been in a quandary over whether or not to improve the road, and had ultimately decided against it. It wasn't a lack of money that settled the issue, but ecology. There simply was no way to widen and surface the lane without causing extensive damage to the root systems of the live oaks that gave the road its name. In the interest of safety, however, the board posted a speed limit of fifteen miles per hour, and warned motorists that they might be sharing the lane with oncoming traffic.

Apparently there are some illiterate drivers, and among their number at least one board member. First, Angus "Red" Barnes nearly sideswiped me in a cloud of dust. Were it not for the grace of God and my antilock brakes, I would have kissed a live oak on my way to heaven. Then, while I sat there still shaking with fear, he had the temerity to back up and roll down his window.

"What the hell are you doing here this time of day? The goddamn place is closed."

"I'm counting on that," I said through gritted teeth. "I've come out to work on Miss Lilah's inventory. What are *you* doing?"

"It's none of your damn business what I do, is it?"

"It is if you run me off the road."

"It sure the hell—" Red stopped, no doubt distracted by the blond head that had bobbed up from the general region of his lap. The tart was rubbing her noggin and moaning, clearly unhappy about her latest encounter with a steering wheel.

I laughed, perhaps cruelly. "The law clearly states that seat belts must be worn at all times, dear. And you, Red, have you nothing to lose?"

Red's face flushed with anger, clashing with his freckles yet again. "You tell Miss Lilah that she and

I are going to have ourselves a little talk. Then we'll see who gets the last laugh."

I brayed like a donkey, but unintentionally, of course. Ladylike laughs have never been my forte.

"Does Miss Lilah know that you use Roselawn Plantation as a love motel? Or your lovely wife, for that matter? I bet the charming Mrs. Barnes would be interested in knowing that her husband doesn't keep his barn door shut when he's away from home."

The color drained from Red's face, exposing his freckles like shells on a beach at low tide. He seemed temporarily incapable of speech.

The tart, who looked familiar, stopped rubbing her head and stuck her tongue out at me. "Bitch."

"Does your mama know where you are?" I asked calmly. The girl looked no older than my daughter, Susan.

"You leave my mama out of this!"

I recognized her then. All Mattie Markham's daughters had distinct lisps. But this wasn't Phyllis Sue, the first of Red's Markham conquests.

"You're Phyllis Sue's younger sister, aren't you?"

"I am not Phyllis Sue's sister." She sounded like a pot of water boiling over on the stove, thereby proving that she was indeed who she claimed not to be.

"For shame," I said gently. "And with a married man, too."

"Red's going to get a divorce and marry me. Aren't you, sweetie?"

Red blanched so white, even his freckles paled. "I didn't say that, Bobbie Jo. I said that I would *consider* divorcing Marsha and marrying you."

"And?"

Red looked at me, and I gave him the best blank stare I could muster. He was going to get no help from me.

"And," he said, "I have decided to stay with my wife. I still love her."

"You said you didn't love her anymore. You said you only loved me."

Even tarts have broken hearts, and it hurt me to hear the pain in Bobbie Jo's voice. She was, in fact, younger than my daughter, Susan. If memory served me right, she was in Charlie's grade at school. Quite possibly she wasn't even eighteen. Still, she was old enough to know better than to play around with a married man. Someone needed to teach her a lesson.

"Seems like I have a dilemma," I said. "Do I, or don't I, tell Bobbie Jo's mama what she's been up to?"

"Please don't tell Mama," she sobbed. "She couldn't take it. Not after what Phyllis Sue put her through."

I shook my head sadly. "Don't young folks have any morals these days?"

She looked up at me through tear-swollen eyes. "But I do have morals," she hissed. "I hardly ever go all the way on the first date."

I sighed. "I won't tell your mama if you promise to straighten up your act. No more 'dates' with married men. In fact, you might try laying off the dates until you've found someone who really does intend to marry you. Preferably someone your own age."

"Yes, ma'am." The edge of defiance to her tone could barely have cut butter, so I felt as if I was making progress.

"But if you simply must date, then please make sure you use protection."

"Yes, ma'am."

I turned to Red. "Now what am I going to do about you?"

"What the hell is that supposed to mean?"

"I would hate to have to hurt Marsha, but you seem beyond redemption. Chances are she is going to get hurt, so maybe sooner is better than later."

"Hey now, little lady, not so fast there. You're talking to a reformed man."

"Since when?"

"Starting now. I mean, I realize now that there is no way to keep these things a secret. Somebody always finds out, right? And hey, I don't want to hurt my Marsha."

"Talk is cheap."

"I swear I won't look at another woman besides my Marsha. I mean it. I won't even watch 'Baywatch' unless you say it's okay."

I was supposed to chuckle, but I didn't even crack a smile. "You're funnier than a screen door on a submarine," I said.

"So you won't say anything to anybody?"

They were both staring at me, their eyes full of doomed hope, like pathetic little puppies at the dog pound. I'm sure if they'd had tails to wag, I would have taken them both home and foisted them on Dmitri.

"Go on, get out of here," I said sternly.

For the rest of my drive up Live Oak Road, I felt like a priest who had just heard confession and given absolution—not that I knew what a priest felt, mind you. A real priest would probably have taken the time to do more active listening, to find out why a middle-aged man was boffing his second teenager, and why the Markham teenagers made such good marks. A real priest would have done a better job of dealing with the chain of events that was about to unfold.

16

It was still quite light out, and the red clay where I parked looked perfectly normal. Uma's blood had been the product of my silly imagination and Miss Lilah's story-telling skills. As for the elusive Maynard, he was probably halfway back to Rock Hill, his blond bimbo bobbing along beside him.

Quite honestly, I was not afraid as I went about my work. Fine furniture, even reproduction, is a joy to behold and, since I am a fairly tactile person, to touch as well.

I ran my forefinger along the surface of a tulip-wood veneer writing table. There wasn't a scratch on it. If I hadn't peeked underneath and seen the screws, I would have believed it to be an authentic Regency table, circa 1810.

"Well, whoever brought you up here had good taste," I said aloud.

The sound of my own words sent a chill up my spine, and I involuntarily glanced up at the door. My heart froze. Standing in the hallway, framed by the door, was a man in blue. Perhaps I blinked or looked elsewhere for a second, but the next thing I knew he was gone.

Think what you will. Call me a coward, and doubt that I ever poked under my bed with a broom. I don't care. In less time than it took Buford to you-know-what, I was out of that room, down those stairs, and out the door. Perhaps I actually flew, flapping my arms like wings, which might explain why I left my purse behind.

Fortunately I keep a spare car key taped to the inside of my gas cap. And I had the nerve to criticize Red for barreling down the lane at breakneck speed! The Japanese have yet to invent a train that could have kept up with me.

"But it wasn't my imagination," I said to Mama. "And would you take me seriously?"

I was, I hate to admit, more than a little annoyed with my mother. She was watching "National Geographic" on TV, something about wild dogs feuding with hyenas, and could barely tear her eyes away from the screen. The wild dogs were ugly spotted things, and the hyenas, although their spots were smaller, were even uglier. I failed to see what the show's attraction was. And it was a rerun, for Pete's sake!

"Oh, Abby, don't be silly. There are no such things as ghosts."

"Fine. Call it a specter—ectoplasm, whatever. I saw it plain as day. It was just as clear as you."

"But no one has ever been able to prove— Oh, Abby, look at those wild dog pups. Aren't they just the cutest things? Now wait! In just a minute that nasty old hyena is going to lope over and snatch one."

That didn't happen. Instead, I loped over and switched off her set.

"Mama! I saw him standing there. He was a Union soldier."

"Nonsense. That's just the stress talking, dear."

"Then I have very creative stress," I snapped. "This soldier was wearing a canteen around his neck and holding a gun in his left hand."

"What about his right hand?" Mama asked just as casually as if we were discussing spot patterns on the wild dogs.

"He was holding his right hand to his head—he had a rag or something in it. Blood was pouring down the right side of his face."

Mama was staring at me just like that time when I was twelve and thought I might be pregnant because I had kissed Jimmy Blattner behind a tree at a church picnic, and his tongue had accidentally touched mine. For at least a split second back then, Mama had entertained the possibility that I might be pregnant. I had seen it in her eyes.

"Abby, maybe it's time for a checkup," she said. Fortunately she had not made the same suggestion when I was twelve.

"Mama! You think I'm crazy, don't you?"

"Of course not, dear." She patted the sofa seat beside her.

Obediently I sat down. I was twelve again. I would let her feel my forehead, hear *my* confession, and I would promise to never kiss Jimmy Blattner again—tongue or no tongue. I would not, however, allow her to convince me that I had not seen a ghost. Of course, being Mama, she had to try.

"You have just seen two murders up close," she said. "It's only natural that your imagination is overworked. How about you and I go down to Charleston for a couple of days? We could have some she-crab soup and poke around the antique shops. Not to mention all those lovely gardens this time of year."

It was a tempting offer. Forget April in Paris; think Charleston instead. There are only two other cities in America (I'm not going to divulge their names) anywhere near as lovely as Charleston, and neither of them can hold a candle to Charleston in April. Paris comes nowhere even close.

Whereas Paris can be cold and drizzling in April, and noses that aren't running are apt to be turned haughtily skyward, Charleston is all sunshine and flowers, with noses pressed admiringly into bouquets. Paris is, of course, much bigger and much older, and can afford to mock the very folk who have journeyed there to venerate her. But Charleston is old too—at least by American standards—although she wears her age graciously, like a prized heirloom mantel.

The fine embroidery on Charleston's cloak is her Greek revival mansions and the many courtyard gardens tucked between them. Tradition has it that visitors may enter any garden with its gate left ajar. Old brick walls covered with creeping fig, roses, and rosemary; a palmetto or two; and a splashing fountain—my idea of heaven is a Charleston garden. *And* an unlimited supply of chocolate–peanut butter ice cream.

April is *the* time to see Charleston. Quite frankly, tourists who swoon in Charleston in July do so because of its excessive heat, not from ecstasy. Some aficionados, however, claim that it is preferable to die from heatstroke in Charleston than it is to live anywhere else.

"I can't go with you to Charleston!" I wailed. "I have too much on my plate."

"Honey, the folks in the Bonanza salad bar line have too much on their plates. You have the beginnings of a nervous breakdown. At least speak to a professional."

That did it. That hiked my hackles. That extra little bit of pressure was enough to transform me from a reactive flibbertigibbet into the proactive, broom-wielding woman I liked to think I was.

I snatched up my car keys. "You coming or not?"

"To Charleston?"

"Nope. Back to Roselawn. I left my purse there, and I'm going back for it."

Mama clapped a hand over her pearls. "But Abby, it's dark out now."

"So? You said you didn't believe in ghosts."

"Well, of course it's not ghosts I'm thinking of, dear. But that place is so isolated—and two women alone—don't you think we'd be asking for trouble?"

"Plenty of folks live by themselves out in the country, Mama. They're probably a lot safer there than we are here in town."

"But that road is dangerous. You said so yourself."

I did my best chicken imitation.

"All right!"

Mama marched off to her bedroom to get her purse. She looked so grim when she returned that I couldn't help but laugh.

"There are no ghosts, Mama, remember?"

She shook her purse at me. "You owe me big time for this one, Abigail Louise. When we get back—if we do—we're heading straight over to Tiny Tim's Tattoo Palace."

I rolled my eyes before glancing at my watch. "Okay, okay."

"And don't think they won't be open, either," she said triumphantly. "I called, and they stay open around the clock."

I rolled my eyes again for good measure.

I'm sure it would be disconcerting for anyone to open their front door and find someone, quite unexpected, standing there. Given the state of my nerves, it was perfectly understandable that I would scream. C.J., however, was not so understanding.

"Lord have mercy!" she complained. "I haven't heard such a racket since Cousin LeRoy saw the light."

"You mean he was saved?" Mama asked politely. "Saved" is not a word that rolls easily off Episcopalian tongues.

C.J. brushed past us and flopped across one of Mama's armchairs. "No, I mean saw the light. He was taking a shortcut between Charlotte and Gastonia along the railway tracks, see, and his shoe got stuck under a tie. Well, it was at night, and Cousin LeRoy was busy trying to pull his shoe out when he sees this bright light coming right at him." She paused to catch her breath.

"Spare us the gruesome details," I said.

"Oh, there aren't any. Cousin LeRoy was a skinny little fellow, and he just lay right down there inside the tracks and let the train roll right over him. Only the tip of his nose was burned. But still, when he saw that train bearing down on him, he screamed so loud they heard it all the way over in Shelby. Even some folks up in Hickory claim their dogs pricked up their ears that night."

Mama is hard to impress. "Why didn't he just take his foot out of his shoe?"

C.J. gave her a funny look. "His feet were never in the shoes. He was carrying them when he dropped one next to the tie."

I offered to punch C.J., but Mama restrained me. "At least let her tell us why she's here."

C.J. sighed. "Oh, that. I'm afraid it's not very good news. Y'all know Frank McBride."

"Of course."

"He was shot tonight in his shop. Apparently he was just getting ready to lock up, because his keys were found in his hand."

"Oh my God!" I sat down in an armchair facing C.J. Mama leaned against the doorjamb.

"Who found him?" Mama asked. "Were there any witnesses?"

"Wynnell heard a noise that sounded like a gunshot. She found him. There weren't any eyewitnesses, but I saw this car cruising back and forth on Selwyn not long before this happened." She looked at me. "That's what I told your fiancé."

"He's not my fiancé."

"What kind of car?" Mama asked sensibly. "Did you get a good look at the people in it?"

C.J. was about as much help as Columbus's cartographers. About the only thing we could conclude from her description was that it wasn't the *Niña*, the *Pinta*, or the *Santa María* that had been cruising Selwyn that afternoon.

"Well," Mama said at last, "if we're going out tonight, we better be going. I have bridge club tomorrow morning at ten."

"Where are y'all going?" C.J. was shameless.

"Roselawn Plantation," Mama said quickly. "You want to come along?"

I was shocked at Mama's invitation, and even more shocked when C.J. accepted.

"I just love haunted houses. There's one in Shelby—"

"On the condition you don't tell us any ghost stories. Abby's scared enough."

I will be the first to admit that it felt downright spooky driving out there that late at night. Rock Hill does not roll up its sidewalks at night, but folks don't congregate to boogie in the streets on Sunday nights, either. The country roads were all but deserted. The one car we passed was most likely a couple coming home from a weekend at Myrtle Beach.

"Or else they were cow tippers," C.J. said.

I wisely let it pass.

"They say cow tipping is gaining in popularity these days."

Mama bit. "What is cow tipping, C.J.?"

"Well," C.J. drawled, "most folks don't know this, but cows sleep standing up."

"Didn't Aunt Eulonia used to do that?" I asked.

"Shh," Mama said. "Let her tell."

C.J. sighed with pleasure. "Now, cows have different stages of sleep, just like we humans. And when they are in their deepest sleep mode, they can't hear a thing around them."

"Abby never could hear her alarm clock."

C.J. giggled. "So the trick is to sneak up on a cow that's in her deep-sleep stage and tip her over."

"How?"

"You just push. The cow will fall over—boom!"

"That's cruel," I said. "And besides, what's the point?"

"It's funny," C.J. said. "They fall over all at once. Like in a cartoon or something."

"I want to see that," Mama said. "Abby, stop if we come to a cow."

"Mama, I will not! Cows weigh hundreds of pounds. I'm sure that hurts them."

C.J. took a deep breath. "Actually—"

Unlike Mama, I have no qualms about interrupting. "Can it, C.J. I'm not stopping for cows."

"Spoilsport," Mama said, and if she had been in the backseat with C.J., I'm sure the two of them would have put their heads together and started whispering.

Uma's blood was flowing fast and deep that night. "I can't even see my feet," Mama wailed.

I grabbed her hand and moved it over a few inches. "It helps if you shine the light on them."

It was like taking Susan and her friends on a Girl Scout camping trip. No, it was like taking Charlie and his friends on a Boy Scout outing. I had never seen such big wusses. Mama and C.J., I mean. At least I didn't have to worry about losing them. They clung so close, we inadvertently swapped shadows a couple of times.

"Y'all aren't even giving me enough room to breathe," I said at the bottom of the stairs.

"I heard something from up there." C.J., who was carrying the flashlight at that point, waved it at the top of the stairs. The entire stairwell, incidentally, was well lit by a lightbulb–studded chandelier.

"Turn your flashlight off, C.J.," I directed her. "There's no need to waste the batteries."

C.J. reluctantly did as she was told.

"Old houses settle at night," Mama said. She sounded more convincing the night she assured me that Santa Claus was real. Of course I was twelve by then, and had begun to have serious doubts.

"Y'all just stay down here and shiver," I said. "My purse is upstairs, and I aim to get it. Be back in a jiffy."

They would have none of it. We climbed the stairs *together*, like some strange six-legged, six-eyed beast, flailing and fumbling, panting and puffing. A real ghost would have fled in terror.

At the top of the stairs we teetered to a halt. "Turn left," I directed.

Even as I spoke the chandelier above our heads went black. Mama and C.J. both shrieked, and they claim that I did as well. At any rate it was a few seconds before C.J. turned the flashlight on. Then we all screamed.

Standing right in front of us, just as real as C.J. and Mama, was a Union soldier. I kid you not. This was no ephemeral apparition. This was a real live soldier—well, you know what I mean. If any of us had possessed ten-foot arms, we could have reached out and touched the man.

Time is not easily measured while one is in a state of terror. Still, I would guess that we stared and screamed for a full minute or so. I know that we all had sore throats the next day.

Who knows, we may have stood there and screamed until Monday's docent came to our rescue if C.J. hadn't dropped the flashlight. Then Mama—although she still swears it wasn't her—accidentally kicked the flashlight down the stairs. God bless the woman in Beijing who put together the damn thing, but it wasn't made to take a licking like that and keep on lighting. We were in total darkness again. Talk about screaming.

Fortunately for the folks up in Shelby, who were undoubtedly holding their hands over their ears, the lights came flooding back on. It took us a few seconds to realize this, however, and C.J. was the last to see the light. She was still shrieking, trying to climb Mama and me to safety, as if we were some flesh-and-blood step stool provided for her convenience.

"He's gone!" Mama shouted above C.J.'s screams. "The ghost has disappeared."

She was right. The hall stretched away in front of us, as empty as church the Sunday after Easter.

"Well, I'll be damned," I gasped. "There really is nothing there."

"Except for that," Mama said, pointing to a blue cap lying on the worn carpet at our feet.

17

"It's real, all right," Mama said, picking it up. "It's even warm."

I felt the cap. "It doesn't feel warm to me."

"It feels like plain old wool," C.J. said. "Kind of greasy."

"What will we do now?" Mama asked. "We don't know where he went, so we can't give it back."

Please believe me when I say that I respect my mother. I honor her as much as possible, whenever possible, but there are times now when I begin to wonder if she's a sandwich or two short of a picnic.

"We'll get my purse," I said, "and boogie on out of here before a rebel soldier comes from the other direction and they start to fight."

At that Mama and C.J. whirled around, taking me with them. Despite our six legs, we nearly fell flat on our faces. To our relief there was nothing to see but empty hallway. We turned again, this time much slower.

Somehow we managed to retrieve my purse and make it downstairs and out to the car without a serious mishap. Thank God the lights stayed on the entire time. As it was, Mama and C.J. had bonded so tight, it was downright obscene. I thought I was going to have to use pruning shears to separate them.

"Well, we're safe now," I said to an empty front seat.

"Not until we're back on the main highway," Mama rasped.

I glanced in the rearview mirror. The Siamese twins were still shaking. In the light from the house they looked like two frightened puppies.

"Oh shit! We left all the lights on in the house," I moaned.

Mama coughed. "Who cares? The thing—the ghost—the Yankee—it may be following us."

"Drive, Abby!" C.J. croaked.

I needed no urging. The way I pressed the pedal to the metal and peeled out of there would have made any teenager proud.

It all seemed rather silly when we were back on the highway. The closer we drew to Rock Hill, the sillier it seemed. At the gas stations there were people calmly filling their tanks. At the fast food restaurants folks were loading up on tacos and cheeseburgers, without as much as a backward glance. It was all so normal.

"The cap? Who has the cap?" I asked.

"Not me," said C.J. "I hope I never see it again."

"Damn! We have to have that cap. It's our only proof."

"Ahhh," Mama sighed. "That feels much better. I was sitting on something."

She held the offending object up, and in the light of a Burger King I could see that it was the cap.

We started to giggle. It was like prying loose the first chink in the Hoover Dam. First a trickle, then a stream, then the inevitable flood. For every action there is an equal and opposite reaction—ask any physicist—but I am convinced that we laughed harder than we screamed. Our relief was greater than our fear.

By the time we got back to Mama's house we were giddy—hoarse, but giddy.

"What do we do now?" I asked. Since we were still on a high without a valley in sight, it was a reasonable question.

"Tiny Tim's Tattoo Palace!" Mama squealed.

C.J. clapped her hands. "Oh goody! I drove by that place on my way into town. I've always wanted a tattoo, but I wouldn't go to a tattoo parlor by myself, of course."

Mama looked at me. "Of course."

I groaned. My first valley was starting to resemble the Grand Canyon. "Give me a break, ladies. We have more important things to do than visit some sleazy shop where they poke you with needles that have been who knows where."

"Like what?" Mama asked.

"Well, uh—for instance, we should take this cap to a Civil War expert."

"It's close to midnight," C.J. said. "All the Civil War experts I know will be asleep."

"Except the real experts," Mama said. "We could pay a visit to Rock Hill Memorial Gardens, but funny, I'm not in the mood."

That sent them into torrents of giggles, and they rolled around in the backseat like fifth grade girls. Perhaps it is petty of me to even mention this, but I found their juvenile behavior more irritating than sand in a wet bathing suit. Mama had never, ever been that chummy with me.

"Well, I'm going home to bed," I announced. "Y'all want to act like children, be my guests."

They tumbled out of my car in hysterics.

I was surprised and more than a little concerned to see the lights on in my house. I had left Charlotte well before dark, and I never leave lights on in my absence. I know, some folks think it deters burglars, but I've been burglarized, and my lights were on at the time. If the truth be known, I live in constant fear that Dmitri will knock over a lamp and set my house ablaze. Something similar happened to my aunt Marilyn when she was in the bathtub. Always somewhat of a recluse, Aunt Marilyn's neighbors suddenly got to see more of her than they ever hoped.

I circled my block three times before pulling into my driveway. A sane person would have called the police. I may have eventually gotten around to doing so, but just as I was beginning my fourth circuit, I caught a glimpse of my son, Charlie, through a window. I was tempted to pounce on the poor kid like a panther with a capital "P," but I sneaked up on him instead. Trust me; Charlie can scream louder than Mama.

"How on earth did you get in?"

"Easy, Mama." He held up a key. "You keep it under the doormat. Everyone knows that's the first place to look."

"Not everyone lets himself in."

Charlie pointed to the phone. "Well, it's a good thing I was here. That woman who called sounded awfully desperate."

"What woman?"

"She had a real high-pitched voice. Kind of like a canary."

"Did you get a name?" I asked patiently.

"She had a motel name. It wasn't Howard Johnson, but it was something like that."

"Could it have been Anne Holliday?"

"Yeah, that's it. Anyway, she wants you to stop by and pick up a book on antiques."

"Why? And did she say when?"

He shrugged. "Anytime, I guess. But soon. Like I said, she sounded desperate."

I made the sternest face I could. "Charlie, I've told

you a million times to take down my messages.
There is a notepad sitting right there next to the
phone. What if—"

"Aw damn. You going to give me a hard time,
too?"

"I beg your pardon?"

"Sorry, Mama, but I am royally pissed off."

"Your daddy?"

"Who else?"

"What is it now?"

"It's our plans. Derek's and mine. You know, to
become vacuum cleaner repairmen."

I had been meaning to talk to my son about that
very same subject, but somehow three murders managed to get themselves in the way. In the future I
would have to eschew potential corpses if I expected
to be a better parent.

"I suppose Daddy is ranting and railing. I bet he
read you the riot act." Who said I couldn't be an
active listener?

Charlie shook his head. There were tears glisten-
ing in his eyes.

"Man, I wish! Daddy doesn't care at all. He actually *wants* me to do it. He said he'd give me the
money to take the repair course." Charlie's voice
cracked. "He said the world could always use another honest blue-collar laborer."

I couldn't believe my ears. Buford had done something right. Buford the Timbersnake had taken a po-
tentially disastrous situation and stood it on its head.
I have nothing against vacuum cleaner repairmen,
mind you, but Charlie's brain deserved to go to college—*then* he could become a vacuum cleaner repairman if he so chose.

"Your daddy's right," I said. "Why bother with
college if you already have a good-paying career in
the palm of your hand? Besides, look at all the temptations you'll avoid."

"What temptations?"

"Girls. Sex. That sort of thing. Winthrop is sixty percent female. There's no point in getting distracted by girls when you've got your life mapped out for you. No, Charlie, you are really lucky. You're not even eighteen and you know exactly what you want."

He stared at me. The tears were drying up faster than dewdrops in June.

"But I don't know what I want. Not *really*."

"Nonsense. Of course you do. You and Derek are going to make a mint taking apart old vacuum cleaners. Real hands-on stuff. You'll like it." I attempted a lighthearted laugh. "In the meantime all those other bozos will be stuck going to fraternity parties and hanging around some boring campus, trying real hard not to get seduced."

His eyes were as dry as Phoenix in July. "That Derek's a jerk. He can really piss me off sometimes, you know? Like yesterday he borrowed my Walkman and then left it at Carolina Place Mall."

"Well, we all make mistakes," I said.

Charlie glared at me. "Yeah, but Derek is an asshole—oops, sorry Mama. He just doesn't want to go to college because he's afraid he won't get accepted. His grades weren't that hot."

"Grades aren't everything," I said. I could learn from Buford if I had to.

"Man, how stupid can some guys get? Fixing vacuum cleaners when I could be a doctor, cutting open someone's gut, or a lawyer—"

"Ripping their guts out through their noses," I said. Hey, I'm not perfect.

Charlie gave me a big hug. "You're the best. Can I call Daddy now?"

I thought about the wonderful thing my lousy ex-husband had done for our son. I thought about the phone waking him up from a much-needed night's sleep. Perhaps he had an important court case in the morning. Then I thought about him sleepily reaching for the phone while Tweetie, her silicone boobs perky even in repose, twittered and twitched.

"You bet. Call him," I said cheerfully.

Many antique dealers prefer to take Monday as their day off, and I am no exception. Most Mondays will find me down at Purvis Auction Barn down in Pineville, bidding on estate items, or if I've really been lucky, privately perusing collections of the recently deceased. I feel high when I'm buying. Even though I can't afford to personally own all the items that come into my possession, just having them temporarily within my grasp is the purest pleasure I know. Sometimes I think my daughter, Susan, is right; money is not the root of all evil, the lack of it is.

I had my usual bowl of Special K and a tumbler of orange juice, but I didn't head out to Purvis's. Both my friend Wynnell Crawford, who owns Wooden Wonders, and Major Calloway, proprietor of the Antique Gun Emporium, keep their shops open on Monday. Wynnell is a dear, and the major is a dolt. Both are experts on Civil War collectibles.

I called on Wynnell first. It is much easier to deal with a "dear" on a Monday morning, and besides, I wanted to talk to her about what happened to Frank.

Wynnell was wearing a skirt and blouse set sewn out of rough weave burlap. I would require a bottle of calamine lotion and a syringe of horse tranquilizers just to touch the thing, much less wear it.

"It's awful," I said, referring to her outfit.

"It is awful," she agreed, but she was talking about Frank. "Apparently he was shot in the back, fell, and hit his head on the counter. Have you ever seen a dead man, Abby?"

Wynnell, of all people, should know that I have. "Just a few less than Jessica Fletcher," I said patiently.

"Why would anyone want to kill Frank?"

"Maybe it was a robbery. He sells guns, after all. Isn't that what most hoodlums are after?"

"Yeah, well, I don't think Frank was robbed. You know what a fanatic he was for neatness. I couldn't see anything out of place."

"The robber might have been a Virgo," I said, just to keep the conversation from getting too depressing.

"A Yankee Virgo, maybe."

"Wynnell, we lost the Civil War. It's time to give it up."

"The War Between the States," Wynnell drawled. "Can't you at least say that?"

"That takes too long."

"My daddy would have whipped me if I had said anything but The War of Northern Aggression."

"Please," I said, "we fired the first shot."

"We had to," Wynnell said. "The Yankees wouldn't turn Fort Sumter over to its rightful owners, and when Buchanan tried to send reinforcements and supplies to the Sumter garrison, we had no choice but to stop him. Buchanan should have left well enough alone."

There was no point in arguing. Wynnell could spend a year with the Hare Krishnas and never buy a single flower. It was this same stubborn streak that was responsible for her intense loyalty. Once she was on your side, you had a friend for life.

I opened the plastic Harris Teeter grocery bag I was carrying. "Tell me, is this authentic?"

Wynnell gingerly picked up the cap. "This is a Yankee cap."

"I know dear. Think of it as a dead Yankee's cap."

"Oh well, in that case." Wynnell examined the cap

carefully, turning it slowly in her hands.

"Where did you get this?"

"Roselawn Plantation. Is it authentic?"

"Very. And it's in remarkably good condition. It's a perfect example of what was called the 'McClellan cap,' which was modeled after the French *kepi*. It was one of the most popular styles among Yankee enlisted men."

"Are you sure?"

The hedgerow eyebrows closed in a frown. "Is that a challenge?"

I hurriedly withdrew the question.

The eyebrows unlocked. "But don't take my word for it, Abigail. Ask the major."

"That won't be necessary," I said emphatically. "How common are these?"

"This is the South, Abigail, in case you haven't noticed. Most of the folks around here fought for our side. There weren't a whole lot of Yankee soldiers living here."

"I was thinking of war souvenirs," I said.

"We lost," Wynnell said bitterly. "Losers seldom collect souvenirs."

"So it's pretty rare to find a perfectly preserved Yankee cap like this around here?"

"Rarer than a virgin at a Yankee wedding."

"Wynnell!"

The woman was incorrigible, and I told her so.

18

I stepped outside and nearly ran into Greg. He was headed for Frank's shop.

"You heard about Frank?"

"Yes. I can't believe it. I told Wynnell I'd seen almost as many bodies as Jessica Fletcher, and that's who I'm starting to feel like. Hanging around me is a surefire way to die. Dr. Kervorkian should just bring his patients shopping at the Den of Antiquity."

Greg chuckled, but his Wedgwood blue eyes seemed to cloud over. "You're not taking this very well, are you?"

I bit my lip to keep from bursting into tears.

"Dinner tonight?" he asked gently.

I nodded.

"I've got kind of a full schedule. Is eight too late?"

I shook my head.

"Abby, there's something you need to know."

I held my breath. The last time Greg and I had an extended fight, he took up with that girl with enormous hooters. He was not the kind of guy to sit at home and twiddle his thumbs.

"I was going to wait and tell you tonight, because there are a few more details I'm trying to clarify," he said with maddening slowness.

"You mean you're running a credit check on her?" I asked sweetly.

The blue eyes stared blankly, then twinkled. "It's not about a woman. There is no other woman. It's about the gun that was used to kill the countess."

"Y'all found it?"

He shook his head. "Not the gun itself, but another bullet from it."

"Where?"

"In Frank McBride's body. The same gun killed both the countess and Mr. McBride."

I let the news percolate for a moment.

"Abby, did you hear what I said?"

I felt an immense surge of relief sweep through my body. "You mean that bullet wasn't meant for me?"

"That's right. The bullet that killed the countess was meant for Mr. McBride. He was standing behind you, remember? Between you and the street where the gun was fired."

I percolated some more while Greg waited patiently. "Why would anyone want to kill poor Frank?" I asked at last.

"It's a good question, and one I was hoping you could help me figure out."

"Me?"

"You're Miss Fletcher, right?"

"I'm afraid I just attract victims, not answers. Frank was a little inconsiderate at times, but I don't know that he had any enemies."

"In what way was he inconsiderate?"

"Well, take the party." I realized that Greg had yet to mention my "date" with Frank on Saturday night. Either he had a lot more self-confidence than I gave him credit for, or else he didn't care.

"Yes? About the party?"

"Yes, the party," I said quickly. "*Both* Mama and I arrived with Frank, but the minute we got there, he deserted us. Spent the entire time yakking up a storm with the hosts. That's inconsiderate, isn't it?"

"Very," Greg said. "I would never do such a thing."

I searched his face for a smile, but found none. "You're making fun of me, aren't you?"

"Absolutely not. A man gets lucky enough to have you for an evening, he'd be a fool to leave you even for a second. Hell, I'd slap a pair of cuffs on you if I had to, but I wouldn't let you leave my sight."

"Greg!"

Greg stooped and gave me a peck on the top of the head. "See you."

"What's the matter? Cat got your tongue?"

I whirled around. "C.J.!"

"It does happen, you know. My cousin Vern back home in Shelby was playing with his cat once, flicking his tongue in and out, letting the cat bat at it. Well, Vern's cat Puffy had real sharp claws—you should see Vern's furniture. Anyway, Puffy accidentally got her claws stuck in Vern's tongue—"

"I don't want to hear anymore," I said.

C.J. sighed. "It was no big loss. Vern never was much of a talker. Then again, neither was Cousin Homer, and he had a cat, too."

"So, did you and my mother succeed on y'all's quest?" I asked dangerously, which just goes to show you how much I didn't want to hear another of her stories. Cat-created mutes indeed!

"Oh Abigail, that place was gross! It smelled like my high school gym back in Shelby, and the tattoo artist was a woman named Dagger. There was no way I was going to let her even touch me, much less with a needle."

"Did Mama get her tattoo?" I was ready to clamp my hands over my ears if the answer was "yes."

"No. Your mother turned six shades of green and backed out faster than a gopher from a snake hole."

I breathed a sigh of relief.

"Anyway, I convinced her there are other ways to

honor Lawrence Welk besides having his name tat-
tooed on your bum."

"*That's* what she wanted?" I shrieked.

"Well, sure. Inside a little heart, of course. My
aunt Mildred had one just like it, but then one
day—"

It was time to cut her off at the pass again. "What
are you doing on Selwyn? I thought you were off
today."

"I am off. I just wanted to see how Wynnell was
doing. She all right?"

"She seems to be doing fine. I showed her the cap.
She said it was genuine."

"Imagine that! Just think, Abigail, what if we were
in England and saw the ghost of a king, and he left
his hat behind. Who would get to keep it? It might
be something worth checking into."

"Maybe you've got a point there. Unless—"

"Unless what?" She sounded as if she were being
forced to throw away half her Halloween candy.

"Unless that was just a sound-and-light show we
saw last night."

A carload of whistling and gesticulating young
men drove by. C.J. ignored them, but I sucked in my
tummy and threw back my shoulders. It never hurts
to look your best.

"Abigail! What more proof do you need? Wynnell
said it was the real thing. If someone was playing a
trick on us, they wouldn't need to wear a genuine
Civil War uniform, would they?"

I shrugged. "Maybe he meant to leave that cap
behind. Maybe it didn't just fall off."

"Oh Abby, you're so silly. The next thing I know
you're going tell me that it wasn't necessarily even
a man. That it was a woman all dressed up."

"It could have been."

C.J. frowned. "Well, there *was* a woman in Shelby

who dressed up like a man pretending to be a woman—"

"That was *Victor Victoria*," I said. "You need to document your sources, dear."

C.J. stomped off to see Wynnell. I stomped off just for the heck of it. Inadvertently I stomped into Bob Steuben, who was unlocking the door to The Finer Things.

"Whoa!" he boomed. "You pack a lot of punch for someone—"

"So short?" I snapped. I'd heard short jokes my entire life, and they have never ceased to irritate me.

"Hey Abigail, come on in," Rob said, running interception for his partner. "We just got back from Purvis's."

The Rob-Bobs gallantly ushered me into their shop in front of them. They both seemed to be in exceptional spirits. High as Himalaya kites.

"Purvis had some good stuff this morning, huh?"

Bob beamed. "We got a seventeeth-century Ushak kilim."

I must have looked particularly vacuous.

"A kilim is a flat-woven rug that uses a slit tapestry technique," Bob said. "Ushak is the village in the Anatolia region of Turkey where this one came from. Only ten Ushak kilims that old are known to exist."

"And we own one!" Bob was bouncing up and down like a schoolboy who'd just found a truly rare and valuable baseball card in a pack of cheap gum.

"So you're going to keep it?" I asked.

Rob glanced at Bob. "That's still up for discussion. There's a lot of money tied up in that thing."

"It's an investment," Bob said.

"Only if we intend to sell it again."

"But we have the perfect space for it." Bob was practically begging. "Abby, you know where I mean. In the den, where we have that hideous Heriz."

"I gave that to you for your birthday," Rob cried.

The last thing I wanted was to be caught up in a domestic dispute about old rugs. When a couple starts to argue about carpets, the magic is beginning to go, if you ask me. I showed them the Union cap as a diversionary tactic.

"I had a great-great-great uncle who fought in the war on the Union side," Bob said. "That might be his cap."

"We'll forgive him," Rob said. I already knew that he had at least two ancestors who fought for the Confederacy.

I told them my ghost story. They were impartial listeners. Both of them were open to the idea of ghosts, but neither had any personal experience with the phenomenon.

Rob laid a comforting arm on my shoulder. "You don't have to go back there, do you?"

"I told Miss Lilah that I would do the inventory for her. I would hate to renege on our deal just because I'm a chicken."

"It would scare the piss out of me," Bob said. It was hard to imagine a basso profundo peeing out of fright. "I've never been there, but I've heard that it can be spooky."

Rob nodded. "Frank said it gave him the heebie-jeebies."

"Frank McBride?"

"Yes. I still can't believe it. Two murders on Selwyn Avenue, and in broad daylight. What is the world coming to?"

"It's already *gone*," Bob boomed, "to hell in a handbasket."

"That's what Wynnell says," I told him gently. "She blames it on you Yankees."

Bob blushed. He now considered himself a southerner—if not by birth, then by the grace of God—and hated being reminded of his Toledo origins.

I turned to Rob. "Did poor Frank go there often?"

He shrugged. "I just know that he went there for some fund-raiser. Maybe about a year ago. Just after the state sold it."

They obviously knew the late Frank McBride better than I did. "Did Frank know June Troyan?"

"I don't know. I kind of doubt it. Frank liked to hang out with the fast crowd. He partied a lot."

Like Bea and Jerry, I thought. "How do you know?" I asked. "Did you party with him?"

They laughed, completely at ease with each other again. "Abby, you're a hoot," Rob said. "Bob and I hardly qualify as part of the fast crowd. But from what I hear, you do. Didn't you party the other night with a jet-setting countess?"

Bob nudged Rob, whose turn it was to blush. Clearly he'd forgotten that I had been standing next to the countess when she was shot.

"Pardon him," Bob said, "while he extracts a size eleven from his mouth."

"No harm done," I said. I wasn't being generous, just fair. Perhaps it is because I have small feet, but I stick them in my mouth so frequently, I wear only slip-on shoes.

"You *sure*?" Rob asked.

I waved a hand to show him that it was already forgotten. "What's going to happen to Frank's shop now? Does he have survivors?"

"Only a brother that I know of," Bob said. "He's a courier or something. Travels all over the place."

"Think he'll take over the shop?"

Rob shook his head. "Frank's lawyer was down at the barn this morning talking to Purvis. There's going to be an auction on May fourth. Open to the trade only."

I felt a fleeting pang of guilt. Poor Frank wasn't even in the ground, and already I was salivating at the thought of his stock being auctioned. Frank's was one of the more upscale shops on Selwyn Avenue, with a lot of European pieces one didn't normally find in Charlotte. Perhaps his roaming brother had something to do with that.

"—had a physique like Arnold Schwarzenegger," Bob said. "What do men see in a woman like that?"

"Or any woman," Rob said. "As a matter of fact, even Arnie is too pumped for me."

Bob grinned. "I was hoping you would say that."

"I beg your pardon? What woman, and what does the Terminator have to do with this?" I seemed to have missed something.

"We're talking about Frank's lawyer," Bob said. "Some woman from Rock Hill who obviously lifts weights. I've never seen such bulging biceps on a woman." He shuddered.

"But with a small head and a little ferret face?" I asked not unkindly.

They nodded in tandem. "You know her?"

"Gloria Roach," I said.

The goose that had taken to dancing on my grave lately was doing a slow shuffle.

19

I called Rock Hill information and was given Gloria Roach's office number. Her secretary, a young woman named Angel, was not as forthcoming.

"Whom may I say is calling?"

Whom? Boy, was I impressed.

"Abigail Timberlake."

The ensuing pause was of such duration that I could have filed my nails.

Angel returned to the phone slightly breathless. "Ms. Roach isn't in at the moment; may I take a message?"

"This is Abigail Timberlake calling. Could you tell me when I might be able to speak to her?"

"I'm sorry, ma'am. I'm not at liberty to say."

"Would it be possible to make an appointment to see her today?" I asked politely.

"I'm sorry, ma'am, but she's booked solid for today."

"Would you be an angel, dear, and see if you have an opening for tomorrow?"

"Just one moment, please."

A bottle of Peach Glow and I could have polished my nails and had them dry by the time Angel got back to me.

"I'm sorry, but Ms. Roach is no longer taking any new clients."

"But I'm not a client, dear. I'm a friend. She was at my mother's house for a party on Saturday night," I said in a foolish attempt to strengthen my position.

Angel sighed. "I'm sorry, Miss Timberlake, but Ms. Roach doesn't wish to speak with you. Perhaps—"

"You have such a lovely voice," I said. "And an impressive command of the English language. Are you an attorney yourself?"

I'm sure that someone with better hearing than I could have heard Angel smile. "No, ma'am, but I have an associate's degree in business from York Technical College."

"That doesn't surprise me a bit. I could tell from your voice that you are a well-educated woman. Ms. Roach is lucky to have you for her assistant."

"I'm just her secretary," she said, her resentment barely perceptible.

I ran with what I had. "That's a shame. Still, it must be thrilling to work for Ms. Roach."

"A thrill a minute."

"I bet. I hear she's kind and gentle, generous to a fault. They say she's a veritable saint. How would you describe her?"

"Well, she's—uh—"

"A ferret-faced, muscle-bound cretin with the personality of a pit bull?"

"She's taking her lunch break today at one." Angel spit out the words as if they were bones in a salmon steak.

"Watkins Grill?" I asked, naming a Rock Hill eatery that was popular with lunching attorneys.

"Tam's Tavern," she said.

I thanked her profusely and urged her to get a law degree. We can always use an angelfish in a profession dominated by sharks.

*   *   *

Tam's Tavern is *the* place to eat in Rock Hill. It's where one goes to celebrate special occasions, to see and be seen by the cream of the "Hill." As a bonus, it serves some of the best food in town.

I would have bet my shop that Gloria Roach was a prompt person, so I pulled into Tam's parking lot at precisely five minutes after the hour. Angel had indeed told me the truth. The black Cadillac with the personalized plate that said SHARK confirmed it.

Marlene, the hostess, gave me a quizzical look when I told her that Ms. Roach was waiting for me, but nonetheless she led me to a round table near the fireplace. Gloria's back was to me, her broad, muscled shoulders straining against the confines of her steel gray business suit.

Taking a deep breath, I quickly skirted the table and slipped into a chair. Gloria's expression was priceless. I never knew so much emotion could be expressed on such a tiny face.

"Did Angel tell you I was here?" she snarled.

"Angel's lips were sealed. I came here because I'm hungry. What looks good today?"

She took a sip from a glass of ice water. "I'm not going to be able to shake you, am I?"

"Think of me as a vicious little terrier hanging on for dear life."

Gloria stared at me, and then grinned. Well, actually it is hard to tell in her case, but the corners of her mouth were at least horizontal.

"You've got chutzpah," she said, pronouncing the "ch" as in child. "Normally I like a woman with chutzpah."

"I swing the other way, and even then I'm not very good at it," I said modestly.

Gloria grimaced. "You're funny, too. However—"

The waitress arrived to take our orders. Gloria ordered teriyaki chicken, and I ordered the chicken quesadillas. We both asked for sweet tea—the Carolina term for iced tea with sugar.

"However what?" I asked, picking up the thread of our broken conversation.

"However, I just don't like you. The moment I saw you, I took an aversion to you."

I was shocked. How could someone not like *me*?

"Ditto," I said when I found my tongue. "You push all my wrong buttons."

"You're petite and pert. I hate that."

"You make me sick," I said. "Big muscles, big mind. You're a caricature. Oh, by the way, you forgot perky."

"Well, at least we both call them like we see them."

"More or less, dear. I may have been holding back a little."

She smiled. I was sure of it. I could see her teeth, tiny pointed things, barely larger than the serrations on a grapefruit knife.

"Truce?" I asked.

"Truce. So, Ms. Timberlake, why have you been chasing me all over town?"

The waitress brought our orders. I waited until she was gone before answering.

"I wanted to ask you about Frank McBride."

Ferret face didn't flinch. "What about him?"

"Did you know he was killed yesterday?"

"Yes, I saw it on the news."

"Did you know him well?"

"No, I did not."

Some truce. I felt as if I were Perry Mason cross-examining a hostile witness.

"But he's your client!"

"I don't know all of my clients well. How well do you know your customers?"

"You can bet I know the big spenders like the back of my own hand."

"Frank McBride was not going to make me rich."

"That's right. He owned an antique shop; he didn't drive an ambulance."

"Very funny. Can you get to the point, Ms. Timberlake? My chicken is getting cold."

So was mine, which was a shame. It really was tasty.

"What was Frank's connection with Roselawn?"

"I'm really not at liberty to discuss my clients. Lawyer-client privilege," she said slowly, for my benefit. As if I had never heard the term before!

"I don't want to know his shoe size, dear. I just want to know what he had to do with Roselawn. Was he ever on the board?"

Her beady little eyes squinted at me over her congealing chicken. "If I give you some basic, unprivileged information, will you shut up long enough for me to finish my lunch?"

"Stick a needle in my eye and hope to die."

"Frank was never on the board of directors of the Upstate Preservation Foundation; however, he was considered for a position at one time. A *certain* member, who shall remain nameless, was insisting that we get an antique expert on the board. We asked around, and Frank's name came up. But Frank didn't want the position—there was no pay, and a lot of work was involved. In the end we decided that five members were all we wanted on the board anyway. A nice uneven but democratic number. Not that the board is even remotely democratic." She bared her serrated gums, so I supposed she was laughing.

"Miss Lilah," I said. "The nameless member, not the expert. And Frank wasn't much of an expert on antiques, if you ask me."

You bet your bippy I was hurt. No one had asked me to serve on the board, and I was a native of Rock Hill.

"If you say so," she said. "Anyway, Frank asked me to be his attorney, so I agreed. You know, routine things, wills, that sort of thing."

I was reminded of the fact that I had yet to get a will drawn up since my divorce from Buford. Every now and then that fact rears its ugly head and strikes terror in my heart. What if I were to die in an automobile crash on the way home? Who would inherit my shop? My personal belongings? The humongous sapphire ring I inherited from a friend that I keep in a bank box because it is, ironically, too valuable to wear? Would Buford get it all? Surely not! But, because I find the subject too uncomfortable to deal with, Buford's name remains on the yellow document I keep in a shoe box on the top shelf of my closet at home.

If he was my heir, that meant that Tweetie was as well. Just the thought of having that twenty-two-year-old bimbo co-owning my business and strutting around with my sapphire was enough to give me heart palpitations.

"You all right?" Gloria asked. "You look a little green around the gills." She moved her plate as far away from me as possible without removing it from the table.

"Your secretary said you aren't taking any new clients. Is that true?"

She licked her lips with a flick of the ferret tongue. "A property settlement?"

"No, but I could order some coffee and spill it in my lap."

She shook her head sadly. "Then you shouldn't have told me of your intentions."

"It's only a goddamn will," I almost shouted.

"Call Angel. Set up an appointment." I have scheduled pap smears with more enthusiasm than that.

"Thank you very much," I said, minding my southern manners.

We finished our chicken in silence.

"Can I get y'all some dessert?" our waitress asked.

"Chocolate mousse," I said without hesitation.

Gloria stood up. "None for me. I've got to be running. I'll be late for my two o'clock appointment as it is."

The waitress and I watched her stride away. "Wow! I bet she was in the Olympics," the waitress said. "I bet *she* leaves a big tip."

I looked down at the table. Gloria hadn't even bothered to pick up her check.

I left a fat tip and paid both bills. Then I swung by the Queen Mum's house to pick up the book she so desperately wanted me to have. She lives several streets back from University Drive. It is a respectable neighborhood, but a definite comedown from Roselawn Plantation. The brand new Oldsmobile Supreme was more impressive than her house.

It was a warm afternoon, but not too hot to garden if one was truly determined. Anne Holliday was truly determined. She was wearing slacks under her dress—for modesty's sake—and an enormous straw hat, bedecked with orange and pink silk flowers, to shade her head. A Mexican hat dancer would die of exhaustion just getting halfway around that thing.

"You can never be too careful," she said, getting slowly to her feet. She was speaking loud enough to satisfy the nosiest of neighbors. "Nowadays, with the ozone like it is, folks are dropping from skin cancer right and left. Still, the gardening has to be done, doesn't it?

"I suppose you're wondering why I don't hire someone to help me with the work. Well, I'll tell you—what with the minimum wage and civil rights laws, good help is impossible to come by anymore.

Things aren't like they used to be, that's for sure. In my day southern ladies had creamy white skin."

"Just some of them," I said. "You told my son you had a book for me?"

She led me inside. "Actually there is no book. I just wanted to talk to you. Will you excuse me for a minute while I clean up?"

She was only gone a minute, but when she returned I hardly recognized her. The hat was gone—although her damp gray hair still held its shape—but more importantly, the dress was gone as well. Of course she was still wearing slacks and a top. But the tan cotton slacks had been replaced by a pair of hot pink spandex ones that left nothing to the imagination, and a bright red tank top that was stretched taut across her sagging but nonetheless straining bosom.

"Oh," was all I said. After a heavy lunch I preferred the taste of blood to shoe leather.

"Have a seat, please."

I sat on an enormous white sofa, and she sat on an identical one across the room. Despite their camelbacks, the sofas were contemporary, as was the glass-and-brass coffee table between us. I suppose I had expected overstuffed armchairs with doilies pinned on them, or at least a clutter of Eastlake mahogany pieces. I certainly hadn't expected a 1990s look.

"Don't judge a book by its cover," Anne said. Her voice was suddenly deep and gravelly, a full octave lower than her usual shrieks and shrills.

I stared stupidly. I was getting rather good at it.

"Had you fooled, didn't I? That flowery little granny routine is just for show. But it's a real pain in the ass."

My mouth, always ahead of my brain, fell open of its own volition.

Anne hooted and slapped her thigh. She was obviously enjoying the effect she was having on me.

"I was his mistress, for chrissakes—I met him at a horse show in Atlanta—but folks would never have given me the time of day if I'd just been myself. Flowery and prissy improved the product in their eyes. Every damn time I went into town to shop for groceries, medicines for *her*, you name it, I put on my getup and pranced around like a churchgoing goody two shoes. That made it easier for them to forget who I was and what I did for a living—not that they really ever knew. The concept of mistress was all they could handle."

"Well, uh—"

"I was damned lucky, you know, getting a break that late in life. I was the oldest one in the stable, but my jockey wouldn't kick me out. Too many good years together, he said. Although face it, dear, eventually he would have had to put me out to pasture. A really old mare can't even earn her feed doing tricks."

I was confused. Things just weren't adding up.

"Were you a horse trainer, dear?" I asked politely.

She thought that was hilarious, and slapped her thighs until mine began to sting out of sympathy.

"I was the *horse*!" she finally gasped.

Surely I had misunderstood her. Okay, so she hung out at horse shows, belonged to a stable, and employed a jockey. But that didn't make her a horse any more than my profession made me a Biedermeier bed. Although she could certainly neigh as well as a horse.

"I'm afraid I misunderstood you," I said. "I thought you said 'horse.' "

"Close enough, dear. Just leave off the 's.' "

I blushed the color of her spandex slacks. "This really isn't my business."

She neighed again. "You're embarrassed, aren't you? Well, don't be. It's just a fact—I was a whore, and a damn good one. Be the best you can be, they say, and I was. I slept with four U.S. presidents, thirteen governors, and more senators and congressmen than I could keep track of. And foreign heads of state, too. Why, there was the prime minister of—"

"Please stop," I begged. No doubt I had turned the color of her tank top.

"You young people are such prudes, but oh well, I'm sure you've gotten my point. I was persona non grata just for being Billy's mistress. Could you imagine what my life would have been like—would be like—if folks knew the whole truth?"

"They'd tie you to the Civitas and pelt you with hymnals?"

The Civitas is a set of four female statues of mammoth proportions sculpted by Audrey Flack. They were especially commissioned to mark the Dave Lyle Boulevard entrance to Rock Hill. They are glorious gals, and the community should have been proud of them from the get go. But, alas, the bronze beauties were created with brazen nipples, a fact that horrified local Bible thumpers, who wouldn't stop thumping until the nipples had been sandblasted to mere nubs. The Civitas is the most likely place to hold a public execution in Rock Hill.

"Exactly."

"Well, in that case, why are you trusting me with your secret?"

"Because I need your help."

That was about as likely as the Charlotte Hornets needing me to score baskets. "I don't even live in Rock Hill anymore, dear. Those Civitas gals have more influence around here than I do."

"I've been keeping an eye on you, Ms. Timberlake, and I've decided that I can trust you."

"My lips could sink a navy, dear."

"Your mother thinks you're the salt of the earth."

"I pay her to say that."

She waved a hand impatiently. "I need your help, and I don't know where else to turn."

I sighed. "What exactly do you want me to do for you?"

"A cousin of mine was recently murdered. I need you to help me find her killer."

Thank God my hair is short, because it was standing on end. I stood up to keep it company.

"Me? Why me? Just because people are dropping like flies wherever I go doesn't mean—"

"My cousin was June Troyan," she said. "She was killed in your shop, Den of Antiquity. She was killed because of you."

20

"**L**et me get this straight," I said. "You and June Troyan were cousins, and that's why she moved here from Florida when her husband died. You were the one who put her up for the docent's job. You and June were as thick as thieves, and she knew all about your past, including your—uh—career in Atlanta."

"You listen well."

"But I don't get it. What does any of this have to do with June's murder? Or with me, for that matter?"

She snorted. "June stopped by here the morning she was killed. She said she was on her way over to see you, but when I told her about the blackmailer—"

"Hold your horses," I said. "What blackmailer?"

"Oh, I didn't tell you yet, did I?"

"Apparently not. You wouldn't have anything to drink, would you, dear?"

Please believe me. I am not a tippler, and I don't usually request refreshments that haven't been offered, but it was turning out to be a rather long and difficult day. A little scotch on the rocks, maybe some mud in my eye, and I might still be sane enough to keep my date.

"Would sweet tea be all right?"

"Preferably something you hide when the preacher comes," I said. I blushed at my inadvertent innuendo.

Anne shook her head. "Sorry, but I don't drink. Never have, never will. It isn't good for you."

"But—"

"That's just an act. Throws them off the scent, so to speak. Give them enough to criticize, and they won't feel the need to dig any deeper."

That had a certain logic.

"Sweet tea will be fine," I said. "On the rocks."

She brought me a huge plastic tumbler filled to the brim. The worst tea I had ever tasted. Even a Yankee wouldn't drink that stuff. But I was raised to be well mannered, so when Anne's back was turned for a second, I shared the vile brew with the pathos plant at my side.

"Tell me about this blackmailer," I said. "Who was he trying to blackmail—you?"

She nodded. "There was a note. It said that if I didn't come up with fifty thousand dollars, my past was going to be dragged through every parlor in Rock Hill."

"May I see the note?"

She shook her head. "I'm afraid that's not possible."

"You do still have the note, don't you?"

"I gave it to June."

"What?"

"She asked for it. My cousin was a real pistol. Very headstrong, but very protective of me."

"Did you at least show the note to the police first?"

"June said to wait until she'd had a chance to talk to you. She said she had a theory."

"Why *me*?" I wailed. The goose on my grave was doing a rumba. "A theory? About what? Did it have to do with a—" I caught myself just in time. I wasn't sure I trusted Madame Holliday.

Anne was leaning toward me. I could feel her willing me to finish my sentence.

"—mahogany sideboard?"

Anne frowned. "June never mentioned a sideboard. As for her theory, I couldn't say. She was going to tell me all about it after she got back from seeing *you.*"

I felt as if I was being accused of something, but of what I hadn't the slightest idea. Anne had no way to know that I had ignored her cousin's first foray into my shop.

"She must have told you something," I said.

"Not one word. The poor woman talked less than a stump post."

Well, she was at least right about that. June hadn't said one word to me—on either of her two visits to my shop. Perhaps if she had I would be at work now, merrily ringing up the register, instead of sinking ever deeper into the mire of murder.

I leaned back against the puffy white sofa. I was beginning to feel a little dizzy. Perhaps there had been something sinister in the tea, something so potent that just one sip was enough to do me in. I glanced over at the potted pathos. It did seem a bit pooped.

"What is the point in telling me all this?"

"I wanted to warn you." My goose had forsaken the rumba and had taken up the tango.

"About what?"

Anne rose from her puffy white sofa and crossed the room to a rather severe chrome-and-glass desk. The drawers were see-through, but even then she fished around in the top left-hand drawer for an interminable length of time. I was beginning to think her hand had gotten stuck—either that or she had found, and was loading, a gun.

I breathed a sigh of relief when she turned around with nothing more than a piece of paper in her hand. "This came in Saturday's mail," she said.

I stared at the paper. Even from where I sat, and without my bifocals, I could tell that the paper had come from my shop. My logo—a lion in a den full of period furniture—takes up almost a third of the page. It is impractical as stationery, but cute, and my customers love it.

"Was the first note written on my stationery as well?"

"No, it was on plain paper. With cutout newspaper letters pasted on it. But it was very neatly done. It almost looked typed."

"Neatness is not my style," I said quickly.

"I didn't think so."

I ignored her insult. "Is this another demand?"

"No. This one has just one word on it."

"Oh?"

"Does the word *Ming* mean anything to you?"

The tango had proved too tame for my goose, who was now doing a rousing flamenco. I shouldn't have been surprised by Anne's question, however. She was not on the board because of her knowledge of collectibles. And Ming is not a household word. What did I know, for instance, about tweeters and woofers, until I heard my son, Charlie, use them in a sentence? Then, rather emotionally, I demanded that he account for his vulgar language. Tweeters, my son patiently explained, was not his nickname for his stepmother. As for woofers, to his limited knowledge they were not, and probably would never be, obtrusions on Tweetie's chest.

I tried to shrug nonchalantly. Instead I must have looked like a condemned woman shrugging off the hangman's noose. Either that or I had a severe itch on my back that had gone unscratched for weeks.

"I don't know. I suppose so. It could be part of a

word—like co*ming*. Or it could be referring to a particular Chinese dynasty."

"Well, it doesn't mean anything to me. Still, I'm taking this one to the police."

"Let me take it for you. I mean, my—well, you see, it just so happens that I'm having dinner tonight with a Charlotte criminal investigator."

"But this is Rock Hill."

"Where was it mailed from?" I asked calmly.

"Charlotte."

I smiled reassuringly. "Then it would definitely be a matter for the Charlotte police."

The old gray mare had a lot of mule in her. "Maybe. But it arrived here in Rock Hill. I'll take it to them myself."

"Fine, suit yourself. But I don't see why you bothered to tell me any of this. Just because one of your so-called blackmail notes was on my notepad doesn't prove anything."

"*So called*?" she brayed. "Are you calling me a liar?"

"Well," I said patiently, "for all I know you were in my shop and swiped the damn thing."

She bristled. It was a good thing she claimed to be a horse and not a porcupine.

"Why, you little witch! I may have broken a few commandments during my career, but stealing was never one of them. You take that back!"

Perhaps it was because she was wearing red. Perhaps it was simply the stress I'd been under, but I forgot my training as a southern lady.

"I will not! And don't you even try to implicate me as your blackmailer, or everyone in York County will know that you used to make your living working as a hoofer."

"You mean *hooker*." She laughed mockingly.

I jumped down from the puffy white sofa. "Whatever! But don't think I'm kidding, because I'm not.

My mama knows everyone who is *anyone* in Rock
Hill. In five minutes flat we could have you tarred,
feathered, and headed south to Chester."

Anne remained seated. "But no one will believe
you," she said calmly. "Anne Holliday, the mistress
with the heart of gold, is a Rock Hill institution now.
Did you know I joined the First Baptist Church? I
sing in the choir, just like your mama."

"My mama is not a piece of white trash," I hissed.

I was shown the door.

Of course I headed straight over to Mama's. If
Anne Holliday, the mistress of disguise, did point
the finger at me, I needed Mama in my corner.
Mama *does* know everyone in Rock Hill, but she
would need a head start rounding up the tar-and-
feathering team. There might well be some serious
convincing to do first. After all Anne Holliday had
indeed managed to fool *all* the people, *all* of the time.

She certainly had Mama fooled. "Give it a rest,
Abby," she said for the third time. "I've known
Anne Holliday for twenty years. I was one of the
few people who spoke to her when she came into
town to shop at the Commons. I ran into her at the
Harris Teeter almost every week. She was always
very polite. And I play bridge with her every week,
for heaven's sake.

"No, Anne Holliday might be a bit fond of the
sauce, but she's no stripper from Atlanta."

"Prostitute," I said.

Mama flinched at the "p" word. "Well, she's certainly not that. She sings in the Methodist choir, you
know."

"I thought it was Baptist."

"Well, it's one of those churches on Oakland Avenue, and it's not the Episcopal church. Not that we
couldn't use another soprano."

"That's only her fake voice. She probably sings bass."

Mama instinctively put her hand up to my forehead, and finding it normal, felt my cheeks and then my neck.

"Well, you don't feel feverish," she concluded, "but to be on the safe side, you should go to bed. It's a good thing Greg canceled your date, because you can stay here and I'll—"

"Greg *what*?"

"He called about an hour ago and left a message. Apparently there's been a new development in one of his cases, and he had to fly down to Tallahassee at the last minute. He asked if he could reschedule dinner for Thursday."

"Mama! Why didn't you tell me sooner?"

Mama's hand flew defensively up to her pearls. "Because you didn't give me a chance, that's why. You were too busy attacking one of my friends."

"I was not attacking her. I was merely repeating what she told me."

Mama clucked sympathetically and shook her head. "You poor dear. Maybe it's something you had for lunch. But don't you worry, Abby, I'll fix you right up. I have some castor oil in the medicine cabinet and—"

I wandered off to use the phone.

21

C alling on Shirley Hall was not just a whim. I'd been meaning to, anyway—maybe to ask her out to lunch—as part of a new plan that I had to make more friends. Although I lived and worked within thirty miles of my hometown, I seemed to be suffering from a dearth of friends now that I was only *half* of a couple.

Oh sure, Wynnell and the Rob-Bobs were great friends, and even C.J. was a friend, if the truth be known, but a body needs more than four friends. Especially these days.

Ask Mama. Her best friend of fifty-five years, Karen Leis, moved all the way to Alaska to be with her daughter and her family—a pitiful excuse in Mama's eyes. Then when Rebecca Thompson had a fatal stroke, and Caroline Crawford died of cancer, Mama was left virtually friendless.

"You've still got your bridge club," I told Mama regularly.

"It's not the same. We play bridge, but we don't share. It's all fluff conversation between hands. Real friendships take time."

"And effort," I said.

"Exactly. Making new friends is like dating. You reveal just bits and pieces of yourself at a time, and hope the other person doesn't run off screaming."

I had to wonder what Mama's dating years were like. How many guys had she sent running, and was Daddy ever among them? The only time I ever sent a boy running was that time when I opened the front door to get the newspaper, forgetting that I was in the middle of a mud facial. You should have heard Larry Janz scream.

Shirley Hall, however, seemed delighted to see me. "Come on in, Ms. Timberlake! Sorry I'm not dressed for company, but I've been relining my kitchen shelves."

"Please, call me Abby."

"Then you call me Shirley."

I nodded gratefully. I never know what to call folks who have their initials along with a diploma.

"When did you move, Shirley? Isn't this the same address that's listed in the phone book?"

"Yes. I mean, no, I haven't moved. I've lived here on College Avenue for the last twenty-two years. Why?"

I couldn't imagine relining shelves unless it was absolutely necessary, and told her so. She laughed.

"Well, when I got done cleaning my oven—"

"You cleaned your oven, too?"

"Every Monday, like clockwork," she said cheerily.

I wasn't about to run away screaming, but these were not bits and pieces I wanted to hear. I cleaned my oven last January, but only because I couldn't decide if the black lump at the back was a chunk of meat loaf or something worse.

Shirley had me sit on an immaculate white sofa that was every bit as big and puffy as Anne's. Where was I when the decorating police decreed that white sofas were in? Well, too bad, I was perfectly happy with my pumpkin orange sofas.

"Goose down," Shirley said.

"What?"

"It's much softer than foam rubber." She giggled. "It feels good on my bottom."

I shuddered at the thought of hundreds of geese having their tummies plucked just to pamper Shirley's ample tush.

"You wouldn't believe how hard it is to find a sofa in this style and with this fabric that has goose-down filler. I spent three days looking up in Highpoint, North Carolina, before I found this style, and then I had to special order the upholstery."

I shuddered at the thought of having so much free time on my hands.

"Care for a glass of fungus?" Shirley asked.

"I beg your pardon?"

She laughed merrily. There was something to be said for merry friends. Wynnell could be a bit of a grouse sometimes.

"It's called Manchurian tea," she explained, "but it's really just a big old fungus. Sort of a pancake-shaped mushroom."

"You make tea out of it?"

"Heavens, no. The tea is what the mushroom grows in. You make a new batch every week, and while the new mushroom is growing, you drink the liquid from the old one. Four ounces every morning on an empty stomach. Although sometimes," she giggled, "if I need a little mid-afternoon pick-me-up, I'll drink a second dose."

"Why? I mean, what does it do for you?"

She bounced up from her end of the white sofa. "Oh, it's practically a miracle drink. It does just about everything but wash your windows." She chuckled. "I do those myself—every other week."

I wanted to gag.

"Look," she said, doing a pirouette like a first-year ballerina, "don't I look five pounds thinner?"

Than what? "Absolutely," I said.

"You see, it speeds up your metabolism and the

weight just drops off. It also erases wrinkles, turns gray hair brown, eliminates age spots, boosts your immune system, gives you extra energy, and heightens your sex drive!"

The last thing I wanted was to look even younger *and* be horny. The boosted immune system and extra energy, however, I could go for.

"My, my," I said politely.

"You want to try some? Only two deaths from it that I know of, and they most certainly weren't following directions. You can tell if it's gone bad by its taste."

"What's it taste like?"

"Vinegar mostly. You see, besides the tea you put in brown sugar and vinegar."

I went for it. I tossed back a juice glass full of the brew. It wasn't bad, perhaps a bit slimy, and with a slightly vinegary aftertaste.

"I feel better already," I said.

She laughed again. I know it is wrong to stereotype people, but Shirley had the sort of tinkling, jolly laugh I associated with overweight women.

"Now you're being silly. It takes a couple of months to get the full effect. Would you like to take a mushroom home with you?"

"Sure, why not?" As long as it didn't get into a fight with Dmitri, I was all for having another pet.

She bounced off into the kitchen—a testimony to extra energy—and I followed. The mushroom, which inhabited a four-quart Corning ware bowl on her kitchen counter, resembled a shiny plastic pancake, except that it was taupe instead of golden brown.

Shirley scrubbed her hands as thoroughly as a surgeon and dried them on paper towels.

"You have to keep it in a sterile environment, otherwise it will act as a growing medium for whatever bacteria it comes in contact with. Never, ever put it on a counter where there's been raw chicken."

"Yes, ma'am, I hear you loud and clear."

"Now look here." She fished out the pancake, which flopped about like a rubber bath mat held on end. "You see, a baby always grows on top of the old one."

I watched her detach the so-called baby from its mother. The two were connected in numerous spots. It was like watching footage of conjoined twins being separated. Carefully she placed the detached baby into a gallon-size freezer bag and slid the mama back into her bowl.

When she was through she washed up again and handed me two sheets of paper. "This tells you all about it, and how to care for it. Follow the rules exactly, Abigail, or you might get sick.

"And here." She handed me a plastic jug, the kind Mama buys her orange juice in. "Take this with you. There's enough Manchurian tea in there to last you until you can harvest your own. Just remember to take it on an empty stomach."

I promised that I would, and I meant it. The stuff hadn't tasted that bad, but after having viewed the mushroom close up, there was no way I could keep its byproducts *and* food down.

We sat and visited for a while longer. She really was a delightful person. Her only drawback was that she disliked the South. Of course, I should be horsewhipped for having asked her the question in the first place. It was very unsouthern of me.

"I'm afraid you're not going to like my answer," she said.

"Nonsense. This is a free country, isn't it?" I was expecting her to complain about the heat and humidity, possibly even the size of our bugs.

"The South is culturally dead," she said.

"What do you mean? Winthrop brings in performing artists all the time. We have community theater and concerts right here in Rock Hill. Even a terrific museum. And if that's not enough, you can find any-thing in Charlotte—even things that are banned in Boston."

"That's not what I mean. I mean intellectual life—the life of the mind."

I still didn't get it. "There are oodles of writers living in the area. Dori Sanders, Gwen Hunter, Mig-non Ballard, oh, and that frizzy-haired blonde—I forget her name—who thinks she's a mystery writer."

She shook her head, no longer looking jolly, but dejected. "That's not it. I mean that people don't en-gage in deep, intellectual conversations. There's no sharing of ideas—one-on-one. I don't feel chal-lenged."

"Ah, I see. Well, Shirley, in the South good man-ners are very important, and it is considered bad manners to contradict someone, unless something very important is at stake.

"But close friends can agree to disagree. I have many stimulating conversations with my friends." Suddenly I wasn't feeling quite as bereft of friend-ship.

Shirley sighed. "I guess I don't have any close friends then. Not here. Back home in Yosilanti—that's just outside Ann Arbor—I had plenty of friends. You might even say I was popular. But now look at me. Twenty-two years at Winthrop and in Rock Hill, and what do I have? Just a mushroom, for chrissakes."

"Now that you're retired, why are you staying?" I asked gently.

"Inertia, I guess. It's too much trouble to move. Besides, I've been away too long—things will have changed. At least here I know my way around. Where to find things on the grocery shelves. Where to buy gas."

"Well, maybe we can be friends," I said, although I was no longer quite so sure, mushrooms and plucked geese aside.

She smiled. I could see the spark again.

"Thanks, Abigail. Maybe we could do dinner sometime. Go to a movie and discuss it afterward."

"I'd like that." I could always make excuses later.

"That's why I agreed to serve on the board of the Upstate Preservation Foundation, you know. I thought I might be able to make friends with the other board members, or even some of the docents."

"And?"

She laughed, this time nervously. "They're all a bit strange."

"Gloria Roach," I said needlessly. Her bad Yankee influence was wearing off on me.

"Yeah, and the others. Take Miss Lilah—such a grande dame, but she's penniless, you know."

"No, I didn't."

"Oh yes. Why do you think she puts on all those airs? Cream of the crop, indeed. If people only knew."

"Shirley, dear, in the South breeding takes precedence over bucks any day."

"Yes, well . . ." She glanced out the window and then back at me. "Not everyone is who they seem."

"You mean Anne Holliday, don't you?"

She didn't bat an eyelash. "Exactly."

"The Queen Mum act, those awful hats—who would have thought?"

"Certainly not me."

"I can understand her position, but playing a Baptist tippler, that's carrying it too far, isn't it?"

"Beyond the pale," Shirley said, wagging her head solemnly.

"At least old Mr. Rose knew what he was getting into, if you'll pardon the pun. He saw a horse and thought he could turn it into a winner."

"Kind of like Black Beauty," she said, and plopped back against the plump softness of her plucked feathers.

I sucked in my breath. It had suddenly dawned on me that Shirley had no idea what I was talking about.

"How tragic for a nun to have her life turn out this way," I said softly. "And all because the bishop died in her arms."

"Really?" She sat bolt upright, a Pillsbury dough girl on a Pillsbury doughboy couch.

"Absolutely. He was blowing up balloons for a church picnic, and he inhaled when he should have exhaled, and well . . . His last word was *screeeeech*. Then he fell right into her arms." I said it all with a straight face, thanks to C.J.

She waved her chubby arms impatiently. Apparently balloon-blowing bishops didn't interest her.

"But a nun? You said she was a nun?"

I fixed an image of Julie Andrews in my mind. There was no need to lie about that.

"Definitely a nun. And a great singer, too."

"The kind of nun that wears a habit?"

"Wimples instead of flowered hats."

She giggled. "And takes a vow of chastity?"

That was a bit of a stretch, even for Julie Andrews. "Your all-around basic nun," I hedged.

"Totally awesome," she said. Her ex-students would be proud of her.

I stood up slowly, stretched casually, and yawned. "Well, I better be going."

She popped to her feet with remarkable agility. "Don't forget to take your fungus home with you. It might get a little carsick—it's very sensitive to its surroundings—so I suggest that you sing to it. You know, lullabies, that sort of thing."

My brother, Toy, unlike Mama, can't carry a tune in a suitcase. He sounds worse than a long-tailed cat on a porch full of rockers. I, however, have inherited a pretty decent set of pipes. Still, I would feel a little foolish singing to a mushroom.

"Won't the radio do? You know, easy listening, that sort of thing? Of course, no hard rock."

Shirley frowned. "It's the radio waves. Sometimes they have bad reactions."

I crooned Righteous Brothers tunes to the fungus on my way home. Halfway through "Unchained Melody" I thought I saw the freezer bag twitch. No doubt the fungus was writhing in agony. So much for my good pipes.

22

I fed Dmitri and I fed the fungus. It was much easier feeding Dmitri. He is fourteen years old, and for the last ten of those years he has refused to eat anything except for one particular flavor and brand of dry cat food.

Although the fungus was no more fussy, it took awhile to boil up its brew, let it cool, and then slip the rubbery sucker into its new home. To the best of my knowledge the mushroom had survived my singing, but I wasn't sure I was going to survive touching it, so I was immensely relieved when Wynnell showed up.

Because she was off duty, my friend felt free to wear a getup that had yet to receive its stitches. All the pieces—and there were at least ten of the brightly colored patches—were held together by safety pins. Another patch served as a head scarf, and yet another, suitably pinned, as a handbag. In all fairness, it was a striking and innovative ensemble.

"Did you get Greg's message?" Wynnell asked.

"Mama told me. And he left a brief message on my machine. And I mean, *brief*—five words. 'Sorry, Abby. Call your mother.' I don't know why, but Greg hates talking to machines."

"Men!" Wynnell said sympathetically. She's been

happily married to the same man for more than thirty years, but she's a loyal friend.

"And it's not like he isn't used to machines," I whined. "He talks on the police—"

"Lord have mercy!" Wynnell shrieked. "What is *that*?"

"That's my ticket to eternal youth. It's a giant fungus, and you drink the fluid that it's been sitting in all week. It's guaranteed to turn you into a whole new woman."

"I like the woman I am," Wynnell said stoutly. "Is this thing alive?"

"I certainly hope so. I plan to name him Freddy."

"Well, I think he's disgusting."

"He's only a plant, Wynnell. A mushroom. You like mushrooms—I've seen you eat them."

The eyebrows fused. "In a salad or on a burger. Nothing that big and ugly. If your Freddy starts hovering over Charlotte, I'm getting out of town. Where on earth did you get him?"

I told her about my visit to Shirley. While we chatted I summoned the courage to remove Freddy from the refrigerator and slide him into a Corning ware bowl. I wanted to just dump him straight from the bag, but Shirley was adamant that I lay Freddy gently on top of the solution. "He needs to breathe," she said. Thank God I didn't need to burp him when he was done feeding.

Wynnell was gratifyingly interested in the details of my visit to Rock Hill. Her daughter, Estelle, had attended Winthrop as a history major, and Wynnell was pretty sure that Dr. Shirley Hall had been one of her professors.

"The woman's a Yankee, isn't she?" Wynnell asked.

I shrugged. "So many people are these days, it's hard to tell."

Wynnell's eyebrows locked together in a frown. "I

don't know why they hired her in the first place. A Yankee woman teaching southern history! Estelle said this woman doesn't even like the South, so what is she doing here?"

Normally I try not to encourage my friend's regional prejudice. I refused, for instance, to sign her petition that the state of North Carolina (Virginia is already a lost cause, in her opinion) erect a fence along its northern border, and require visitors from north of the Mason-Dixon Line to show their passports when entering. The fact that Wynnell got more than three thousand other folks to sign was a bit unsettling. This time, however, she had a valid point.

"Did you know she's retired?" I asked, living dangerously.

"*What*? And she's still here?"

"Not only that, but she claims not to have any friends in the area. That's what's so odd. Of course, Anne Holliday doesn't have any friends, either, and she stayed on after Old Man Rose died."

"That's different. At least the woman is from Dixie."

There are times when I should have my lips stapled together, and this was one of them. But Wynnell is my very best friend, and I had to tell *someone* who would believe me.

"Trixie Dixie," I said. "Before she met Rose, Anne Holliday did tricks for a living."

"She was a magician?"

"For some, I imagine. Most of the time it was probably routine. She was a prostitute."

The hedgerow eyebrows arched up to meet her scalp. "No kidding? How did you find out?"

"Straight from the horse's mouth."

"Wow," she said, "and this woman's on the board of the Upstate Preservation Foundation?"

I nodded. "Of course, the others don't know. She

only told me because she wanted to make sure I understood that the real Anne Holliday was not the churchgoing tippler with a garden on her hat, but someone to be reckoned with. The real Anne has been around the block several times."

"I'm sure she has, and all in a night's work. But why did she need to impress you?"

"Because she thinks she has something on me." I filled my friend in on the unfortunate disappearance of my notepad, and its subsequent reappearance in bits and pieces.

"Someone's framing you," she said solemnly, "just as sure as you're a picture that needs hanging."

"Could it possibly be her? Trixie Dixie, I mean?"

Wynnell closed a pin that had come open in a strategic place, thereby sparing me a glimpse of her unmentionables, which in her case really are unmentionable. No word in English exists that adequately describes the undergarments Wynnell makes with the scraps left over from her outfits.

"Anything is possible, I suppose, but I'd bet my money on the Yankee."

"De Camptown race is five miles long," I said. "You'd be better off putting your money on the bobtail nag, and let somebody else bet on the bay. Shirley Hall might hate the South, but she likes me. She wants us to be friends."

"Traitor." She pointed to Freddy. "And no offense, Abby, but besides being a Yankee she sounds a little weird."

I helped Wynnell adjust a pin that was digging into her left shoulder. "Okay, so she's unconventional. Eccentric even. Isn't eccentricity a quality we southerners cherish?"

"What about the Roach lady? You said before you didn't like her. Maybe the feeling is mutual."

"It is for sure; she told me to my face. I had lunch

with her today, you know. At Tam's Tavern down in Rock Hill."

"You don't sound like bitter enemies to me."

I laughed, remembering the expression on Gloria's face when she saw me. "I invited myself. Ms. Roach was not amused. She's tough as nails, and I don't mean just her body, but I can't picture her plowing into a little old lady with her car. With her fists, maybe, but she wouldn't want to scratch that black Caddy. Besides, the woman is obviously a control freak, and a control freak wouldn't try to shoot someone with a Civil War pistol."

Wynnell cringed but didn't correct my nomenclature. "That's a gut reaction, isn't it?"

"Yes, I guess so."

"Your gut has been wrong before, Abby. It could be Ms. Roach. It could be that redhaired letch you were telling me about. It could be any one on the board, or any of the docents."

"Et tu, Brutus?"

"My point is you are too trusting, Abby."

She was right. When Buford told me he had run out of gas on our first date, I should have at least leaned over and examined the gauge. To my credit, I didn't buy his story that he was dying from a rare form of cancer that struck only males, for which sex was the only cure.

"I wish Greg were back in town," I wailed.

"There, there," she said, and gave me a big hug. It was a short-lived hug, however, because the monstrous pin that held her bosom together was poking me fiercely in the nose.

I don't know why the networks switch over to their summer programming as early as April. No doubt they're in cohoots with the fashion industry, which insists on selling bathing suits in January, but never in July. Santa Claus is undoubtedly the mastermind behind this fiendish scheme. Last year I saw Christmas decorations going up in some stores in late August. If somebody doesn't put a stop to St. Nick and his accelerated calendar, we're going to get so far ahead of ourselves we'll lose an entire year.

There was nothing but reruns on TV that evening, I didn't have the oomph to go out and rent a video, and I was fresh out of unread books. Frankly I was relieved when the phone rang.

"Greg?" I asked hopefully.

"This is Shirley Hall. I have to see you right away."

The static was terrible, and I could barely make out what she said.

"There's no need to worry about the fungus, dear. I've named him Freddy, and he's doing just fine."

There was a moment of pure static.

"Ms. Timberlake, this is very important. I need to see you. In person."

"It's after nine, dear, and we just talked this afternoon. Can't we make it tomorrow?" I was definitely going to reconsider a friendship with the Yosilanti Yankee.

"This can't wait. I think I know who killed June Troyan and Frank McBride."

"Who?" If the receiver had possessed vocal chords, it would have screamed in pain.

"Oh, I can't tell you over the phone. I have to show you—" The phone crackled so badly, I momentarily lost her altogether.

"What?"

"This has to be seen to be believed. It's awesome."

"I'll be right over, dear." There is nothing like a little adrenaline to put the zig back in my sagging zag. Freddy the fungus had a hard act to follow.

"Oh, no! Don't come here. Meet me out at Rose-lawn."

"Now? Like I said, it's kind of late and Rose-lawn—well, I mean—"

"That it's haunted?"

"Yes." I felt like an idiot saying that. Especially to a retired college professor.

"That's why you have to meet me there."

"Couldn't we at least drive out there together?" The broom-wielding Abby had been swept away by the ghost of Maynard, and in her place was a spine-less jellyfish.

"I'm down in Great Falls, Ms. Timberlake. Rose-lawn is halfway between here and Charlotte. See you there in about forty minutes, give or take."

I called Wynnell's house, but nobody answered. Surely she hadn't gone anywhere else in her pinned-together frock. Then I remembered the time Wynnell attended a church picnic in a pinafore made out of recycled paper bags. The forecast had called for sun-shine, but this was the Carolinas. Thunderstorms pop up as unexpectedly as spider veins. In just one minute Wynnell's pinafore dress was reduced to soggy pulp; the next minute Wynnell was wearing less than even her husband had seen her wear in several years. There was simply no telling where that woman would go in a cloth dress held together by sturdy metal pins.

The Rob-Bobs were my second choice as ghost-buster backups. Good buddies both, they were al-ways there to lend a helping hand when needed.

"Sorry, no can do," Bob boomed.

"I'll let you cook supper for me again," I promised rashly.

Rob got on the extension. "Sorry, Abby, but we're having a little get-together here tonight. It would be rude if we left our guests."

"A party? And I'm not invited?"

"It's a support group for gay adult southerners whose partners are Yankees. GASPY. Tonight the partners are included. We're trying to teach them how to make proper biscuits and gravy, but *some* of them are proving to be slow learners."

In desperation I called C.J.

"Hello?" she said sleepily.

"I didn't wake you, dear, did I?"

"Actually, you did."

I glanced at my watch. It wasn't even ten.

"You're too young to go to bed with the mockingbirds," I chided her. "You should be out having a good time, and I've got a great idea."

"I'm tired, Abby," she said crossly. "I've had a hard day. I just want to go to sleep."

"Nonsense, dear. You haven't even heard my idea. Remember that nifty adventure we had the other night?"

"Abby, I'm not going back to that horrible haunted house, so you can just forget it."

"We won't be alone, dear. A friend of mine will be meeting us there. She's a big woman, not like me or Mama. I'm sure if there's any trouble, she could protect us."

"Never go to a haunted house at night with a big woman," C.J. muttered.

"Excuse me, dear?"

"My uncle Billy-Bob was dating this big girl back home in Shelby—"

"How big was she?" I asked politely.

"Huh? Abby, do you want to hear this story or not?"

"You could tell me on the way over to Roselawn," I said sweetly.

There followed a moment of silence during which I feared I'd lost her. "C.J.?"

"Are you ready to listen?" she asked at last.

"Yes, ma'am."

She took a deep breath. "Well, Uncle Billy-Bob took this girl—Betty Jo, I think her name was—to this vacant house on the edge of town. He was planning to make out with her, you see. Only neither of them had a flashlight along. So they're sneaking around in this empty house—which was as dark as a well digger's ass, you see—when all of a sudden a bat or something comes flying right over their heads. They both scream and jump, but the next thing you know Uncle Billy-Bob can't find Betty Jo. Not anywhere. He even goes home and gets a flashlight, but no luck."

"Lord have mercy!" I gasped loudly, just to cheer her on.

"Well, the next day Uncle Billy-Bob and his brothers, Uncle Bobby-Bill, and Uncle Bibby-Boll, go back out there to help him look for Betty Jo."

"You're making that up," I said. "I mean about the brothers' names," I added quickly.

She sighed. "Yes, you're right. There is no Bobby-Bill. *His* name is really Bolly-Bib, but he was arrested for dancing too closely with a sheep at the Harvest Moon Ball, and the family is ashamed. I'm not supposed to mention his name. You won't tell on me, will you?"

"My lips are sealed. So what happened to Betty Jo?"

"That's the awful part, Abby. They searched all day long, and every day for the next three weeks, but they didn't find her. It wasn't until a year later, when the house was being torn down to build a Harris Teeter, that they discovered Betty Jo. Of course she was dead by then. Hardly more than a skeleton."

"Ugh!"

"Apparently there was a secret trapdoor, and she had accidentally stepped on it and landed in a soundtight little room. Ever since then Uncle Billy-Bob has been a couple of horses shy of a herd—if you know what I mean."

"Indeed I do, dear. So will you come with me?" I asked brightly.

"Lord no! Haven't you even been listening, Abby?"

I hung up and called Mama. There was no answer.

23

I did not go out into that dark night alone. I made Dmitri come with me. I would have taken Freddy, too, but I couldn't find the lid for the Corning ware bowl, and I wasn't about to have fungal fluid sloshing all over my car.

Dmitri hates riding in cars. He associates them with veterinarians and long glass thermometers that are plunged up places the sun has yet to shine. He stiffened as soon as I opened the car door, and by the time I turned on the engine, he was yowling like a rock musician with his hair caught in a wringer.

"Settle down, dear," I said soothingly.

Dmitri settled into my lap, his claws embedded to their hubs. I yowled along with him.

By the time we got to Roselawn, we were both hoarse. When I got out of the car, it took me a few minutes to separate cat from pants leg. A light shower had commenced, and Dmitri was not enthusiastic about experiencing its charms.

"April showers bring May flowers," I crooned.

Never an avid gardener, Dmitri was not amused.

I suppose I could have worn Dmitri like hairy yellow chaps, but he's a rather corpulent cat, and I was worried that it would put too much strain on his claws. Personally, at that point I didn't mind the pain. With my eyes blinded by tears I wouldn't be able to see the dark mist—no doubt Uma's blood—that swirled around my car, like something out of a B movie.

It was now an hour since Shirley's call, but her car was nowhere in sight. Any normal person would have turned around immediately, or at the very least remained locked securely in the car. A glutton for terror and pain, I dashed to the rear entrance, carrying Dmitri in my arms.

Roselawn Plantation, like any respectable southern home, had a back porch. Dmitri and I, only slightly dampened by the shower, took refuge under its generous roof to wait for Shirley. Poor Dmitri was still upset, but the frantic yowls at last subsided into low, throaty growls. Unlike Billy-Bob and Betty Jo, I carried a flashlight, and the twirling patterns I created with its beam along the porch floor seemed to distract my cat—for a while.

I suppose we had been standing just outside the back door for about ten minutes when Dmitri made it quite clear he needed to use the litter tray. A normal cat might well have been content to piddle on the porch, given that the grass was wet, but Dmitri was strictly an indoor cat that had no prior experience with porches or lawns.

"All right, all right," I snapped, "there's a linoleum floor just inside that door. But don't you dare put one paw into the parlor until Shirley gets here. There's a Yankee ghost in there who's not just whistling 'Dixie.' I have his cap to prove it."

I unlocked the kitchen door with my left hand. My right hand was holding the flashlight, and my right arm was wearing a cat. Just as the fingers of my left hand found the switch, the bulb went out. Mine and the flashlight's.

I regained consciousness in utter darkness. I'm not talking about the dark of a moonless night, or even the dark of a well digger's ass. I'm talking about pitch-black, the color of Buford's soul.

Only once before had I seen such darkness, when Buford and I made a valiantly feeble (the valor was mine, the feebleness his) attempt at a family vacation with our children. That was the summer Buford took up with Tweetie, and perhaps I should have suspected something even then, but that's another story.

At any rate, the four of us took a motor trip to Tennessee. One of our objects was to visit the Lost Sea, which is really a small lake deep within a cavern. While on the tour our guide turned off all the lights so that we could have the thrill of experiencing total darkness.

But that night at Roselawn, the lights never came back on. Even the light in my head flickered only intermittently. In that utter darkness it was impossible to tell if I was conscious or unconscious. With no visual clues to guide me, my thoughts and dreams blended together like coffee and cream. Thanks to Dmitri's claws, even the old reliable pinch test was useless. I hurt *all* the time.

I may well have remained in this state of sensory-deprived confusion had it not been for Mama's powerful genes kicking in. My shnoz can't hold a hanky to hers when it comes to smelling trouble, but it is more than adequate in the scent department. And I smelled something.

Sometimes I dream in color, sometimes I feel things, and I always hear things in my dreams, but I have never smelled anything. This then was reality, not a subconscious flight of fancy, because there was no mistaking the scent of decay.

It wasn't a musty smell. It was dry and slightly acrid, like old gym shoes found in the back of a closet years after they were worn. It was the odor of dead bacteria and stale air.

With the return of olfaction, my other senses began to sort themselves out. In utter darkness the only way to tell up from down is by one's sense of touch. Gradually I realized that I was lying down on my side, and not only had my body been clawed by Dmitri, but it was badly bruised as well. I was lying on some of those bruises.

I found my fingertips and felt the surface beneath me. It was earth, probably clay, but dry and covered with a layer of fine grit. With a great deal of difficulty, and not a little noise, I sat up. My head felt like a watermelon that had been bounced to market on washboard roads in the back of a truck. Make that a truckload of battered melons.

"Oh God!" I said aloud. I know I spoke aloud, because in moving my lips I inhaled some of the grit. There was, however, no echo or resonance of any kind.

Perhaps I should court your rational nature and tell you that I realized I was in a pit of some sort, and that I had been placed there by the person, or persons, who had obviously conked me on the head upon entering the kitchen. But that simply wasn't the case. I *didn't* know where I was. Despite my pain, I didn't even know if I was alive or dead.

Even Episcopalians believe in an afterlife, and since I had never experienced one (not to my knowledge, at any rate), how was I to know it didn't include pain? Surely not heaven, but that other place—the one whose name I had bantered about carelessly ever since I learned it was not a polite word. Perhaps I was there. Perhaps this was my punishment for hating Buford, snapping at my kids, neglecting Mama, ignoring C.J., mocking Wynnell's outfits, and making fun of that frizzy-haired blond mystery writer who lives in Rock Hill.

"I'm sorry!" I wailed.

Either God didn't answer, or I couldn't hear him

above the throbbing in my head. At any rate my circumstances didn't change. To cover my bets, I decided to try a full confession. Loudly, and slowly, I enumerated, in detail, my manifold sins—at least the ones I could remember. Contrary to public opinion, I have transgressed on more than a few occasions. I began with the time I was five, when I willfully drew on Auntie Marilyn's white walls with Mama's bright red lipstick because she wouldn't give me a second piece of candy. I ended with dragging Dmitri, clawing and yowling, on a trip he clearly didn't want to take.

Then it hit me like a ten-pound bag of cornmeal. Dmitri! If this wasn't the *other* place—and I was beginning to doubt it was—my youngest and hairiest baby was missing. Perhaps he was lying somewhere near me, at the end of his ninth life.

Frantically I called his name. Like God he didn't answer. That was no surprise. The greater the urgency in my voice, the less likely he is to come. I called again and again in a much gentler voice, but to no avail. It was quite possible the feisty feline was not dead after all, but merely refusing to acknowledge my existence. It would not have surprised me to learn that he was crouching not a foot away, and was perfectly well.

Although it was painful to do so, I slowly began to expand the perimeter of my known world. Inch by inch I explored with my fingertips. I was dreading what I might find. Call me a sentimental old softy if you will, but the discovery of a cold, crumpled cat would have broken my heart. As battered and bruised as I was, what difference did another scratch or two make, as long as it meant that my precious hair ball was still alive?

My heart stopped, and then began pounding faster than a madman on a xylophone. My fingers had encountered something, but it wasn't a cat. It was round and smooth except for one rather noticeable dent, and it had three holes in it, just like a bowling ball. I put my fingers in the holes, and with the fingers of my other hand to lend support, I picked it up. It was much lighter than a bowling ball, and it wasn't round after all. Just below the thumb hole was a rough, protruding edge. I ran the index finger of my left hand along the edge. It was definitely perforated, and the strange part was, the perforations felt like teeth. Although it took me a few seconds, I concluded I was holding a human skull.

I let out a scream that would have scared the horns off the devil had he been lurking anywhere nearby. Of course it was pointless. With no one to hear me but myself, it was almost like that proverbial tree falling in an empty forest. *Almost.* The tree, however, can't hear itself, and consequently can't be frightened by its own noise.

Ask any psychologist; fear and anger are reverse sides of the same coin. While both emotions can be debilitating, both have their value as well. My fear was obviously not getting me anyplace, so it was time to give anger a try. This was not a conscious decision, mind you, but something instinctual. At any rate my coin flipped, and I was suddenly as mad as hell.

"Damn you!" I screamed to whoever was responsible for my circumstances.

Abigail the timid had become little Abby with the flailing broom again. Nor more flight for this bird. From now on I was ninety-eight pounds of pure fight.

My transformation was not only amazing; it was complete. I didn't have a shred of fear left in my soul. If the devil himself—now rendered hornless—tapped me on the shoulder, I would slap him silly. And it wasn't bravery, mind you, because bravery can only exist in conjunction with fear; it was pure primordial adrenaline.

I fumbled crazily for the skull, and when I found it I flung it as far as I could. I heard it shatter against a hard surface, perhaps a distant wall, and was elated.

"Take that, you anorexic Yankee!" I shouted.

My shaking hands located more of Maynard's remains: ribs, spinal vertebrae, an ulna, or was it a radius? It mattered not. As much of Maynard as I could find was sent flying in the darkness.

It became a game that was almost fun. "Hipbone connected to the leg bone, connected to the foot bone," I chanted.

Maynard, if that's indeed who he was, had remained remarkably undisturbed since the onset of decay. He was still dressed, in fact, but his wool uniform had not fared so well. Some buttons and a few handkerchief-size fragments here and there that fell apart in my hands were all I could account for. His bones, on the other hand, all seemed to be there, and lined up in the correct order as far as I could tell.

I was surprised, therefore—but not scared—when my groping fingers grasped another skull. I turned it over slowly in my hands. It was smoother than Maynard's skull, and smaller. Perhaps it was a child's skull, or that of a small woman. Uma?

Turning it over again I discovered a flat plane about four inches across. The skull tapered on the opposite side, forming a small neck. There were no eyeholes or nostrils. No sign of teeth.

"Well, I'll be damned," I said aloud. "It's a ceramic vase. So, Maynard, you were a Yankee looter, were you?"

Maynard, Yankee that he was, didn't have the courtesy to answer. It was time to insult him back. Still holding the vase, I groped for another bone to fling, but instead of encountering a metatarsal, or perhaps one of his phalanges, I stubbed my fingers on what felt like yet another vase.

"Greedy bastard!"

I set the first vase down and felt for the second. It wasn't a vase after all, but a small ceramic bowl about the size of the one I eat my Cheerios out of every morning. It was upside-down, and I wondered if my harsh treatment had overturned it or whether it had been intentionally placed that way. At any rate I was beginning to feel like a bull—albeit a small one—in a china shop. Who knew what else lay in the blackness just beyond my reach? Had either of the ceramic pieces been broken, I might have cut myself. Bleeding to death in the dark was not how I had ever imagined my demise. It was a far cry from dying in Greg's arms at age ninety-six, with the second slice of chocolate cheesecake only half eaten beside my bed.

"Be careful," I admonished myself, huffing and puffing. "Walk your hands across the ground like giant spiders." Of course I spoke aloud. When one is alone with a hundred-and-fifty-year-old corpse, talking aloud *is* a sign of good mental health.

It was good advice, and fortunately I took it. My pair of giant spiders danced lightly across the grit, and within seconds each had discovered another piece of ceramic. Then another, and another. I counted nine pieces in all. Some were vases, some bowls, but one was a small ceramic box with a lid. And they were all bunched together in a space barely more than a yard square. Who knew what lay in the nether reaches of my black space?

"Jeepers, creepers, Maynard," I gasped, "planning to set up your own store back in Boston?"

Maynard refused to answer again. As soon as I caught my breath, I would search out a big bone, maybe a nice fat femur, to fling at the darkness.

My breath! I inhaled deeply. Was it just my imagination, or was the air staler than before? Was my ragged breathing a result of exertion, or a real lack of oxygen?

I realized with a start that I had been taking my oxygen supply for granted. It is not, after all, a topic that comes up with any frequency. But I was now in a space that was entirely devoid of light, which meant it was tightly sealed, making it impossible for fresh air to enter as well. Or did it?

It had been as black as Buford's heart in the Lost Sea Caverns, but we had still been able to breathe. The same long winding cave that had led us deep into the bowels of the earth, away from the light, had also admitted air. Perhaps there was a tunnel connecting this space with the outside; or perhaps I was doomed, trapped in a pit more tightly sealed than Mama's lips when it comes to giving out compliments.

One thing was certainly clear, however. Unless I stopped being reactive and started using the noggin the good Lord gave me, there were going to be *two* skeletons and nine pieces of ceramic for the next visitor to count.

24

There is nothing heroic about struggling to save one's own life, therefore I shall spare you the litany of the agonies I endured over the next several hours, or at least what seemed to be that length of time. My advice to anyone so foolish as to ignore C.J.'s sage advice concerning haunted houses is to at least wear a watch with an illuminated dial.

At any rate I was eventually able to determine that I was in a man-made (surely God would have been more concerned with symmetry and quality of materials) pit or cellar. The space measured approximately eight by ten feet, although it could have been much larger. Frankly I am terrible at estimating the size of anything, and believed Buford's ten-inch lie for years.

My pit, as I now thought of it, had apparently been dug into the hard clay subsoil. Two of the walls were unfaced clay, while the other two were covered with fieldstone. As far as I could tell, the stones were simply stacked, not mortared.

The floor was clay, and the grit I had been feeling was undoubtedly its dried, crystallized surface. It was nowhere near level. When I tipped a ceramic bowl on its side, it rolled away out of my reach, and I didn't find it again until I almost sat on it.

I didn't expect the ceiling to be so low. I could touch it everywhere I tried, without having to stand on tiptoes. I had expected to feel voluminous swags of cobwebs, but there was only the feel of rough-hewn wooden beams and chinks of crystallized clay.

My most interesting discovery, however, was that my pit was a veritable treasure chest. In addition to the nine ceramic pieces, I found four metal pitchers, three large, heavy candelabras, two metal tea sets, a wooden chest brimming over with flatware, and a smaller wooden box containing sundries, several of which felt as if they might be pocket watches. I am not a kleptomaniac, but when Maynard failed to protest, I pocketed one of the small, round objects. It would be a small down payment on the damages I hoped to collect from the Upstate Preservation Foundation.

"Well," I said aloud, "that's not so bad now, is it? At least you're not in Hell with a capital 'H,' and Maynard here isn't about to try anything fresh. Are you, dear?"

Maynard was mum.

"Typical man," I said. "Just lying around, while I, who have put in a hard day already, am expected to wait on you hand and foot. Oops—better make that hand or foot. I just stepped on something and it cracked. What's that? Did you say something, dear?"

Maynard remained mute.

"Okay, so I'll figure this one out on my own. Just don't expect any help from me when I do. And believe me, dear, you're going to need help. All the king's horses and all the king's men aren't—" I clapped a gritty hand over my mouth. Just to be on the safe side, perhaps it was better not to remind Maynard of what I had done to him.

"Let's see," I said to divert his attention, "there has got to be an entrance to this joint somewhere. I may be small, but I wasn't shoved down between the beams."

Or was I? Not between the cracks, of course, but what if there was an overhead opening of some kind? A trapdoor, maybe.

"Think, Abigail, think!"

If there was a trapdoor, it was likely located above the spot where I had regained consciousness. Much simpler to throw a body down a hole than to carry it down a ladder. Maynard, I bet, had not ventured far from where he was dumped, and I surely hadn't moved much while I was out of it. It was a fine theory if one didn't take into account the treasure trove. Clearly it had not just been dumped from the floor above.

I did my best to relocate my first position. It would have been a lot easier, I grant you, if poor Maynard had been allowed to rest in peace *in* one piece. Nonetheless my spider fingers did a thorough search of the ceiling, and just as I was about to succumb to the mother of all neck cramps, my nails found a crack that ran crosswise along several beams, a crack too straight to be coincidental.

"Eureka!" I screamed. "Maynard, old boy, I think we've found it!"

Although Maynard was not effusive with his enthusiasm, I'm sure he shared it. It would have been helpful if he'd gone a step further, gotten off the floor, and helped me push the damn thing open. The trapdoor—for that's what it was—was stuck, and there was nothing I could do to force it open.

The flatware knives I inserted in the cracks and used as wedges all bent or snapped blade from handle. It was a wonder none of the flying blades hit me in the eye, not that I could have been made any blinder. I considered using one of Maynard's larger bones as a battering tool, but discarded that idea in shame a moment later. Maynard and I had become buddies. True, I had treated him shabbily, but he would no doubt have forgiven me had he been in the position to do so. After all he was in far greater need of bonding than I.

"Think, stupid!" I berated myself. "There has got to be something else you can use."

Indeed there was, but until I had a chance to appraise them, I was loath to use one of the heavy candelabras, or even one of the metal pitchers. It was only an educated guess, and my fingers have been wrong before—just ask Buford—but the items in question felt like silver.

"Try one of the stones, silly," Maynard muttered.

"What?" I spun around, dropping the mangled knife I was holding.

Either Maynard was the tight-lipped son of a bitch I'd been accusing him of being all along, or it had been my imagination. He said nothing more.

Still, it was a good idea. I willed my legs to function, and as soon as they started taking orders, I directed them over to the nearest stone wall. When I bent over to begin the arduous task of prying loose a stone, I first felt the fresh air. It was barely more than a suggestion at that point, like a fluffy bit of down brushed along a callus. It was so slight, in fact, that I all but ignored it at first. Like Maynard's muttering it was probably just a figment of my imagination.

"Come to Mama," I said, and tried to pry loose a stone about the size and shape of a homemade loaf of bread.

It wouldn't budge. I tried another, which was as stubborn as the first, but that's when I felt the whisper of air for the second time. I dug my nails in around the stone next to the one I'd been working on, and tugged. It was as loose as a six-year-old's tooth, and I fell backward, clutching the rock to my chest.

I was surprised but unhurt, and was back on knees in less time than it takes my son, Charlie, to quaff a quart of cola. That it took so long was only because a stream of decidedly fresh air was pouring over my body, filling my nostrils with its heady scent and my lungs with its revitalizing power.

There were four loose stones in all, and the dimensions of the space left by them was approximately eighteen by twelve inches. I felt around inside with one of my exploratory spiders. The depth appeared to go on forever.

"It's a tunnel," I explained to Maynard. "A very narrow tunnel for a very small person. I don't think it's how I got here, but it's how I'm leaving."

"What if the tunnel leads to nowhere?" Maynard asked me—in my imagination, of course. I might have been missing a marble or two, but not the entire collection. "What if you get lost?"

"So what if I get lost? What's the worst that could happen? If I stay here I'm guaranteed to go on your crash diet, and no offense, dear, but it's a little extreme."

"What if the tunnel collapses?" Maynard was a sensible guy.

I stuck my head and arms back into the tunnel and felt the sides, roof, and floor again. They were composed of the same heavy wooden beams that supported the roof of the pit.

"I'll take my chances, dear."

Poor Maynard. We had been so close, shared so much during our brief time together—indeed, there were parts of him with which I had made an acquaintance that I wasn't even sure Buford had. Like a backbone, for instance. Now it was time to leave my good buddy behind.

"So long, Maynard," I said solemnly.

With my arms out in front of me to function as feelers, I began wiggling my way to freedom.

* * *

Unless you are fond of spiders, roaches, and the biggest centipede north of the Amazon, you won't want to hear about the next stage of my great escape. What you need to know is that it was extremely painful scooting along on my stomach. Not only did I have Dmitri's scratches, and a myriad of bruises to contend with, but the tunnel floor was a minefield of splinters. Even Mr. Bowling, my seventh grade math teacher, should be spared an ordeal that painful.

It was also extremely tiring, and I stopped to rest several times. At least one of those times I drifted off to sleep. My guess is that I was asleep only a few minutes when the giant rat began sniffing at my fingers.

Under normal circumstances rodents and I do not cohabit peacefully. Suffice it to say I was the last mother in my neighborhood to take her kids to Walt Disney World. A kingdom presided over by a giant mouse does not meet my definition of magical.

To my knowledge, there had been no rats in the pit. Therefore, a rat this size in front of me could only mean one thing—the tunnel *did* lead somewhere.

"Go away, nice rat," I groaned, and scrabbled my fingers at him.

The rat was every bit as friendly as Mickey, and didn't budge. In fact, he began to lick my fingers.

"Shoo, you hairy son of a Dumpster!"

"Meow."

"Dmitri?" I bumped my head on the tunnel roof in my excitement.

"Meow."

"Dmitri!" I affectionately scratched my feline friend under the chin. All was forgiven.

Dmitri forgave me as well. As usual, he purred like a well-tuned engine. In that confined space, however, he sounded like a lawn mower without a muffler.

A few minutes later, our bond reestablished, it was time to move on. Alas, poor Dmitri did not get the picture. He would have been content to have his chin scratched until one or both of us resembled the hapless Maynard. Animal lovers will have to forgive me if I confess that I had to pinch him in order to get him to budge, and even then he only reluctantly turned around and heroically led me to freedom.

The tunnel, I was soon to learn, exited under the wooden floor of the old kitchen. There was a crawl space there, approximately three feet high, and I was able to sit up for the first time in what must have been hours. I can't describe what a relief that was. Now it was my turn to procrastinate, but Dmitri wouldn't have it. If I wasn't going to scratch his chin, I at least had to feed him. To convey his message, he nipped my ankles several times.

"Okay, boy, let's go," I said.

Frankly I didn't have much hope that Dmitri knew where he was any more than I did. Any animal that chases his own tail has got to be spatially challenged.

Dmitri led me to a hole in the floor that was barely cat size. From its rough edges I surmised that Dmitri had done a little remodeling of his own. It still needed to be improved on, and while Dmitri nipped impatiently at my ankles, I worked at expanding the hole. Unfortunately at this end of the tunnel there were no loose rocks, candelabras, or human bones to aid me. I did manage to find a small stone about the size of my fist, and I used it as best I could.

Several fingernails later I was a free woman, except for the minor inconvenience of being trapped in the plantation's old kitchen. The door was securely locked from the outside, the windows painted shut. Fortunately my assailant had no appreciation for the tenacity of a Timberlake—even one by marriage. They would have to pay for the broken window, not me.

They were going to pay for something else as well. It is one thing to throw a middle-aged busybody into a pitch-black pit to let her die of starvation, if not fright. Perhaps, in some small way, I deserved it. But to starve a helpless cat was unconscionable. One thing I knew for sure—Dmitri had not come willingly. Hopefully his tormentor had experienced a little torment as well.

At any rate it was dark when we got outside, and I assumed that it was no longer the night of our arrival. It seemed probable that it was the next night, but it may have been several nights later, for all I knew.

My car was missing. I had expected that. My assailant had misjudged my will to survive, but he or she was no idiot.

The mansion was, as I expected, locked. There was however, an outdoor garden spigot by the back door, and Dmitri and I made that our first stop. I gulped, he lapped, and vice versa. It was the longest drink on record. You would have thought we were a pair of small, misshapen camels, fresh in from a six-month trek across the Sahara.

I was considering breaking and entering the mansion to use the phone—I had become something of an expert, after all—when I heard the distinct sound of rap. I don't mean a knocking noise, either, but that sort of staccato entertainment in which today's young people openly and unabashedly shout obscenities, denigrate women, and malign minorities. Oh, for the good old days when innuendo and allusion were an art.

It wasn't difficult tracking down the source of the rap: a beat-up pickup on the front lawn of the plantation. The cab, as far I could tell, was empty, but the vehicle was bucking up and down like a bronco with a burr under its saddle.

There was no need for Dmitri and me to sneak up on the ardent lovers. Lightning, an earthquake, and a volcanic eruption all happening simultaneously could not have gotten their attention. In fact, I drove almost a mile before they realized they were moving horizontally as well as vertically.

25

I politely turned off the radio as soon as the young man began pounding on the rear window. I will spare you his exact words, but they were taken from the lyrics to which we had just been listening.

"I'm only borrowing it, dear," I shouted.

He put together another string of invectives and pounded harder. I calmly responded by braking sharply, then gunning the engine. There was a great deal of horizontal movement in the bed of the truck, none of it happy. From then on the young couple clung to each other morosely. They didn't even have the decency to be afraid, and shame was out of the question.

I hung a right on 901, and another right on Cherry Road, which is the main drag. The clock above Nations Bank read two A.M., and there was not another car in sight. Contrary to the stereotype of a small southern town, folks in Rock Hill do not roll up the sidewalks at sundown. There are plenty of cultural events to enjoy in the evenings before the sidewalks are taken up, and they are never rolled but folded neatly and stored in giant drawers lined with sachets.

Any thinking, responsible person would have driven straight to the police station or Piedmont Medical Center, but not yours truly. I was battered

223

and bruised, and craved the bosom of my mama. It was as simple as that.

I pulled into Mama's driveway, put the truck in park, but left the engine running. Dmitri graciously allowed me to pick him up, and I jumped down. Every fiber in my body screamed in agony; some screamed twice.

"Thanks for the ride," I told the kids.

The boy stood up shakily. "You ain't going to turn us in to the police?"

His question gave me a start. I hadn't but for a second considered that they might be responsible for the condition I was in. I didn't think the two of them together could change a lightbulb without a manual.

"Should I?"

"Dewayne said the truck was his." The girl pouted. "I didn't know it was stolen, I swear."

"Shut up, Yolanda. It ain't stolen."

"Does your mother know where you are?" I asked her.

"Man, we don't need this shit," Dewayne said. He hustled Yolanda into the cab, and they were off in a squeal of tires that woke half the neighborhood, including Mama.

"Lord have mercy!" Mama said, opening the door just a crack. "Police Chief Larry is going to hear about this. There is supposed to be a curfew in this town."

"Mama, it's me!" I cried, wanting nothing more than to fling myself into her comforting arms.

"Abigail! What in heaven's name are you doing here this time of night? Was that Greg who dropped you off?" She craned her neck to look down the street in the direction of the vanished truck.

"Mama! Look at me."

She looked, and did a double-take. "Lord have mercy, Abby. You look like something the cat dragged in." She must have seen that I was holding Dmitri. "No offense," she added.

Dewayne and his truck were now a faint buzz in the night. A mosquito receding into the distance. She turned, and I followed her inside.

"I'm sorry, Mama, that I worried you so. I guess I should have gone straight to the police so they could start their investigation. I'll call them now. We don't want my kidnappers to get away."

Mama looked as confused as she did the first time she tried to open a bottle of childproof pills. I hastened to explain.

"I was supposed to meet Shirley at Roselawn but she didn't show and I got conked on the head and tossed down a hole with a dead Yankee and a pile of treasures and only just now escaped through a tunnel the size of a heating duct where I met Dmitri who'd been locked in the old plantation kitchen but we had to steal a truck first." I said it in one breath, a feat that would have been impossible in the thin air of the pit.

Mama instinctively felt my forehead. "Well, you're not burning up, so I don't think it's fever talking. Have you been drinking, dear?"

"Mama!"

Both hands flew up to caress her pearls. "You're serious, Abby?"

"Look at me, Mama. Would I do this to myself? And smell me! I—" What I did was burst into tears. I smelled like a Port-O-John in August.

"I've had a bad cold," Mama said. "I haven't been able to smell a thing since Sunday night."

"Didn't you care that I was missing?"

The pearls were a blur. "You were missing?"

"Since Monday night. What day is it now?"

Mama glanced at the clock above her TV. "Wednesday morning. *Early* Wednesday morning." Eight-millimeter tears had formed in her eyes. "I didn't know you were missing, dear. I've had a real humdinger of a cold. I was in bed all day yesterday. I called your shop twice, and your house three times, but you didn't return my calls. I didn't think *you* cared."

I threw myself into my mother's arms, and we both sobbed like babies. Good mother that she is, she allowed us just enough time to dwell on our mutual failures before putting a pragmatic spin on things.

"You need to eat," she said. Her nose began to twitch. "You go take a nice hot bath while I rustle up some pork chops, mashed potatoes, collard greens, fried okra, biscuits—and for dessert some piping hot peach cobbler with vanilla ice cream."

Mama was fully capable of rustling it up, despite her cold. Besides, she needed to feel useful. Still, all that food on a long-empty stomach might not be such a good idea.

I shook my head. "Just some peach cobbler."

"That does it," Mama said sternly. "I'm taking you straight to the hospital. No ifs, ands, or buts."

The doctor who examined me at Piedmont Medical Center was very kind, but he plugged me into a labyrinth of plastic tubes and forced me to stay overnight for observation. Every time I blinked, a staff of thousands shone flashlights in my eyes, and I got prodded and poked with thermometers more times than a Thanksgiving turkey. And of course I had to give my statement to the police. I was finally left alone just as the morning food trolleys began their rounds, and I fell asleep to the sound of clanking cutlery.

I woke up in mid-afternoon to find Mama sitting by my bed, her face grim. My first thought was that she had been the victim of an intense religious experience.

"Mama?"

Her face brightened upon hearing my voice, and I breathed a deep sigh of relief. She would no doubt continue to sing in the Episcopal choir and sit on washing machines.

"Abby! I was so worried. We all were. Greg was just here, but he didn't want to wake you up. He said you looked just like a—uh—"

"Sleeping Beauty?"

"An unraveled skein of yarn."

"Thanks, Mama. Tell him I love him, too."

Mama and I had sound-bite conversations, interspersed with periods of dozing. We both dozed, as much as she denies it. When the supper trolleys rolled around, Mama fed me as if I were a baby. She made me clean my plate, too, and then I fell into a deep sleep and didn't wake again until the next morning. Upon awakening I felt like a million bucks. After a sponge bath and a little makeup, I looked like a thousand.

"Jeepers, creepers," I said to Mama, who was back on duty again, "where did that giant bouquet come from?"

She surveyed the room, which contained more flowers than either of us had ever seen outside a funeral home. She pointed to an arrangement the size of a Volkswagen bug, and I nodded.

"That's from the Upstate Preservation Foundation. They're afraid of a lawsuit, if you ask me."

"And so they should—well, one of them, at any rate."

"Do you know which one?"

"I have a hunch, but I can't prove anything at this point."

"If I didn't still have my cold, I could help you smell out the culprit," she said loyally.

I asked her to bring me the card attached to the behemoth bouquet. It was signed by all the board members, except for one.

"Aha! Just as I thought. Shirley Hall's name isn't on the card. No doubt she's down in Rio by now, with a suitcase of stolen loot—"

"Abby—"

"No, Rio is too hot. Shirley likes it cold. Where do cold-loving criminals go when they're on the lam? The Yukon? Siberia?"

"Abigail!"

"But, Mama, she tried to poison me. I've got the brew at home to prove it."

Mama hoisted herself up on the bed and gently patted a battle-scarred arm. "Abby, dear, Shirley Hall is dead."

"What?"

"Her body was found in the Catawba River, not far from Roselawn. It was discovered by two boys who were hiking in Landsford Canal State Park."

"Oh, Mama—"

I began to cry, for Shirley, of course, but for myself as well. It was time to let it all out, to cry myself dry. I could have cried for weeks had the nurses not been so inconsiderate and unhooked my IV the day before.

Poor Mama did her best to comfort me. I have always been sure of her love, but cuddling and coddling do not come naturally to her. Patting gingerly seemed to be her forte, and I graciously allowed her to do this. The pain would eventually ebb away.

"She called and left a message for you," Mama said suddenly, just as I was catching my second wind and working up to another good blubber. "She couldn't get you at home, so she decided to try me."

"What? When?"

"Monday evening."

I gripped Mama's patting arm. "What did she say?"

"She said she was running late for your meeting, but would be there as soon as possible. Oh, Abigail,

I didn't realize that the 'there' she was referring to was Roselawn Plantation!"

"Did she say anything else?"

"Some Bible verse, I think. I didn't know Shirley was religious."

"Mama, what was the verse?" I asked with remarkable patience.

"Something about the last being first, and the other way around," Mama said. "It was hard to understand her; the static was terrible. That is a Bible verse, isn't it? Or is it from the *Kama Sutra*?"

"It's a Bible verse," I said.

I chewed on its meaning while Mama dutifully dabbed at my blotched face with a napkin soaked in water. We were both so preoccupied that neither of us heard Greg knock and enter.

"Hey," he said almost bashfully.

I looked up to see a sight for sore eyes, and everything else for that matter. He had never looked so handsome. The Wedgwood eyes, thick dark hair, classic nose, straight white teeth—Greg was perfect Hollywood leading man material. He had, in fact, once worked as an extra in the cult classic *Romancing the Kidney Stone*. Why Hollywood had not snatched him up could only be a testimony to its lack of good judgment. Well, its loss was my gain, and I meant to tell Greg so just as soon as I settled another small matter.

"I know who killed June Troyan, Frank McBride, and then tried to kill me," I said.

26

It took every one of my feminine wiles to persuade Greg to go along with my plan. Perhaps if I hadn't looked like an unraveled skein of yarn, the job might have been easier. Nonetheless, just after the supper trolleys had been wheeled away with their empty cargo, the entire board of the Upstate Preservation Foundation trooped in. Frankly I was so nervous, I had scarcely eaten a bite.

"This better be damned good," Red growled. "I already shelled out big bucks for the bouquet."

"Shhh," Marsha said.

I frowned at her. She wasn't invited. I was considering telling her so when the Roach burst into my room. At least the pecking order was preserved.

"Make it fast," Gloria snapped. "I have to be in court in twenty-five minutes."

I gave Miss Muscles the critical once-over. She was wearing a purple spandex tank top and lemon yellow sweatpants. Either her hearing was on a racquetball court, or courtroom etiquette, along with just about everything else these days, had gone to hell in a gym bag. At least she was carrying a briefcase.

"Have a seat," I said pleasantly.

Of course that was easier said than done. Marsha had taken the only chair, and Mama was the only person—besides Greg—I would allow to perch on my bed.

I might have made an exception for the elderly lady who stumbled in next, had I not known that Anne Holliday, in addition to being a mistress of Rose, was a master of ruse. She was in fine fettle that day, too, with a flowered hat that shamed some of the arrangements my well-wishers had sent.

"What a cheery little room," she chirped. She pretended to admire my botanical garden, but her shrewd little eyes were boring holes in me. Squeal and you'll pay, they said.

I smiled at Marsha. "Would you be a doll, dear, and let Miss Holliday have the chair?"

Marsha sighed, and with all the speed of a teenager jumping up to mow the lawn, relinquished her coveted seat. Anne staggered convincingly over to the chair, but gave no indication that she appreciated my complicity.

The door opened one more time, and in swept the grande dame herself. As usual, Miss Lilah was impeccably dressed, this time in muted spring colors. Her linen suit was ecru, and her long-sleeved silk blouse was robin's egg blue. True to character, her skirt, though it was linen, showed not a wrinkle. Either the woman had walked to the hospital or had mastered the art of driving while standing.

"Why, Lilah, what have you done to your hair?" Anne Holliday was sitting bolt upright and sounding twenty years younger. If she wasn't careful, she was going to blow her own cover.

We were all, in fact, staring at Miss Lilah. Gone was the immaculate chignon. It had been replaced by soft silvery waves that brushed across her cheeks and spilled down to almost shoulder level. I'm sure there are some who would consider that length to be too long for a woman of Miss Lilah's maturity, but frankly it was flattering. Not all of us can afford plastic surgery—or even want it—which doesn't mean we enjoy being seen in public with turkey necks. Not that Miss Lilah had pronounced wattles, mind you. I'm just saying that a woman has a right to cover her deficits with her assets.

Miss Lilah graced us with one of her beneficent smiles. "This time of year I always feel the need for a little change," she said. "I hope I haven't gone too far."

"Well, frankly—"

I shot Anne Holliday a warning look, which she wisely heeded. My ice pitcher was within reach, and her English perennial garden was an easy target.

"I think it's lovely," I said.

"Ladies, please," Red grumbled. "I didn't come here for a fashion show. I've got three building sites that need my attention."

"Hear, hear," the Roach said as she flexed her arms in an isometric exercise that made her muscles bulge obscenely.

Greg glanced at me, and I nodded.

He cleared his throat. "Thanks for coming. I know it was rather short notice, and y'all have busy schedules—"

"You can say that again." Gloria Roach's right biceps had assumed the size and shape of a leg of lamb.

Greg, Mama, and I frowned at her. "The sooner you hush up and listen, the sooner you can leave," Mama said.

Gloria's left biceps swelled to the size of a small ham, but she said no more.

"As y'all know," Greg said calmly, "Ms. Timberlake here was accosted out at Roselawn Plantation on Monday night."

"I already told the police that I have an alibi," Red growled. "Marsha, tell them where I was."

"I have an alibi, too!" Anne warbled.

Red turned viciously to her. "Mr. Johnny Walker or Mr. Mogen David?"

Greg held up a restraining hand. "We are not here to make accusations. We are here to listen to a statement from Ms. Timberlake."

All eyes fastened on me. I swallowed deeply, trying desperately to remember everything Greg and I had agreed on.

"Go on," Mama whispered.

"Well, uh—I—uh—"

"She wants to tell you a ghost story," Mama said.

Red grabbed his wife's hand. "Hell, I don't have time for this."

Greg, my hero, took a step forward. "You'll make time."

"There're no such things as ghosts," Red snarled.

"Maybe that depends on your definition, Mr. Barnes. From what Ms. Timberlake tells me, there most certainly is something that goes bump in the night."

"What the hell is that supposed to mean? He can't make us stay and listen to this shit, can he?" Red turned to Gloria.

The Roach looked as if her body had sprung a fast leak. Her muscles drooped, and her little brown ferret face had turned the color and texture of cottage cheese.

"I knew there was a ghost out there," she whispered, barely audible. "I could feel its presence. Once I even saw it—a little girl standing on the landing with a rag doll in her hand. One second there she was; the next thing I knew she was gone."

Anne twittered. "You and I should do happy hour together. I lived in that damn house for thirty years and never once saw a ghost."

"Did this little girl ghost have a name?" I asked pleasantly.

Gloria shrugged. "How should I know? She was only there for a second."

"Miss Lilah," I said, "have you ever seen a ghost out at the old plantation?"

"Of course not, dear."

"How about a ghost named Uma?"

"I have no idea what you're talking about."

"No ghost named Uma? Then how about one named Maynard? I seem to recall you telling me about him."

"Why, that's pure fiddle-faddle," she said, just as cool as a cucumber in January. Believe you me, politicians about to undergo a Senate investigation would do well to tear a page from her book.

"Perhaps the complete name will ring a bell," I said, and reaching underneath my pillow, withdrew a round object.

Red took a step forward. "What the hell is that?"

I pushed a little button, and the object popped open, revealing a pocket watch. "I found this is at the mansion," I explained. "It reads: 'To my son, United States Army Corporal Samuel Eugene Maynard III, on his twenty-first birthday. Love, S.E.M. II, April 10, 1862.' "

I snapped the watch shut. "I'm sure that by now y'all have heard about the secret trapdoor under the china cabinet. I'm sure that you also heard that I was not alone during my interment in that horrible pit. My companion didn't say much, but I have since learned that he was Corporal Maynard.

"This," I snapped the watch shut for dramatic effect, "was his. I found it in a box with several other watches—all of which, I am told, belonged to the Rose family, and have their initials engraved on them."

I turned to Greg, who nodded.

"There was other loot, too," I said. "Silverware, tea sets—oh, and vases. Ming vases, I hear. Lots of beautiful vases. Some of them very rare and valuable."

"Shame on you, Anne," Lilah said sharply.

"Me?" Anne's voice was a full octave lower now. "I may be lots of things, toots, but I'm no thief. I didn't even know there was a trapdoor beneath the china cupboard. You, on the other hand, have been spending an inordinate amount of time out there since the foundation took over. Of course most folks would think, just looking at you, that you have all the money you need. But I happen to know that you were raised as poor as a church mouse on welfare."

Miss Lilah was standing ramrod straight. Rage did not detract from her class act.

"How about you, Anne, would you like to share your past with our friends?"

I jumped to Anne's rescue. "Well, I wasn't accusing you of being a thief, dear," I said. "The loot I was referring to was hidden there during the war— the Civil War—to keep it safe from the Yankees. I'm sure that was before even your time."

Rather than express gratitude for getting her off the hook, Anne Holliday had the nerve to glare at me. Then she turned on Miss Lilah like a bear with threatened cubs.

"So it was *you* who was blackmailing me?"

Greg and I possessed the only pairs of eyes that weren't in danger of popping out. Even Lilah and Anne looked as if they had thyroid problems.

"Ladies, please," Greg said. He had stepped between the two women, although I'm sure Miss Lilah would never have raised a hand in public. "It was Shirley Hall who wrote that letter. She seemed to have a nose for sniffing out things."

"I do, too, when I don't have a cold," Mama whined.

"Tell us about the blackmail," Ferret Face urged.

She had whipped a legal pad out of her briefcase and was busy taking notes.

"Maybe it's none of our business," Red growled, and I instantly suspected that he might have been the recipient of one of Shirley's letters. "Miss Timberlake, is there more to your story?"

I glanced at Greg, who nodded.

"Yes, well, of course the plantation was never burned, but at least one Union soldier found his way there. The unfortunate Corporal Maynard. Mr. Rose was off fighting the war, but someone in the family—probably Mrs. Rose—killed him with a blow to the head and hid his body with the family treasures.

"One would think that after the war the valuables would be recovered, except that life got in the way. Mr. Rose, fighting as a Confederate soldier, was killed in the Battle of Petersburg. Mrs. Rose, it is said, went stark raving mad. There were several little Roses, I've been told, one of whom eventually inherited the estate, but the legal heir never knew about the murder or the treasure.

"Only one other adult besides the Roses knew the secret, and that was the house slave who helped Mrs. Rose hide her most portable valuables. This slave was, of course, freed soon after the war. It is my belief that a descendant of this slave—quite possibly a Rose herself—has returned and made it her business to collect what is rightfully hers."

I had expected Miss Lilah to be shaking like a paint mixer at Home Depot, but she was as cool and calm as ever.

"You can't prove it."

"No, but Shirley Hall could. She was blackmailing you, too, wasn't she? She traced your family tree and discovered there were a few ripe fruits on it she could easily pick. Shirley figured she could earn more from you than she ever had as a professor at Winthrop. So you killed her, and then you called me and pretended to be her. It was you who asked me to come out to the plantation Monday night, where you tried to kill me. That static on the phone was a clever trick."

"You can't prove that, either."

"Of course I can, dear. Would you be a doll and pull your hair back from your face?"

"I'll do no such thing."

"I wouldn't blame you," I said quietly. "Those scratches Dmitri gave you must look pretty nasty. I've been handling him since he was six weeks old, and even I"—I shot a glance at Greg—"look like an unraveled skein of yarn."

It was finally all over. Miss Lilah didn't even bother to bolt for the door. She had far too much class for that.

27

"**S**o you see," I said to Wynnell a week and a half later at a party she was throwing in my honor, "it wasn't a Yankee after all. Miss Lilah was pure southern. Rose was her great-great-granddaddy. The house slave who helped hide Maynard was her great-great-grandmother. Lilah's great-grandmother was raised in Atlanta, where she passed for white and married a white man. Her grandfather moved to Rock Hill at the turn of the century. Miss Lilah is as southern as you are."

Wynnell was wearing a dress that looked for all the world like a wrinkled quilt that had had its backing removed. A shmatte, as Rob would say. It was not something Scarlett O'Hara would have worn, even in the most dire of times.

But let it be known that my friend is not a racist, merely a regionalist. "Miss Lilah is actually more southern than I," she said, hanging her head in shame. "My great-grandmother on my father's side was born in Chicago, but moved to Charlotte when she was three."

We all gasped.

"Next to Bob, you're the most Yankee person here," Rob said sympathetically. He turned to Wynnell's husband, Ed. "Too bad my support group is only for gay partners of Yankees. Otherwise you'd be welcome to join."

Ed smiled bravely. "Thanks. It's been horrible keeping Wynnell's secret all these years. It feels great just getting it out in the open."

I gave Ed a big hug. The burdens some folks have to bear.

"I'd like to change the subject," C.J. said.

We all groaned.

She glared at us, but a good-natured glare, I am sure. "This is serious. Abigail, I want to know if there really is a ghost out at Roselawn Plantation."

I shrugged. "All I know is that I didn't see one."

"But the one we saw upstairs—who dropped his cap—that was Miss Lilah?"

"You betcha. But the cap did indeed belong to Maynard, as it turns out. It was the real thing, all right. So was the gun. Miss Lilah's ancestor kept the items after helping to dispose of Maynard. The gun and the cap were handed down from generation to generation with the story of the loot."

"But we didn't see her car that night," she insisted stubbornly.

"That's true, and I didn't see it the night she clobbered me over the head with a table leaf. You see, our dear Miss Lilah was hiding it in the summer kitchen—she was the only one who had keys to the outbuildings. The ironic thing is, it was the weight of her car that made one of the old floorboards buckle, thereby exposing the other entrance to the dungeon—the one Dmitri crawled through after she locked him in the kitchen. It's a wonder she didn't notice it."

"What I want to know," Bob boomed, "is who gets to keep all that beautiful stuff? Some of those Ming vases are museum quality."

We looked at Greg.

"They're part of the estate, and as such belong to

the Upstate Preservation Foundation," he said. "Gloria—I mean, Ms. Roach—can fill you in on the details."

"Not bloody likely," I mumbled.

Greg's dark eyebrows lifted in amusement. He looked exceptionally handsome that night, in cream-colored slacks and a red polo shirt that was open at the neck. He was my date for the evening, but he had done nothing but talk about the Roach. I knew he didn't go in for women with bulging biceps, or did he? He had been spending an inordinate amount of time with the woman, and had even gone so far as to hint recently that my tummy could use a little toning.

"What did you say?" Greg asked loudly. The man could be maddening.

Mama came to my rescue. "It was me. I said, I still don't get it. Lilah Greene confessed to killing June Troyan, who had accidentally stumbled on the trapdoor when she was rearranging furniture. But why, pray tell, did she kill Frank McBride?"

"Frank started out as her fence, Mrs. Wiggins." Greg had it in him to be gallant to Mama *and* to two-time me with the ferret-faced Hercules. "But it wasn't just the stuff in the pit they were selling, but all the best pieces in the house. Apparently, with his contacts Frank knew where to buy convincing reproductions."

I gasped. "So that's why Miss Lilah agreed to let me do an inventory. She wanted to see if they'd gotten away with their little scheme."

"Exactly, only it wasn't such a little scheme. Miss Lilah saw the plantation and its contents as her birthright—but of course she needed Frank to help sell the stuff. Their operation was running real smooth until June Troyan moved the china cupboard one day. If that hadn't happened, they may never have been caught. None of the others on the board knew the first thing about antiques."

Mama shook her head. "That doesn't make a lick of sense. Why would Miss Lilah purposely invite an antique expert in to appraise a house full of fake furniture? Isn't that asking for trouble?"

I raised my hand. "Ooh, ooh, can I answer that?"

Greg smiled. "Go for it."

"Because, Mama, at that point it was too late. I suspected something fishy was going on out there, and so did the police. By inviting me to help her, she was very cleverly shifting suspicion away from herself."

"The woman has balls," Rob said, and then immediately apologized to Mama.

"She had chutzpah," Greg said. He pronounced the "ch" as in China.

We all laughed.

"No, I mean it. In one of the locked outbuildings—an equipment garage for mowers and such—we found a blue van."

"*The* blue van?" I asked excitedly. "Didn't I tell you in my shop, on the day June Troyan was killed, that it had to be the blue van?"

"That you did. And the reason it took us so long to find it is that after that day she hid it in the outbuilding and never drove it again."

"I thought y'all checked the vehicles registered to all the docents and board members," I said, risking his ire.

He flashed me a broad, self-righteous smile. "We did. The van didn't belong to her—it was an old work van that belonged to Old Man Rose and came with the estate. The gardener used it to haul bales of pine straw and bags of manure. It was obviously not his primary vehicle, and even Miss Holliday forgot about it."

"But of course Miss Lilah didn't," I said. Much to

my chagrin I found my admiration for her was actually growing. "When the foundation bought that property she made it her business to go over every square inch."

"She was lucky she didn't get stopped for driving with expired plates," C.J. said. "I can't drive one block without having a siren pull me over. Once in Shelby—"

"We do our best," Greg said evenly, "but we can't be everywhere."

Mama jumped gallantly to his rescue. "What I want to know is, why did she kill Frank?"

"Because after she killed Miss Troyan, she got worried that things might have gone too far," Greg said. "Apparently Frank didn't have her—well, she thought he might cave in and expose her. So she shot him with Maynard's gun, which she thought would be impossible to trace. It's a wonder it didn't blow up in her face."

The sun rose in my clobbered cranium. "Ah, so it was Frank who was pestering me."

Greg nodded. "Miss Lilah was right. Frank was panicking. He was trying to find out how much you knew. Apparently he stole the Ming from your shop to test the water, so to speak. Finally, he just couldn't handle the pressure, so he dumped the vase at C.J.'s door. It was his pitiful attempt at a smokescreen."

"Oh, Abby, the things I do for you," C.J. whined.

Bob turned to me. "And it would have been easy for him to swipe your notepad," he boomed. "Abby, you really need to keep better track of your things."

"I've been telling her that for fifty years," Mama said.

"I'm forty-eight, Mama."

"I thought you were at least fifty," Greg said without cracking a smile. "I've always liked older women."

Mama patted her pearls playfully, Wynnell

smoothed her shmatte shamelessly, and I fumed.

"You must be thinking of Ms. Roach," C.J. piped up. That child has all the sensitivity of a numb armadillo.

Greg grinned. "No, but speaking of Miss Roach—"

"I'd rather not," I snapped. "That woman is like a summer storm cloud. Her name keeps popping up all over the place."

Greg had the audacity to smile broadly. "Well, to every cloud there is a silver lining, and Miss Roach has found a very pretty silver lining to this one."

"What did she do, wrestle the cloud down to the ground and line it herself?" I'm pretty sure those words came from my mouth.

Still smiling, Greg excused himself, and returned a moment later carrying the same Ming vase June Troyan had tried to leave with me.

"Rubbing salt in my wounds, are we?" I snapped.

The Wedgwood eyes danced gleefully. "Abby, this is for you. Miss Roach said that possession truly is nine tenths of the law, and since this was found in your shop, and the case is now closed, it belongs to you."

"I-uh-I—"

"Here." Greg thrust the vase at me.

I took the vase, too stunned to apologize.

"Look inside," Greg said.

I did. At the bottom of the vase, in an open black velvet box, was a ring. In the ring was a modest, but very bright, oval stone. Like Greg, it was winking at me.

"Ooh," C.J. gasped, "never take a vase from a tall man wearing a red shirt. My cousin Fuzzy in Shelby—"

"Shush, dear," I said, and winked back at Greg.